"Jessie hasn't got caller ID on that phone," Owen said. "I'll get it. And put a recording device on it. In the hope that Mimi—if it's her—calls again. I've already called about a security system."

"I don't need your help," she countered. "I can take care of myself—I always have."

"I promised your grandmother," he repeated.

Then he startled her by reaching out and gently straightening the collar of her blouse, his fingers lingering as if he was reluctant to do such a thing, and even more reluctant not to.

Eden's breath stopped, seemingly stuck in her throat, and warning rippled her nerves. But she did not tell him not to touch her, and she did not move away from him.

She gazed up into his unwavering blue eyes and realized, *Damn, he wants me. And I want him. This is a complication I don't need. Damn. Damn. Damn.*

HEAR
NO EVIL

—◈—

BETHANY
CAMPBELL

BANTAM BOOKS

NEW YORK TORONTO LONDON SYDNEY AUCKLAND

HEAR NO EVIL

A Bantam Book / November 1998

ISBN 0-553-57688-7

Published simultaneously in the United States and Canada

PRINTED IN THE UNITED STATES OF AMERICA

OPM 10 9 8 7 6 5 4 3 2 1

To Dan, with love, as always

If you can look into the seeds of time
And say which grain will grow and which will not,
Speak then to me.

—SHAKESPEARE

HEAR NO EVIL

ONE

—◦◦◦—

THE MIAMI AIRPORT, SHE'D ALWAYS THOUGHT, LOOKED AS if it had been designed by Alfred Hitchcock.

It was full of eerie angles and curves that led the eyes astray and set emotions on knifelike edge.

She had always thought so, and to remember it now, doing what she must, seemed both frivolous and macabre.

The hell with it, she told herself silently. *You wanted to do this. You said you could do this.*

Taking a deep breath, she hoisted the shoulder strap of her leather duffel into place and walked more quickly.

She was a slim woman, wearing no makeup, and her most striking feature was her brown hair, straight and gleaming, cut to shoulder length. Behind slightly tinted glasses, her eyes were brown and serious. She wore baggy

silk slacks of navy blue and a lightweight tan jacket. She
glanced at her watch. It was twenty-five minutes until
noon.

Her destination, the Nassau-Air baggage check-in
counter, was located in one of the airport's more peculiar
corners, and she had nearly reached it.

She turned right and was startled, as always, at how
abruptly this lobby loomed into view. Instead of offering
an air of spaciousness, it seemed choked and awry.

Directly in her path stood a dark metal structure the
size and shape of a burial vault. It was a large vending
machine, set at a skewed angle, and it blocked her path.

Beyond the vaultlike machine, a strip of restaurants
and bars, bright with neon, veered down a corridor to
the left. To the right zagged a long row of check-in count-
ers with names like Gulfstream, Paradise Island Airways,
AeroJamaica.

She headed for the farthest cubicle, with its blue and
orange Nassau-Air logo. Her heart pounded, but her
stride was steady and her hands did not shake. She had
taken four milligrams of Xanax, which was eight times
her normal dose. She felt at once an intense fear and a
godlike detachment.

Drace said there was the possibility that the bomb
could go off accidentally at any time; she tried not to
think of this. It was like looking down from a dangerous
height and paralyzing oneself with terror.

What if it goes off? she thought bitterly. *My troubles
would be over, wouldn't they?*

Yes. But the job would not be done. Do the job.

The round-faced Hispanic man at the Nassau-Air
counter spoke poor English, seemed bored, and as he
checked her passport, his stomach gave a loud growl.

"Anna Granger," her passport said, "Duluth, Minnesota." The photograph showed her unsmiling, her glasses sitting crookedly on her nose.

Her name was not Anna Granger nor had she ever been in Duluth, Minnesota. Drace had arranged for the passport. Drace had arranged everything. She tried not to think of what was in the leather duffel as the clerk tagged it. She tried not to wince as he threw it unceremoniously on the floor behind him.

I could die right now, she thought. *So could he. I won't think about it. La, la, la.*

"The plane's on time?" she asked, nodding at the flight announcement board.

Nassau-Air Flight 217 was to depart at one-thirty. More than an hour away.

"Won't be boarding till one-twenty," he said, hardly glancing up from his computer screen. He squinted at it with a scholarly air, then, at last, handed her a boarding pass. "All set."

"I've got time to grab a bite of lunch?" she asked brightly.

"What?" He frowned.

"I have time?" she asked. "To go to a restaurant?"

"Oh, yes," he said. To her ears, it sounded as if he said "Oh, jes."

Don't talk any more than you have to, Drace had warned, so she smiled stiffly, adjusted the strap of her oversized handbag, and turned from the counter.

Her knees felt weak and insubstantial, like two bubbles floating beneath her, magically bearing her away. Her head was light, her stomach hollow.

"You're sure you can do this?" Drace had asked. She had seen something like reluctance in his beautiful blue eyes. She'd seen doubt.

"Yes," she'd said. *"I'm sure."*

Now she made her way to the nearest women's rest room. She was grateful to see no maintenance woman. She locked herself into the toilet stall farthest from the entrance and hung her big handbag on the hook inside the door. She took off her glasses, put them inside the purse, and took out the case for her contact lenses.

She removed one colored lens, then the other. "Don't it make my brown eyes blue," she said under her breath.

She snapped the case shut, put it away. As she pulled off the brown wig, she thought of flushing it down the toilet.

But no, Drace had told her not to get rid of anything in Miami. She thrust the wig into a plastic bag and stowed it, too, in the handbag. From the coin purse in her wallet, she took a ring and put it on the third finger of her left hand. It was silver, set with a small greenish turquoise.

She drew out her makeup kit and did her face. She'd always been skilled at makeup, and the transformation took barely five minutes. Foundation, eyebrow pencil, eyeliner, mascara, powder, blusher, lipstick. She worked using only her compact mirror, but her movements were quick and sure.

She pulled off the shapeless silk slacks and tucked them too into the bag. Beneath them she'd worn sky-blue leggings, skintight. She slipped off her tan jacket, turned it inside out, and put it on again. It was now sky-blue and matched the leggings.

She zipped shut the handbag, slid its strap over her shoulder, and opened the door of the stall. She moved to the bank of sinks and washed her hands, examining her image in the mirror. She was a short-haired blonde now, with a Dutch bob and eyes as blue as her jacket.

She studied her makeup critically, the subtle blue eye shadow, the glossy red of her lips. Not perfect, but it would do. She ran a brush through her hair.

When she left the rest room, she headed for the moving walkways that sped passengers from one concourse to another. She traveled until she reached the concourse farthest from Nassau-Air. She went through the security check and quickly made her way to Gate E16.

She arrived at E16 with time to spare and checked in for Flight 458 to Dallas. "Boarding in about thirty-five minutes," said the dark man at the desk.

She nodded. She walked to the nearest pay phone and dialed the Nassau-Air desk. "Is Flight 217 on time?"

"Is right on schedule," said the Hispanic clerk, still sounding bored.

She hung up, went into a neighboring shop, and bought a copy of *Vogue* magazine. She'd once loved *Vogue* and wondered if it would give comfort to her now.

She returned to her gate and sat in one of the plastic chairs. She drew her gold pillbox from her handbag. She took out two more tablets of Xanax and swallowed them dry, not bothering to find a water fountain. She pretended to read the magazine, and she waited.

Five minutes before boarding time, she rose and phoned the Nassau-Air desk again, asking if Flight 217 was still on schedule. The clerk said yes. Again it sounded to her as if he said "Jes."

She returned to her departure gate just as the public-address system announced that the Dallas flight was boarding. She waited until her seat row was announced, then made her way through the boarding corridor with a deceptively light step.

She was traveling coach class and found her seat on the aisle, next to a priest with a clerical collar. The priest gave her a start, and she wondered if his presence was some sort of omen. He looked into her eyes as if it were.

I'm beyond omens, she thought fatalistically. She nodded to him as she sat. *La, la, la.*

The priest was a heavy man with thin hair and a nose full of broken veins. He held a rosary in one hand. "God has to be my copilot. I don't do well flying on my own."

She smiled and fastened her seat belt. She glanced at her watch with seeming nonchalance. It was one thirty-two. Nassau-Air Flight 217 should be taxiing down the runway now, speeding for takeoff.

Her mouth was bone dry, dry as the mouth of a skeleton. Mentally she counted to sixty while beside her the priest seemed to be silently saying his rosary. She thought, *Pray for us sinners now and in the hour of our death.* She did not know how she knew these words. She was not Catholic.

She took a deep breath and stared at the inflight phone on the back of the seat before her. She opened her purse and withdrew the credit card Drace had provided. She put the card into the slot next to the phone, which released the receiver.

"You're making a call?" the priest said, as if she were about to perform a miracle.

"I didn't get a chance to say good-bye to my brother," she said. "He'll be surprised when I phone from here."

"Will wonders never cease?" the priest marveled and watched with interest as she punched in the number she had memorized. For a split second, she wondered if she wanted the plan to work.

Yes, she thought. *Let it work. Let it work.* She listened and waited.

The leather duffel bag should be aboard the Nassau-

Air flight now, and the small plane should be airborne, just barely. Within the duffel bag was a brand-new cellular phone, a blasting cap wired to its ringer terminals.

When the cellular phone rang, the voltage to the terminals would set off the cap and detonate an explosive charge powerful enough to blow Flight 217 to bits, turning it into a giant peony of flame.

If everything went as planned, she would hear only silence from the phone. No ring, only silence.

There was no ring at the other end of the phone.

The priest watched her with interest. In her mind, she heard a ghostly echo, as if from a detonation far away. She wondered if she would hear this echo for the rest of her life.

Her hand steady, she put the phone back in place.

"Nobody home?" the priest asked.

"Nobody home," she said and smiled. She leaned back in her seat.

Now I've murdered, she thought numbly.

She imagined calling Drace from a pay phone in Dallas, although such a thing was forbidden to her. *How many did I kill?* she would ask him if she could.

She imagined him saying, *Everybody. All of them.* But it was, she told herself, only a small plane. A very small plane, after all.

She felt oddly detached. Her head buzzed. *I am damned,* she thought. *La, la, la.*

She opened the copy of *Vogue.*

Eden Storey was a tall, slender woman of thirty-three who had an unusual, but highly marketable, talent.

She had a skilled, versatile voice that could make her sound like a crone, a seductress, an ingenue, or a child.

Although neither her name nor face were famous, most of the public had heard her voice—on radio, television, children's recordings, even in films.

She worked steadily and loved her small town house on the edge of Brentwood. Her life was simple, uncluttered, and it satisfied her.

Today bright California sunshine fell through the glass patio doors of her living room, but Eden didn't notice. She was lost in imaginary snow.

She sat curled up barefoot on her couch. Loose pages of the script and sheet music of *The Snow Queen* lay scattered around her. Frowning in concentration, she pored over the lyrics of "Song of the Northern Lights."

The animation artists would endow the heroine, Gretta, with a face and body; they would draw her fantastical adventures. But it was Eden who would give her a voice.

Gathering up the scattered pages, she rose from the couch. The sunlight glittered on her short brown hair, which was streaked with gold. Her face was too thin for true beauty, but it was an arresting face, full of character. Her eyebrows had an arch that gave her a natural air of skeptical amusement.

She wore faded jeans and a simple shirt of white cotton. Her only jewelry was a pair of diamond ear studs that she had bought for herself.

She tried a few scales, glad that no one was home in the town house next door; she could sing as much and as loudly as she liked. In a voice that she made innocent yet yearning, she began Gretta's theme song:

Roses will grow again,
Winter won't last—

The telephone's discordant ring struck through the melody like a knife, stabbing once, then twice.

She tucked the script under her arm and picked up the receiver. She was certain the caller was her friend Sandy Fogleman, phoning to tell how her audition had gone. Sandy had promised to call at noon, and it was six minutes past.

"Hi," Eden said cheerfully. "How'd it go?"

To her surprise a man replied, a man with a distinctly Southwestern accent.

He said, "Miss Storey, you probably don't remember me. This is Owen Charteris from Endor, Arkansas."

Owen Charteris. She stiffened. The name jogged unpleasant memories. Years ago, in what now seemed like another universe, he'd been a figure of dazzling privilege to her, a handsome golden boy from a very "good" family—unlike hers. Why in God's name would he call her?

Charteris said, "I'm calling about your grandmother."

Eden's thoughts skidded into a wild spin. *My grandmother? What's he got to do with my grandmother?*

"I'm sorry," Charteris said. "She's had an accident. A fall. She's in the hospital. Here in Endor."

Shock flooded her in an icy wave. "An accident? How—bad?"

Once again Charteris said he was sorry, but no emotion seemed to touch his cool drawl. "She has a broken leg and some cuts. She fell down her front stairs, it was a kind of fainting spell. Brought on by your sister. Nobody knows exactly where your sister is—"

He paused. Numbed, Eden stared at the sunshine merrily spilling its gold across the white carpet.

Why was he talking about Mimi? Of course, nobody

knew exactly where Mimi was. Nobody had known for years.

Eden communicated little with her grandmother and not at all with Mimi. Yet the thought of Jessie's accident shocked and bewildered her. Jessie had always seemed immortal to Eden, as indestructible and permanently set in place as the Great Wall of China.

"We need to find your sister," said Owen Charteris. "It's imperative."

My God, Eden thought, *Jessie's hurt so bad she's dying, and they want to get in touch with Mimi. Oh, God. Oh, God.*

"I—I don't know what to say," Eden stammered. "The last I heard she was in Michigan. But she and my grandmother—"

She couldn't finish the sentence. She didn't want to tell Owen Charteris about Mimi's everlasting broken promises and how they had split the family.

"Miss Storey?" he said. "Are you all right?"

Eden closed her eyes, rubbed her hand across the lids. Tension throbbed in her temples, and her body was tight with conflict.

"Is Jessie dying?" she asked. "Is that what you're trying to tell me?"

"No. Not at all. Her condition is good."

Eden caught her breath and held it, her emotions too complex to sort.

Charteris rode on over her silence, and vaguely she realized she disliked his voice. It was too calm. "Your grandmother wants you to please come home," he said. "Those are her own words. She said she needs you."

Eden's defenses, already unsteady, faltered and fell like the stones of a breached wall.

Jessie was frustrating, often impossible, and so proud

she was contemptuous of help. For Jessie to say "Please come home" was as unlikely as the sun rising out of the west.

"She actually said that?" Eden asked. "That she needed me? She *said* that?"

"I went to the hospital with her. We're neighbors, Jessie and I. You might say I'm her landlord."

Eden pressed her fingertips against the drumming pulse in her temple. Charteris was Jessie's landlord? Since when? Jessie had never told her this.

"I'll get there as soon as I can," Eden said, dashing away her tears with the back of her hand. "I'll have to rent a car, mine's in the shop. But if I start this afternoon, I can drive it in—"

"Don't take the time to drive. Fly. The quicker you're here, the better."

Damn! Eden thought in sorrow and guilt. She hated flying. But Jessie wanted her and Jessie needed her, and it was the least that Eden could do.

"All right," she said. "I'll get the first flight out. I'll rent a car there. I need to tell my director, my agent—rehearsals start in two weeks . . ."

She pressed her lips together, forcing herself to be silent. She'd been babbling, thinking aloud.

"I'll pick you up when you get here," the Charteris man said firmly, as if he were used to taking charge of things. "Call me when you know your flight. Have you got a pencil? Take my number."

Dutifully she obeyed, too dazed to resist. She felt as stunned as if someone had struck her on the head with a brick.

"The sooner you're here the better," Charteris told her. "There's the child to think of."

A dark cloud of apprehension rose in Eden's mind.

"Child?" she said, knowing she sounded stupid. "What child?"

For an instant he didn't reply, as if her question surprised him. "Your sister's daughter," he said. "Her six-year-old. Peyton."

Child? Eden thought in disbelief. *Child?*

"A child? Why does Jessie have her?"

"Mimi's child," he said coolly. "She sent her to Jessie. Today. We don't know why."

Oh, Jesus, Mimi, what have you gone and done this time?

"Sent her? I don't understand."

"We don't, either. Maybe I'll know more by the time you get here."

"This child—where is she?"

"I've got her," Charteris said. "My sister's helping me, but she can't stay past tomorrow morning. The sooner you get here, the better for the kid. She's shaken by all this. She doesn't understand, either."

"Of course," Eden said mechanically. But she felt as if a second brick had struck her. She'd known nothing about a child—nothing. Had Jessie known? If she had, for God's sake, why hadn't she told Eden?

She didn't realize she'd let the script of *The Snow Queen* slip from her fingers. The pages lay in a drift of white about her as if she stood barefoot in an icy drift of snow.

"Call me as soon as you know your flight number," the man ordered.

"Certainly," Eden said. She hung up, too stunned to say good-bye or thank you.

"A child," she muttered to herself in disbelief. "Mimi has a child."

•   •   •   •

Owen Charteris hung up the hospital pay phone.

With a sigh, he sagged against the wall and tiredly rubbed his knuckles across his jaw. He was a tall, lean man of forty with prematurely gray hair and ice-blue eyes.

Nightmares of Laurie had wakened him shortly after midnight last night; he hadn't gone back to sleep. He'd stayed up, drinking black coffee and gazing into the rainy darkness.

Now he glanced at his watch and set his jaw. He leaned back his head and stared at the sterile white ceiling of the hallway. Under his breath, he cursed.

Three years ago to the day, almost to the very hour, his wife had died in this hospital. Three years ago, shortly after two in the afternoon, Laurie Anne Charteris had been pronounced dead.

Now by some obscene coincidence, he was here again, where she had slipped away from him forever. Christ, he was tired of death.

At least tough old Jessie Buddress was going to make it. It would take more than a broken leg and mere bruises and contusions to stop the life force that was Jessie.

Her prodigal granddaughter Mimi was another matter; wherever the hell Mimi was, she was probably in trouble.

The woman who'd brought the child, Peyton, to Jessie's house had been tight-lipped to the point of rudeness. She'd handed Jessie an envelope in which there was a one-sentence note from Mimi: "Please take care of my baby."

There was also a copy of Peyton Storey's birth certificate. Her birthplace was Holland, Michigan. Her father was listed as "Unknown," and the kid herself was stubbornly not talking. She seemed afraid.

Where in hell had Mimi been for the last seven years? And what in hell had she been up to? He'd asked the police to work on it, but they had no zeal for it; it was not a high-priority case.

In the meantime, he was stuck with Mimi's bastard kid. Back at Jessie's place, his sister was holding the fort, taking care of her. Thank God Shannon had been in town, thank God she could stay for at least one night, and thank God she, not he, was dealing with the kid.

Owen couldn't help himself; he avoided children, and from the start he hadn't been able to take to this one. With her ageless eyes and unsmiling expression, she reminded him of some hobgoblin child out of a Stephen King novel.

The first time he had seen her was late this morning. He'd been walking the dog past Jessie's house, when, frantic, Jessie had called him in, and there, inside, was the source of her dismay—the kid.

The kid had a thick mop of black hair and oversized hoop earrings of fake gold. She'd given him a long, somber, dark-eyed stare. Without taking her thumb from her mouth, she announced, "Your dog is dying."

Owen had felt his lip curl in distaste. He didn't answer her, but he'd looked down at the old dog. It had been Laurie's when they married, only a pup then.

During Laurie's final illness, she worried obsessively about the dog. Owen had promised her he'd always take care of it. But the dog was sixteen years old now and dying of old age: instinctively the kid had known.

The child's innocently cruel words echoed in his ears: "Your dog is dying."

Yeah, kid. Right. Go to hell. If the child hadn't been connected to Jessie, he never would have volunteered to watch over her. As much as he despised the hospital, he found himself strangely reluctant to go back to Jessie's house, his sister, and the child.

He shoved himself away from the wall and strode down the hall to Jessie's room. The old woman thought that the stranger who'd dropped Peyton off had Missouri plates on her car; she had been rattled, but she was observant as hell.

Jessie lay propped up in bed, her leg elevated and encased in white. She was seventy-one years old, a big woman, and she had a badly bruised nose, a bandage on her cheek, and three stitches in her forehead from the accident.

Her dander was up, because she'd been told she'd need to stay in the hospital at least nine days—her fracture was that serious. Even though her body was battered, her spirit was defiant, and her voice was still strong and hauntingly sonorous. "Did you get hold of Eden?" she asked.

"She's flying in as soon as she can," Owen said.

He thought he saw an expression of relief in Jessie's eyes, but she thrust her chin up and looked as if she weren't surprised. She made her living as a psychic, a phone psychic primarily, and seldom admitted to being surprised by anything.

How she would rationalize Peyton's unexpected appearance or her own accident he had yet to hear, but he knew she would have an explanation, mystical or practical or both, and she wouldn't back down from it.

With a shaky hand, she took a sealed envelope from her bedside table and held it toward him. "Give this to Eden when she comes."

Owen nodded and thrust the envelope into the pocket of his nylon jacket.

"She ain't going to be happy when she reads it," Jessie warned in her sibyl's voice.

Owen raised a dark brow and gave her a questioning look.

"She'd never come if she knowed the whole truth up front," Jessie said darkly.

She gave Owen a sharp look. She had strangely colored eyes; he could never put a name to what color they were.

"The whole truth?" he asked. "What's the whole truth? That you'd been worried about Mimi? About those calls lately?"

She ignored the question. "Did you tell her what I said? That I wanted her? That I needed her?"

"Yes," Owen answered, suddenly wondering what secrets lay beneath those simple words.

"Well, that's truth enough," Jessie said. "She'll probably raise hell. She usually does. Pay her no mind."

He had misgivings, but he said nothing. "When you go home," she said, "I want you to unplug my business phone line."

Owen nodded. "I'll do it."

"And don't let Peyton in my office," ordered Jessie. "She's too curious by a damn sight."

"I'll lock the door."

"Have you seen that new doctor?" Jessie demanded. "He come walking in here with a can of RC Cola in his hand, wearing jeans. He looks twelve years old. He asked me about my *ovaries*. I said, 'You tend my leg, not my private parts.'"

Owen patted Jessie's thick hand. "Be nice. Maybe they'll give you time off for good behavior."

Jessie's expression changed. She gave him a wary

glance. "It's good of you to watch out for Peyton. I know it's hard for you. That you don't take to children."

He shrugged one shoulder. "It's not for long. Your granddaughter'll be here soon. She'll take care of everything."

Jessie crossed her arms. She gave him a curt nod. "She better," she said, a hard glint in her eye.

TWO

~~~~~

Eden's commuter flight to Endor was not only late, it hit turbulence, which soon mixed with a witch's brew of lightning and violent rain.

The plane made a particularly nasty lurch, and the woman behind Eden started to weep, plea-bargaining with God. Eden hung on to the arms of her seat, gritting her teeth and vowing to be brave. She sang under her breath.

Then a blinding bolt of lightning turned the air of the cabin a crackling blue, thunder shook the fuselage, and she bit her lip so hard it bled.

Eden crushed a paper airline napkin against her mouth. *No more singin' in the rain,* she thought miserably and wondered if they all were doomed. But at last, as the flight approached Endor, the tempest gentled into mere autumn rain.

The plane landed on a wet black strip that shimmered with rainbow reflections of the airport's lights. When Eden descended the narrow steps, her knees were still jellied, her stomach still queasy.

The sky was pitch-black, and the thin, steady rain chilled her as she crossed the tarmac, lugging her carry-on bag. It was three-thirty in the morning, and she felt like very hell.

She pushed open the glass doors into the terminal and wondered, dimly, if Owen Charteris had kept his promise to meet her. She hoped not; she was in no mood to be grateful.

But almost immediately she heard a male drawl that she recognized as his. "Miss Storey?"

She looked up and was taken aback to see a tall, lean man with jutting cheekbones. His hair was thick and silver-gray now instead of brown. He was unsmiling, and a frown line was etched between his dark brows. He was taller than she remembered.

She was jolted by the surprise that, after all these years, she recognized him: the startling blue eyes, the high-bridged nose, the angular line of his jaw. He'd been a handsome bastard all those years ago; he still was, perhaps even more so.

"Owen Charteris," she said numbly, without pleasure.

"Welcome back to Endor." His tone sounded sardonic.

She was too shaken to exchange pleasantries, even false ones, and could think of no reply.

He said, "Maybe 'welcome' is the wrong word."

He reached to take her carry-on. She clutched it

more tightly and eyed him suspiciously. "You turned gray," she accused, as if he'd committed some sort of betrayal.

What a stupid thing to say, she thought, but she found herself focusing on his gray hair, as if it were a fascinating illusion. The golden boy had become a silver man, and her words had simply tumbled out.

A cold smirk flickered at the corner of his mouth. "Thanks for pointing it out. Do you want to give me that bag or do we keep fighting over it?"

"I can carry it," she protested, drawing back. It was as if by keeping hold of the bag she could keep a grip on herself as well.

He shrugged as if he didn't care. He was dressed casually, Arkansas style. His faded jeans were not designer jeans, his cowboy boots were scuffed from use, and he wore a belt with a silver buckle shaped like a coiled rattlesnake.

How Freudian, Eden thought sarcastically. Yet she was surprised and displeased to feel a tremor of sexual awareness run through her. Guiltily, she willed it to go away, and it almost did.

He had the Charteris family height and leanness, and the Charteris air of ironic detachment. She stared at him rather defensively, as if he were a prize exhibit in the museum of a past she'd tried to forget.

The high school hero's grown up and gone gray, she thought. *And Mimi's left her child on Jessie's doorstep, and Jessie's in the hospital—*

The thoughts of Mimi and Jessie struck her anew, driving all her other crazy thoughts away. She grasped her carry-on more tightly. "Has anybody heard anything about Mimi?"

"Nothing," he said.

Her throat tightened. "What about my grand-mother? Should I go see her right now?"

Without emotion he looked her up and down. "I'll take you if you want. But it wouldn't do any good. And frankly, you look green around the gills. Maybe you should rest."

She brushed a strand of damp hair from her eyes and forced herself to stand straighter. "Jessie—how is she?"

"Asleep. They gave her a sedative. She was raising hell."

Imagine that, Eden thought wearily, but said nothing.

"Who gave you the split lip?" he asked.

"God," she said.

"Rough flight?" he asked in his laconic way.

"My life only passed before my eyes two or three hundred times."

He seemed to try to smile again, but his mouth only twisted slightly. "I'll take you home, give you a drink."

"I don't drink," she said more sharply than she meant.

She thought she tasted blood in her mouth again, but ignored it. Lord, she was tired, but she had to keep her priorities straight. "How's the child? Mimi's daughter?"

For some reason mention of the child wiped the forced smile from his face. He looked downright grim. "We finally got her to sleep. You'll see her in the morning."

His words sounded more like threat than promise. She struggled to muster up a modicum of politeness and said, "You and your wife, it's very good of you to take care of the child. Very kind."

His eyes weren't kind. They were the cold blue of ice. "My sister," he said. "Not my wife."

He bit the words off so acrimoniously that Eden sensed she'd made some sort of inexcusable blunder. "I'm sorry," she said, not knowing what she was supposed to be sorry for.

His expression didn't change, but something in his mien had gone harsh, even more aloof than before. He said, "On the phone, you sounded surprised when I mentioned the kid. You didn't know about her?"

Eden made a gesture of frustration. "No. It's a long story. No. I didn't know about the child. That sounds terrible, I know, but it's—a family matter."

"Yes," he said. "It is. That's one reason Jessie wants you here. To take care of the kid. She's not going to be up and around for a while."

Eden's jaw dropped in surprise. "She wants me here for *that*? My God, I don't know anything about children. I've never been around them. I hardly remember *being* one."

"Me, either," he said. "But she's all yours now."

She stared at him aghast, not wanting to understand the full import of his words. "W-why," she stammered, "did this happen? Why did Mimi send this—child?"

"It's a family matter," he said, echoing her words. "I don't know. But Jessie's been nervous lately about Mimi."

She swallowed hard. "Nervous? Why?"

His eyes held hers. "She thinks she's in trouble. It involves some calls Jessie's been getting. I don't have all the details."

"Trouble? With the law?"

"I don't know."

Hellfire on a stick, Eden thought. *What now?*

Owen Charteris raised his brows in an expression that might have been sympathy or merely resignation. "Did you have luggage checked aboard?" he asked.

She nodded. "If it didn't get thrown out for ballast."

"Why don't you go clean up," he said. "You've got blood on your lip and your blouse. I'll wait for your luggage. It won't be here, but I'll check for it."

"Won't be here? Why?"

"It'll be lost," he said matter-of-factly. "Luggage coming to Endor always gets lost. We're sort of the Devil's Triangle that way."

"Devil's Triangle," muttered Eden. "That's how I remember it, all right."

If he felt she had insulted his hometown, he didn't show it. He gazed toward the luggage carousel, as if it were far more interesting than she was.

Absently he reached into the pocket of his windbreaker. "Jessie wrote a note. I'll let you read it in private. The ladies' room is that way."

Not bothering to look at her, he offered her a somewhat crumpled envelope. She took it reluctantly, careful not to let her fingers touch his. A queer sense of foreboding twisted in the pit of her stomach.

Inside the rest room, she couldn't bring herself to open the envelope immediately. She set it on the shelf over the row of sinks and stared at herself in the mirror.

Sleeplessness had carved dark circles under her eyes. Her skin was pallid, and her lower lip was as swollen as if a wasp had stung her. The front of her silk blouse was flecked with the scarlet of her own finely spattered blood.

So what? she thought, splashing cold water on her

face. She was back again in this despised town, supposed to baby-sit a niece she hadn't known existed until this morning, and so far her only ally in this mess was Smiley out there, the patron saint of lost luggage, who seemed bitter over something, possibly everything.

She washed her face, brushed her limp hair, and halfheartedly applied a swipe of lipstick to her upper lip. She didn't bother trying to clean the blouse, it was ruined, she knew.

Full of a sense of impending disaster, she forced herself to pick up Jessie's note and open it. From childhood she remembered that Jessie didn't write greetings or endearments; she wrote orders, made pronouncements, issued proclamations.

The paper glared yellowy beneath the flicker of the fluorescent lights. Eden read Jessie's familiar scrawled misspellings with growing disbelief and distress.

I have never askt you for help or Money and I aint about to do it now but what I askt is you do your Duty. Blood is thicker than water.

I need you do two thing for me. One you take Care of that Baby. Its the leest you can do for your Sister.

Two you take Care of my phone Bidness until I get Home and to do it myself. You know how to do it and you are the Only one who can. Its the leest you can do for Me and I dont askt no more of you than That.

My list of Steddy Callers in the file box. Tarot and such is in rite desk drawer. It hurts my heart to know my callers is trying to get to me and can not do it. It is like watching Money

wash down the sink. Now you hook up fast as
possbel. There is more I will tell you latter.
                    Your Grandmother Jessie Maye Buddress
                    God's gifted Spiritual Adviser

Anger rose in Eden like a jet of lava. This was why Jessie
wanted her? This was why she *needed* her?

Watching over Mimi's daughter was one thing—
Eden even felt a certain reluctant responsibility for the
child.

But Jessie had spent over half the note detailing how
she wanted Eden to take charge of the damned psychic
hot line—because money was going down the drain.
Money! No mention at all that Mimi might be in some
sort of trouble.

Eden resisted the desire to rip the note to shreds and
flush it down a toilet. For somebody who was supposed
to be "sensitive"—endowed with psychic powers—Jessie
was the most insensitive creature Eden knew. No wonder
she had driven off first her daughter, then both grand-
daughters.

Yet at the same time, a sickening sensation contracted Eden's stomach, worse than any the pitching
plane had caused. She *did* owe Jessie. If she was honest, it
always came down to that: she owed Jessie a great deal.

Jessie had lived by her wits alone, but she'd managed
to raise Eden and Mimi. "I take care of my own," she'd
always said, and she'd done exactly that.

She loved money because she'd known poverty and
feared it with all her heart. Security was as precious to
her as life's blood, and she was fiercely proud of her
work, questionable as Eden found it.

Her trade demanded a bold mix of intuition, observation, guile, and pure chutzpah. She was good at it,

damned good. And she was right: no one could replace her—except Eden.

Eden could imitate Jessie's voice to perfection, and Jessie had made her learn the fortune-teller's trade. Eden could so expertly impersonate Jessie on the phone that no one could tell the difference.

She had done it twice in high school, once when Jessie had suffered complications from a gallbladder operation and again when she'd had surgery on her hand.

Back then, Jessie had simply ordered her to take over the phone business; they had to have money, and Eden did as she was told. She'd hated every duplicitous moment, and she had hated Jessie for making her do it.

She clearly remembered the hate—and humiliation, as well. Being Jessie's granddaughter was not easy. Jessie was different from other people, not merely eccentric, but flamboyantly so. She could be loud and bossy and full of embarrassing pretension.

Yet Eden could also remember being eleven years old and waking up with an earache so agonizing that she was helpless to do anything except cry. Jessie stayed up and held her in her arms all night long, trying to comfort her.

Jessie had nursed Eden and Mimi through croup and flu and chicken pox. Somehow she'd found the money to get braces put on Mimi's teeth, and, although she'd grumbled endlessly, she'd paid for Eden's voice lessons. And Eden had often grudgingly admitted to herself that she loved Jessie.

She'd loved and hated her, a hopeless, helpless mix. In California she had thought she'd left Jessie far behind, but now she realized that she hadn't. The old woman could still exasperate her and make her dizzy with guilt.

She reread Jessie's words.

". . . you take Care of my phone Bidness until I get

Home and to do it myself. You know how to do it and you are the Only one who can. Its the leest you can do for Me and I dont askt no more of you than That."

Tears of frustration sprang into her eyes. "Dammit, Jessie," she whispered through her teeth.

Once again she tasted blood in her mouth like an omen.

By some sort of cosmic accident, the woman's luggage had arrived. Owen had thought the probability of this to be on a par with the sky raining goldfish, but her bags heaved into view on the creaking carousel. A suitcase, not weighing much, and a suitbag. She didn't plan on staying long, obviously.

This actress wasn't what he'd pictured. She wasn't glamorous, she wasn't even blond. Her brown hair was boyishly short, and she wore little makeup. But she was slim and trim and pretty in a fox-faced sort of way. She also had an air of razor-sharp intelligence, which was the last thing he'd expected.

Now she came bursting out of the rest room, and she had fire in her eye. For the first time she looked as if she were related to Jessie, all right.

She stalked up to him and waved the envelope at him. "Do you know what this says?" she demanded.

"No," he said, and he didn't care. He was tired of trouble. It had taken him and his sister until two in the morning to get Peyton to sleep. Now Shannon was passed out on Jessie's bed, and he himself hadn't slept for twenty hours.

"She hardly mentions my sister," Eden said. "She's not that concerned about my sister's *child*. She wants me to take over her damned phone business."

He was vaguely surprised, but he only shrugged. He noticed the longer he looked at her, the prettier she seemed, so he stopped looking. "Is this all your luggage?"

She ignored him. "I came all the way from Los Angeles to read tarot cards over the phone? What's she thinking of?"

He picked up the luggage. "She's built herself up a tidy little business. It's about all she's got."

Eden's eyes flashed. "I don't want any part of it."

"I've got nothing to do with it," he said, and headed for the doors to the parking lot.

"I've got a mind to get back on a plane and go home," she threatened, but she followed him.

"You're forgetting about the kid," he said. "I like Jessie, but I'm not a baby-sitter. The job is yours."

She seized him by the elbow, trying to slow him. "Mine? I could hire somebody who could do a better job than I can. I could have done that by *phone.*"

Her touch startled him, came close to disturbing him. But he was in no mood to argue, so he shook off her hand and walked on. "I see it as a family matter," he said.

He shouldered the door open and held it for her. The rain had weakened into a cold, clinging mist. She swept outside, her head held high. "What about this child? Who's her father?"

"Ask Jessie," Owen said. Jessie was the one who'd been sent the birth certificate, not him.

"Does *she* know?"

"You'll have to ask her," he said shortly.

"Oh, hell," she said, her shoulders sagging again.

Owen thought she suspected the child was illegitimate, but he didn't intend to be the one who told her.

He led Eden to his black Blazer, unlocked the

hatchback, pushed his hunting paraphernalia aside, and pitched her bags inside.

She shivered and said, "It seems wrong that a child's mixed up in this."

"But there is," he said, "and she's a handful. You're welcome to her."

He held the door open for her on the passenger side, but she only stood staring up at him. "What do you mean, she's a handful?"

"I mean she's a handful," he said. "Get in, will you? It's wet out here."

Eden got into the car, and when he slid in beside her, she gave him a pointed look. "You're telling me that Mimi's child has a behavior problem?"

He switched on the ignition, turned on the windshield wipers. "Her name," he said, "is Peyton. She marches to a different drummer."

"Oh, great," Eden said. "A different drummer. Why do I sense volumes of trouble in that phrase?"

She put her hand to her eyes, rubbed them tiredly. "I'm sorry," she said. "I shouldn't be sniping at you. This is between Jessie and me."

"Yes," he said. "It is." He was uncomfortably aware of her nearness.

She kept her hand over her eyes. "I suppose she's terribly upset over this. God. What a mess."

He glanced at her, was vaguely surprised at how vulnerable she looked. "She's having trouble admitting how much it bothers her," he said quietly.

Eden shook her head. "This child—when did she get here? How? Can't you tell me anything?"

He sighed tiredly and brushed his knuckle against the cleft in his chin. "Jessie didn't know the kid existed. Yesterday morning a woman knocked at her door. She had the kid by one hand, a beat-up suitcase in the other. She pushes them both toward Jessie. 'This is your grand-daughter's girl,' she says. 'Mimi's girl, Peyton. Take her. She's your responsibility, not mine.' "

Eden's hand dropped from her eyes. She stared at him, shock in her expression. "Just like that?"

He nodded. "Just like that. She handed Jessie a note from Mimi saying to take care of the kid—that's all. Then she got in her car and drove away."

"But my God," she said. "Who was she?"

"She wouldn't say."

"But if she had a car, she had a license plate—"

"Jessie's in shock. The kid's in tears. Jessie thought the plate was from Missouri—she's fairly sure; it was muddied."

"Deliberately?"

"Very probably."

Eden sighed in exasperation. "What kind of car?"

"Hell," Owen said, "Jessie doesn't know cars. It was blue. A blue car. That's all she or Peyton could say."

"Did the woman say anything else, anything at all?"

He rubbed his burning eyes. "That she didn't want any part of the mess. That she refused to be involved."

"Mess," Eden repeated miserably. "Mess! What the hell's Mimi gone and done now?"

"Hell would probably be a good place to look for an answer to that."

She gave him an irritable glance. He shrugged and started the motor.

"What about Jessie's accident?" she demanded. "How did *that* happen? A comet dropped out of the sky and hit her? It was just generally a bad day?"

The windshield wipers made their monotonous, melancholy sound. He backed out of the parking space.

"The kid arrived at about ten in the morning," he said. "I wasn't around. Later I was walking the dog, and Jessie yelled at me to come in. She was upset."

"Well, naturally she was upset," Eden countered. "But what *happened* to her?"

"I told her we should go to a lawyer. I called one. I went back to my place to lock up the dog. I drove up just as they were coming out of the house. Jessie just swayed and fell. The kid got pretty upset."

"But did she faint—or what?" Eden persisted.

He shook his head. "The doctors aren't sure. She's got high blood pressure. Maybe she fainted, maybe just got dizzy, maybe it was a small stroke."

"A stroke?" Eden echoed, horrified.

"Her mind seems fine," he said. "Sharp as ever, if that's what you're worried about. Her leg got the worst of it. It's a serious injury for a woman her age. But she's strong. Very strong."

"Yes," she said tonelessly. Then she covered her eyes again. "Mimi," she said in a weary voice.

They drove the rest of the way in silence. When he pulled up in the drive, she dropped her hand and stared dully at the little white house. At first, it seemed to sit alone, surrounded by the darkness of the woods, but then, through the rain, she saw another, taller house a hundred yards distant, almost hidden by the trees.

"It's a nice place," she said, looking at the little house. "Jessie's finally done well for herself. You live around here, too?"

He nodded. He remembered when Jessie had lived in a sorry, rusted-out trailer on the edge of town. It was, he supposed, where Eden and Mimi had grown up. He had given Jessie a break on the rent for this house. Jessie didn't know, and her granddaughter didn't need to know, either.

The rain had started to come down in earnest again. "Come in and take a look at your niece," he said.

"Peyton?" she said, as if trying to convince herself the child was real and had a real name.

"Yeah," he said. "Peyton."

THREE

~~~~~

SOMETHING UNCUSTOMARY TRIED TO TUG EDEN FROM THE safety of her dreamless sleep, but she was not ready to waken.

Everything was normal, fine, and warm. Polonius, Ted's cat, curled up next to her, his silky hair tickling her chin.

"Bad cat, Polonius," she muttered. "Move."

No.

This could not be Polonius. Eden had parted amicably with Ted months ago. He was gone and had taken the cat with him.

She was not even home in California, she was in Arkansas. Jessie had sent for her because there had been an accident. Jessie was hurt, and Mimi couldn't be found, which was important because—

Eden's eyes snapped open. What was in bed with her was a *child*. She tensed, automatically drawing away from the alien touch. Rising on her elbow, she stared down.

The little girl slept with her thumb securely in her mouth, and her hair was a wild tumble of curls, black as ink. Her lashes and eyebrows were just as midnight dark, the brows drawn together in a sleeping frown. She wore large gold hoop earrings that seemed too adult for her. This dark, exotic child was Mimi's daughter. Peyton.

Last night the child had been sleeping soundly in the room's other twin bed. Eden, still shaken from her flight, had stared at her numbly, too exhausted for emotion. All she could think was, *She doesn't look like Mimi.*

Eden had undressed, clambered into her well-worn nightshirt, and collapsed into the scratchy, lavender-scented sheets. Sometime during the early hours of the morning, the child must have climbed into bed with her.

Now Peyton sighed in her sleep and her mouth twitched restlessly around her thumb. She frowned harder. Eden found herself oddly touched and saddened by this childish frown. Did the girl know why Mimi had abandoned her? Was she frightened? Homesick? Sorrowing?

Tentatively, almost against her will, Eden touched the little girl's face, brushing an errant curl from her cheek. "You need a haircut, kid," she whispered softly.

She was startled by the slow, almost surreptitious opening of the bedroom door. Turning from Peyton, she looked up in alarm at the lean face of Owen Charteris.

A lock of pewter-colored hair fell across his forehead. With his right hand he tucked his blue work shirt into the front of his jeans, as if he had just thrown on his clothes.

His hair might have turned gray, but his body still

looked hard and tautly muscled, and under his dark brows, his eyes were ice-blue. His wide shoulders seemed to fill the doorway.

"Your grandmother's phoned twice," he said quietly.

Eden suppressed a groan, rose higher on her elbow, and held up her wrist to see her watch. It was nearly ten.

"Oh, rats," she muttered inelegantly. "She's probably wondering where I am."

"Yes," he said. "She is." He gave her a measuring look, his eyes lingering without expression on her breasts.

Eden glanced sleepily down at herself and was shocked to see that she hadn't bothered to button her nightshirt; her breasts were half-exposed.

She clutched the shirt's front together, rebelliously thinking, *So he got an eyeful—he couldn't have enjoyed it. I must look like a Gorgon. He should have turned into stone.*

"You could have knocked," she said coolly.

He shrugged. "I didn't want to wake you. Or the kid. Get dressed and I'll take you to the hospital. Jessie wants me to bring her some things. My sister can baby-sit, but she has to leave by afternoon."

She clutched her nightshirt together more tightly. "How's Jessie?"

"The same," he said with no emotion.

Eden forced her gaze to fall back to Peyton, who frowned more worriedly in her sleep. The child was warm and pink-cheeked, her upper lip slightly sweaty. She stirred drowsily and snuggled nearer to Eden, sucking her thumb harder.

She smoothed the child's tumbled hair again. "What am I going to do with you?" she breathed.

•   •   •

The rain hadn't ceased. It drizzled down from a gray sky so bleak that it seemed designed to mock the brightness of the yellowing leaves.

Thank God for Shannon, Owen thought as he drove Eden to the hospital. This morning his sister had bustled quietly around Jessie's house, putting things in order, brewing coffee, and packing a suitcase for Jessie. Most important, she had made comforting small talk with Eden Storey.

Owen had lost any talent he'd ever had for small talk. His ability to comfort a stranger had long ago dried up like a dead thing, turned to dust, and blown away.

Shannon knew this. She had kept up a stream of chatter that was amiable, practical, and just sympathetic enough. She was as smart as she was tactful and had avoided the most difficult subjects facing the Storey woman.

The most difficult, damn it, was the question Eden had whispered to Peyton in the bedroom, the question he didn't know how to answer: *What am I going to do with you?*

He could tell by the expression on Eden's face that she was deeply troubled. She stared numbly at the windshield wipers as they carved their glassy portal into the rain.

When he stopped at a red light, Eden gave an almost imperceptible sigh. He rubbed the cleft in his chin and stole a sideways glance at her.

He wished like hell he hadn't caught that lovely chance glimpse of her breasts this morning. The sight had given him an unexpected twitch of hardness in the groin.

She had a good body: long-legged with flaring hips, a trim waist, and flat stomach. Her breasts were well

shaped and firm, and her white sweater clung subtly to
their thrust.

She was simply dressed in the sweater and a pair of
gray slacks and black low-heeled shoes. Her only jewelry
was a pair of diamond ear studs, and she wore little
makeup. Her lower lip was still slightly swollen and
looked tender.

He felt an unbidden and unwelcome stirring of desire and, almost simultaneously, a sick wave of guilt. He
was trying to get through the anniversary of his wife's
death. Goddamn and double goddamn and triple goddamn the stirring of any hard-on for this anxious
stranger.

He allowed himself a grim moment of self-loathing.
Then he forced away all thought of Eden Storey's disturbing breasts and her tender mouth.

He pushed away any sympathy for her, as well. Sympathy was for people who had emotion to spare. He had
none. But he would warn her of some unpleasant facts
before they caught her off guard. He could do that much.

He said, "I filed a missing person's report on Mimi.
Jessie asked me to. The police haven't found her but
they've found out things about her. She's got a record."

Eden turned to face him with an abrupt jerk. He
read dismay in her eyes. "A record?"

He kept his voice harsh, as noncommittal as he
could. "Hot checks, petty theft, passing stolen goods. Jessie doesn't know all this yet."

Eden stared at him, her lips parted as if she wanted
to speak but had no words.

He set his jaw and squinted through the rain. He'd
been around long enough to know some people were
born to trouble, and Mimi was one. He said, "She did a

stint in prison, too. Two years in Michigan. Jessie doesn't know that, either."

From the corner of his eye, he saw Eden flinch as if she'd been struck. "Prison?" she asked tightly. "What for?"

"She got mixed up with a guy who dealt in stolen guns. And drugs. She apparently did a pretty good job of frying her brains."

"Oh, hell," Eden said miserably and dragged her hand through her bangs. Mimi had once had intelligence and talent to burn, and she had burned it. Eden stared at the windshield wipers as if they might hypnotize her into a better, more sensible world.

Slowly she said, "If she was locked up for two years, where was Peyton?"

"A foster home. Some people in Holland, Michigan, named DeBeck."

"But when was this? How old was Peyton?"

"Six weeks when the DeBecks took her. She was a little over two when Mimi got out. Mimi took care of her awhile, then gave her up to another foster family. Named Murdoch."

Eden's face tautened. He thought he saw a tear rise and glitter like a shard of glass, but she blinked it back. "Why did she give her up again? Didn't she want to be tied down?"

"She claimed a welfare counselor pressured her into doing it. Within the year, she wanted Peyton back."

Eden muttered something under her breath.

He shrugged. "It seemed to be her pattern. She wanted the kid. She didn't want her. Different excuses. Once a bad car accident."

"Had she been drinking?" Eden asked, her jaw

tensed. Mimi's addictions had finally driven the splitting wedge between them.

He nodded. "Then one day, two years ago, she said she and Peyton were going to Wisconsin, for the weekend. They never came back. Nobody knows where they went."

"How hard did they try to find out?" Eden challenged.

"Probably not too hard. That's how it goes."

"That's how it goes," she echoed bitterly.

He adjusted the windshield wipers to their highest speed. It was raining like a very bastard now.

Eden's body looked as tense as a tautly drawn bow. "So now what happens?"

"The police keep trying. But they won't try hard. The case isn't urgent. It'll get swept under the rug."

She turned to face him. "How do you know so much about what the police think?"

"I used to be with them," he said tonelessly. "Detective. State police."

"Oh." Then she brightened. "What about Peyton? What does she say? Didn't you ask her about Mimi? About the woman who brought her here?"

"Of course I asked her. She won't answer any questions about her mother. Or the past."

"Not at all? But why?"

He didn't like telling her this part, so he said it bluntly, with nothing to soften the blow. "She says she's not supposed to talk. She says if she does, somebody will come hurt her, kill her."

"*What?*" Eden demanded, clearly horrified. "Why would she even think such a thing?"

He pulled into the lot of the hospital, put the car into park, and pocketed the keys. He gave her a level look, taking in her pale face, her bewildered blue-green eyes, her swollen, very, very tender-looking lip.

"She's probably saying what your sister told her to."

She looked more stricken than before. "My God, what was Mimi mixed up in? She couldn't believe that—could she?"

He said, "I've got no idea what was going on in your sister's life or in her mind. And neither does your grandmother. None."

When Eden had been a child, Dr. Dennis Vandeering had seemed impossibly ancient to her, a white-haired old man on the brink of senility or death.

But neither death nor dementia had yet claimed him. Small, wizened, troll-like, his dark eyes were magnified by his thick glasses until they looked like toy, oversized eyes. His white hair was sparse, his face carved by wrinkles, but his teeth, which were large, perfect, and artificial, gleamed almost luminously.

He took Eden's hand in his own, which was small and monkeylike. "So," he said, his magnified eyes widening, "little Eden Storey. All grown-up. Ha. Ha. Ha."

Eden could not even try to force a smile. "Yes," she said. "I remember you."

His leathery little fingers curled around hers. His huge teeth gleamed. "I took your little appendix out. Ha."

"What about my grandmother?" she said tightly.

The smile slowly died. "Her leg's badly broken. At her age, that's serious. Also, her blood pressure's high."

Eden's composure fluttered unsteadily for a moment.

"Now," Vandeering said, his fingers playing over hers. "Are you ready to see her?"

Eden drew back her hand, squared her shoulders. "Yes."

"You don't need to steel yourself, my dear. She's her old self completely. Ha."

Ha, indeed, thought Eden. *Her old self is what worries me. Her old self is hell on wheels. With fuel injection.*

"I know this is difficult," Vandeering said. "Would you like someone to go with you? Me? Mr. Charteris?"

The doctor's tiny hand was on her shoulder now, massaging and plucking at the fabric of her sweater. Owen stood discreetly apart, leafing through an old copy of *People.* Now his blue eyes met hers and held them.

"I—I—" Eden stammered. She meant to say she'd go alone, but the words would not come out.

Owen set down the magazine and came to her side. He put his hand on the small of her back. Her skin prickled strangely, as if in warning.

"I'll take you to the room," Owen said.

Together they walked down the hall, breathing its antiseptic air. Eden had forgotten how much she hated hospitals, their quiet, nervous atmosphere. Memories of Jessie and Mimi swarmed through her mind with almost supernatural clarity.

She remembered Mimi, six years old, lying in the dirt under the chinaberry bush, crying because she had just learned their mother had died. She remembered herself crawling in after her, holding her in her arms, trying to comfort her, but crying, too.

She remembered Jessie coming for them, taking them from Little Rock by bus, clear up to the north of the state and the strange town of Endor. Mimi burst into tears the first time she saw Jessie's run-down, rusting trailer house. *"I can't live here!"* she'd wailed. *"Don't make me live here!"*

So many memories—Mimi laughing, giggling, smiling, crying. Mimi singing her heart out, off-key, to a pretend microphone, imagining she was a country-western star. Mimi and Jessie, clashing like Titans, over and over again.

Eden's knees began to feel shaky, insubstantial. A hard knot formed in her throat, threatening to choke off her breath. And then she found herself standing outside Jessie's hospital room.

"Go in without me," Owen said. "I'll join you after you've had time to talk."

He dropped his hand from her back and stepped away from her. With a pang, she realized she didn't want him to leave. He handed her the valise his sister had packed.

As she took it from him, nervousness teased through her system, stinging and unpleasant. She hadn't seen Jessie face-to-face for fifteen years.

She took a deep breath, rapped at the frame of the open door for the sake of politeness, then entered. She said, "Hello, Jessie. I'm sorry I wasn't here sooner. I got in late last night."

Jessie sat propped up in bed watching a soap opera on television. Her leg was elevated and in a white cast. Slowly, like a queen, she turned her head to look at Eden. She had bandages over her nose and on both cheekbones and stitches in her forehead, but they did not make her look pathetic or silly. She seemed somehow more formidable.

Jessie was a large woman, five foot seven and weighing almost two hundred pounds. She wore a hearing aid in her left ear. Her iron-gray hair was swept up in an elaborate crown of braids, and she had a broad, strong face, unremarkable except for her eyes.

Jessie had raised Eden, but to this day Eden couldn't say what color the woman's eyes were. They were not blue or gray or green or hazel or violet or amber. Mimi had said it best when she called them "ghost-colored."

Jessie wore a ring on every finger, each with a mystic stone or an occult symbol. Silver Gypsy bracelets circled her thick wrists, and she had one earring shaped like a cross and one shaped like the Star of David. Around her neck was a chain with a silver figure of a dancing Hindu goddess.

She did not smile at Eden or open her arms to her. She simply looked her up and down, a critical glint in her eye.

"Well," she said. "You decided to come home at last."

I will not feel guilty, Eden vowed silently. But she did feel guilty, just as Jessie had intended. *God, God, why'd I ever come back?*

Eden kept her head high. "I was told you said you needed me."

Jessie's battered face grew even more haughty. "Your little sissie's baby needs you," she said. "It's good of you to come from high-and-mighty Beverly Hills."

"I don't live in Beverly Hills," Eden said. "Exactly."

"All California's going to sink into the sea," Jessie said with a superior sniff. "Like Sodom and Gomorrah."

"Sodom and Gomorrah didn't sink into the sea."

"In the end it amounts to the same," Jessie said. "You didn't come all this way to argue with me, I hope."

For a moment, the two women regarded each other, their faces stiff with control. At last, Eden sighed. There was no such thing as staring down Jessie, there never had been, and why was she foolish enough to try?

"I'm sorry about—all this," she said, making a helpless gesture. "I really am. I brought your things."

Jessie's cool gaze settled on the suitcase in Eden's hand. She beckoned for Eden to bring it to her.

"If I'm going to stay here," Jessie said, "I want a nightgown that covers my backside. I hope everything's here. I wanted my hairbrush and my toothbrush and my plastic tortoiseshell combs and my slippers and my bathrobe and my medication. I need some different support hose for when I come home, I got runs in my other ones when I fell down the steps, though I paid nine ninety-nine for them and they's supposed to be runless, and—"

"Slow down," Eden said. "If anything's not here, I'll bring it later."

She moved to Jessie's bedside and wondered if she should kiss her grandmother's cheek. But Jessie seemed interested only in snapping open the suitcase and rummaging through it. "Ain't you going to ask me how I feel?" she asked querulously, not looking at Eden.

Eden decided against the kiss. "How do you feel?"

"Rode hard and put up wet. My leg's swelled up like a watermelon and my ribs feel like they been beat on with hammers."

"I'm sorry," Eden said. "I really am. I just saw Dr. Vandeering. He says—"

Jessie cut her off. "Dr. Vandeering is a pipsqueak and a Pisces. He's got watery blood and watery ways. Don't talk to me about Dr. Vandeering."

Eden set her jaw and thought, *I can't tell her anything. This is how it always was between us. This is how it always will be.*

"All right," she said, struggling to be patient. "Then you tell me how you are."

"I'll be fine," Jessie said. "These doctors don't know squat."

"But—"

"Squat is what they don't know. I passed out because I needed to rest in my etheric body awhile, that's all. Now change the subject."

So much for adult, rational, practical conversation, Eden thought. "All right," she said. "What do you want to talk about? Peyton?"

Jessie raised her chin righteously. "You shouldn't make me ask about her. You should have said right off."

"When I left this morning, she was still asleep. The Charteris man said it took her a long time to fall asleep last night. I guess she was *very* upset."

"Of course she's upset. Her mama's gone, and her granny's locked up in this hellhole. You take good care of that child. She's your own blood, your own kin."

"Who else's kin is she? Have you any idea who's the father of this child? Or where Mimi is?"

"The poor child's got no father," Jessie said. "She's a woods colt. What did you expect?"

Eden winced. She supposed she had expected precisely that. "You're sure?"

Jessie glowered. "Mimi sent me a copy of the birth certificate. That and a one-line note. One line. No wonder I had to rest in my etheric body."

"Couldn't you rest in your etheric body without bouncing your real one down the stairs?" Eden asked and immediately regretted it.

Jessie narrowed her eyes. "You always had a smart mouth. Always."

"I'm sorry," Eden said. "We're both upset, that's all."

Jessie looked unmollified. "I want you to plug in my

business phone and handle my calls. Hospitals is expensive."

Eden crossed her arms. "Now, listen, Jessie. Somebody's got to take care of that little girl, and I'll do what I can. But as for your business, I don't want to get sucked into it."

"Sucked into it?" Jessie demanded. "You didn't mind it when it put a roof over your head and fed you and clothed you. You didn't mind when it paid for your fancy singing and dancing lessons."

Damn, thought Eden. *This isn't just a guilt trip. It's an entire world cruise of guilt.*

She said, "Keep the phone unplugged for a while. It's not much more than a week, and money isn't everything. Right now you've got more important things to worry about."

"Indeed, I do," retorted Jessie. "And one of them's your sister. So plug in that phone, miss, and do as I say."

Eden cocked a dubious brow. "What's the phone got to do with Mimi?"

Did she imagine it, or for an instant did Jessie's expression grow less imperious?

"There's been calls," Jessie said. "Calls from somebody that is close to her. My vibrations is not good."

A frisson tingled through Eden, as if her nerve endings had been touched by frost. "What do you mean?"

Jessie's eyes, with their unnameable color, fastened on hers. "I think this time your sister's in big trouble. I think this time she's opened a bag of snakes. I've heard their tails rattle. I seen the gleam of their yellow eyes."

FOUR

⟨—∼⟩⟨∽—⟩

THE CLICK OF BOOT HEELS ON THE TILE MADE EDEN turn. Owen Charteris stood in the doorway. He gave Jessie a measured smile. "I'm going over to Archie's Archery. Can I get you anything while I'm out?"

"What I want is you," Jessie said. "Come in. I got something to say, and I can tell by the expression on her face she don't want to hear it."

Owen gave Eden a wary look that said, *What's this?* But he stepped inside, as if Jessie's wishes overrode all else.

Eden said, "Jessie, please don't involve him in this—"

"I want him to hear," Jessie insisted. "Owen, this girl ain't been here ten minutes and she got my blood pressure up. She needs to hear this, and so do you."

Owen's expression was one of grudging resignation, but like a courtier he moved to Jessie's bedside. Although he didn't touch her, his stance seemed to say he was her protector, her ally. "What is it, Jessie?"

Jessie looked up at him, her gaze softening into something like affection. "I told you I been having calls from somebody that knows Mimi. I think Mimi's in trouble."

Owen raised a dark brow as if in scientific interest.

"You phrased it a bit more dramatically to me," Eden said, remembering the image of snakes. "Is this some vision you had? Something your spirit guide told you?"

"I *told* you, somebody's been calling. For the past three-four weeks."

Eden turned to the window so she wouldn't have to look at her grandmother and the Charteris man; they seemed to have some bond that eluded and challenged her.

"All right," said Owen. "Who was this person? What did they say? And what kind of trouble do you think Mimi's in?"

Last night he didn't want any part of this, Eden thought resentfully. *Why's he butting in now?*

Jessie said, "Her name's Constance. She won't tell me no more except her birthday, and I ain't sure she told the truth on that. She's got a voice all breathy and ragged. Like she gargled glass."

Eden kept staring through the window glass at the drowning day. She tried to harden herself for whatever was to come. "So what did this Constance say about Mimi?"

"She claimed she knowed about me from somebody

that sounds like Mimi. She was feeling me out for some reason. I could tell. My ears perked up."

"Go on," said Owen.

Jessie continued. "I tried to get her to talk more about it, but she wouldn't. And right then I got a bad feeling—a *psychic* feeling—that something was going on."

Eden forced herself to speak carefully. "You had a feeling? That's all?"

"No, it's *not* all." Jessie looked queenly, but grim. "I says to her, 'Where is this friend of yours?'

"And she says, 'I don't want to talk about her. I want to talk about me.' Then she asked me to read her tarot cards, and I did. And a darker spread of cards I never seen."

Eden allowed herself the ghost of a bitter smile. "The cards are pieces of paper, Jessie. That's all."

"The cards is windows—for them with wit enough to see through them," Jessie retorted.

Owen gave Eden a cold glance that told her to stop being contentious. He put his hand gingerly on Jessie's shoulder. "How many times has she called you?"

Jessie seemed comfortable with his touch. She looked up at him, not Eden. "Three-four time. She's up to something, and she's not alone. She always wants to know about somebody. She'll tell me birthdays, but she won't give me no names, she just wants readings. She's nervous."

"It's not a crime to be nervous," Eden objected.

Jessie ignored her and kept speaking to Owen. "One of them birthdays I recognized. It was Mimi's."

"Lots of people have the same birthday," Owen said, but his face had hardened, as if he believed what she said and didn't like it.

"Another one, I didn't recognize," Jessie told him. "It was a child. I didn't know any such child. Until yesterday. And there that birthday was—on Peyton's birth certificate. I checked it against my note cards. This here Constance knows them. I suspected it before, but I *know* it now."

Eden winced in disbelief, but Owen looked grimmer than before.

Jessie said, "This Constance, she's with at least four other people, and they are *up* to something, I tell you. She kept asking about dates—she says, 'I got something to do. When should it happen? This day or that?' "

"Did you give her any dates?" asked Owen.

"I did," said Jessie. "Yesterday was one. At the time it didn't seem no better nor worse than any other."

Owen frowned. "And yesterday Peyton showed up."

Jessie sank more deeply into her pillow, as if wearied. "Yes. And scairt to death to talk, poor little tyke."

His frown deepened. "You think this woman was feeling you out on Mimi's behalf?"

Suddenly, without warning, Jessie put her face in her ringed hands. "Snakes," she said miserably. "I keep seeing their yellow eyes, their wiggling tails. I hear 'em go rattle and hiss. Sweet Jesus, protect that child."

Owen leaned nearer to her, concern etched on his lean face. "Jessie, calm down. It doesn't help anything, you getting into a state."

"Who's going to protect little Peyton?" Jessie asked. "Who's going to watch out for her?"

"*I'll* watch out for her," Owen said from between clenched teeth. "I promise. I won't let anything happen to her, I swear."

Jessie kept her eyes hidden with one hand, but with the other, she clutched his, making him look acutely uncomfortable. "You always been good to me," she said. "Better than family."

"Look," he said, disengaging his hand from hers, "I'm going to get a nurse. I don't want you worked up like this."

His blue eyes locked for a cold instant with Eden's. "Help her, will you?" Then he left, and she heard his booted footsteps hurrying down the hall.

Eden felt alarmed by Jessie's tears, but suspicious of them, as well. Never had she seen Jessie cry; she did not think she was crying now.

She moved to the old woman's side and put her hand on Jessie's shoulder, as Owen had done. But Jessie twitched away from her and sat upright again. She snatched a tissue from her bedside tray and made as if to wipe her eyes, but they were perfectly dry.

"All right," Eden said in unhappy surrender, "just what do you want me to do?"

Jessie crumpled the tissue and stuffed it down into her bosom. "You go home and plug in my phone line. You take my calls for me, just like the old days. And you take care of Peyton. You tend to her and tend to business."

She shook her finger at Eden. "And you keep a watch out for that Constance. She'll call again, I feel it. Find out what you can from her. Think smart. Pretend you're me."

"Yes, yes," Eden said. At this point she'd agree with anything if it meant escaping from Jessie.

"You treat my other callers with respect, you hear?" Jessie warned. "I got important people depending on my advice. And troubled souls needing my guidance."

Eden nodded, looking as obedient as she could.

Jessie turned her attention back to the suitcase's contents. "Where's my hearing-aid batteries? Where's my rayon apricot-colored nightgown?"

"I don't know," Eden said. "I'll bring them next time. I'll bring anything you want, but—"

"I specifically said my rayon apricot-colored night-gown with the matching lace on the yoke," Jessie said, displeased. Her face had grown red, her voice shook. "*Who* packed this?"

"It doesn't matter," Eden said, alarmed that Jessie was growing upset again. "Calm down. Dr. Vandeering said your blood pressure—"

"Bring me that nightgown," Jessie ordered. "No, send it with Owen. You stay home. Stay put and take care of that baby and that phone. Can you remember that, my rayon apricot-colored nightgown with the matching lace?"

"Yes, yes," Eden said. "I'll make sure you get it. Just settle down."

"And the matching slippers and robe," Jessie added. "If I have to be in the hospital, I might as well do it in style. Maybe that's why I bought that nightgown. I knew something like this was going to happen. I had a presentiment. Damn, my heart is hammering like hell's best carpenter."

"Lean back again," Eden told her. "Please—"

Jessie leaned back, but her eyes were rebellious. "You do as I say. You need any help, ask Owen. He lives at t'other house. He's remodeling it."

"Who is this man?" Eden asked. "Why are you so chummy?"

"And don't handle my crystal ball," Jessie instructed. "It's highly charged right now. You never could use it right. That gift wasn't given to you."

Exasperated, Eden wanted to say, "Jessie—none of

this will work. I can't take care of Peyton. I don't know how. I'll hire someone to take care of her. And I can't stay here and work your phone because of some wild hunch about Mimi. I've got my own work in California."

But she thought of Jessie's blood pressure. She said nothing. *Tomorrow,* she thought. *I'll tell her tomorrow when we're both calmer. We have more important things to do than bicker.*

By the time Owen drove the Storey woman back toward Jessie's, the rain had stopped. The sky turned from gray to vibrant, autumnal blue. Sunlight gleamed on the yellowing leaves of the walnut trees, the muted orange of the oaks.

None of this sunniness touched Owen's heart. He frowned to himself. He and Shannon would officially introduce Eden to her goblin of a niece, then Shannon was free to go home to Hot Springs. He envied her, wanting to escape himself.

He wanted to go to the river to bow-hunt deer. He was troubled, and he needed the silence and sounds of the deep woods: the splash and rush of the river as it surged over ancient stones, the lonely moan of the wind in the trees.

The crossbow, in its sling, was already in the back of the Blazer. He'd been ready to take off yesterday, just spend a few days by himself. He'd meant to lose himself in the pure, intricate ceremonies of hunting. But, instead, Jessie had fallen down the stairs.

Now he was thinking of losing himself otherwise, in other ceremonies not so pure. He had the urge to go to Tulsa, where a man could have a degree of anonymity. He knew a place called Cosette's where the girls were clean and careful, and where he could keep relationships simple and impersonal.

Too often lately, a dark hunger gnawed at him, all lust, no love. He had no love left, wanted none. His body didn't need love, only release. He did not like these sexual transactions in Tulsa, but he needed them. His body was like a horse that needed to be run from time to time, so that it wouldn't grow wilder or meaner than it already was.

Against his wish or will, Eden Storey brought out the meaness, the wildness, and the old, dark hunger in him. He didn't like it, he resented it, and he intended to keep his distance from her.

"I'll get you settled with the kid," he said, not looking at her. "Then I'll leave you alone. I'll be at the other house if you need me. I might go hunting a few days."

"Fine," she said. There was fatigue in her voice, as if her visit with Jessie had exhausted her in ways he didn't understand. Now he was going to throw her to Peyton, the wolf-child. It couldn't be helped.

"Jessie's got a Ford Escort. She doesn't drive it much anymore, but it still runs. The keys are on a nail beside the back door. If you have any trouble with it, let me know."

She held her head high and stared moodily out the side window, watching the dappled light dance on the colored leaves. "Thank you," she said. "You've been very kind."

Resolutely he tried to keep his attention on the road. He wasn't being kind, and he knew it. Still, he was obliged to provide for her to some extent; she and the kid were, after all, concerns of Jessie's, and he owed Jessie.

"If you need anything else," he said, "money, whatever, just tell me."

"I don't need money," she said, almost sharply. "I've been taking care of myself just fine for years."

You certainly have, he thought, studying the elegance of her profile. He looked away from her and made his voice harsh. "Mimi's probably guilty of abandonment. But it doesn't become a criminal matter unless you or Jessie press charges. You can keep the problem in the family."

Eden put her hand to her forehead and sighed tiredly. "Family," she said, as if it were the name of a particularly cruel curse.

He kept his eyes on the highway. "What about Jessie's feeling that Mimi's in trouble? And this caller she thinks knows her, this Constance?"

Eden rubbed her forehead, then let her hand fall back to her lap. "Mimi's always in trouble," she said, staring at the trees again. "And Jessie always sees omens and portents in everything."

"You don't believe her?"

"Do you?"

"A lot of people do," he said evasively. "She's done all right for herself by them."

She raised her chin higher. "She *has* done all right. She kept telling me she had. I thought she was exaggerating. We used to scrape by on so little. And after I left here, she'd never accept money from me. Never. If I sent it to her, she sent it right back, insulted."

"She's independent."

"There's such a thing as being too independent."

"She's got a lot of pride, that's all."

"There's such a thing as too much pride."

He said nothing. A silence fell between them, and he was content to let it grow.

But he felt Eden's eyes on him, studying him as if he

had answers she wanted. She said, "Just exactly how has she done so well? That little house—it's very nice."

"Psychics got more popular in the last ten or twelve years. The phone business has been good to her. She's built up a clientele."

Eden cocked her head and crossed her arms. "I hope it's saner than the 'clientele' she used to have."

He gave her a brief, dubious look.

"For instance," she said, "the man who traveled around with space aliens. The other crazies. The drunks. The poor people looking for a miracle and hoping she's it."

He shrugged. "She provides a service."

"She also takes their money."

He heard the bitterness in her voice, and it irked him. "You don't sound like you have much respect for her."

"But you, on the other hand, do," she said. "Why?"

He thought a moment. The truth was too complicated to go in to, and too personal. He said, "I think she's an extraordinary woman. That's all."

Eden's smile was small and sardonic. "Extraordinary's one way to put it. What did she do? Read your stars and tell you how to break the bank at Monte Carlo?"

"Let's skip it." He rounded a curve edged with cedars and Jessie's house and his own came into view. He was glad. He wanted to rid himself of this woman who both excited and irritated him.

"Your loving niece is probably up by now," he said. "Waiting to meet you."

Eden's little smirk died into nothingness, which gave him a petty pleasure. Then an almost haunted look came into her eyes, and his pleasure vanished.

•   •   •

Peyton was awake, but still had a sleepy, sullen expression. She lay on the floor in the living room, her left thumb firmly in her mouth, drawing crayon pictures in a Big Chief tablet.

The television blared before her, tuned to a cartoon show. Beside her lay a mangy-looking toy bear whose stitched mouth had unraveled almost into nothingness.

Owen smiled down at the child, but his smile seemed forced. With unnatural heartiness, he said, "Peyton, this is your aunt, Eden Storey. Aunt Eden."

Peyton turned her face, giving Eden a dark, unreadable glance. "I know," she said. "I got in her bed. She thought I was a cat."

Eden, too, smiled, and her own smile felt stiff and false on her lips. "Hello, Peyton," she said. "It's nice to meet you in the daytime."

Peyton refused to look up. "I'm not a cat. I'm a person."

Helplessly, Eden looked at Owen. He gazed down at the child with his expression so controlled that she knew it concealed dislike.

Shannon came into the room from the hall. She looked a good deal like her brother, tall and lean with piercing blue eyes, but her thick hair was still brown.

She took Eden's hand in hers and squeezed it warmly. "How's your grandmother?"

Eden was grateful for the simple human contact. This woman was far different from her chilly-blooded brother. "My grandmother's—feisty."

Shannon nodded sympathetically and put her other hand on Owen's shoulder. "Owen, I'm packed, and I'm going. If I leave now, I can stop by the home and see

Mama one more time. I can be on the road and back to Hot Springs before dark."

Owen gave his sister the hint of a sardonic smile. "Anxious to leave?"

"Eager to see my own kids, that's all." She gripped his shoulder more tightly. "And, Owen, help take care of this little girl. I have the feeling she's been through a lot."

Eden's heart contracted at the words. Owen frowned. "Did she say anything?"

Shannon shook her head worriedly. "Not really. She talks so strangely. And the pictures she draws—I found these in her room, under her bed."

She released Eden's hand and reached for another tablet beside a lamp on an end table. "Here," she said, handing the tablet to Owen. "Look at this."

Owen held the tablet so that Eden, too, could see. He lifted the cover. A child's crude drawing filled the page.

A woman's stick figure wore a skirt and had long, frazzled hair—like Mimi's. Mimi had always worn her curly hair long and in a flyaway style. The woman held a stick child by the hand, and the child's scribbled hair was black, like Peyton's.

Both woman and child seemed to be fleeing from a large house with a fierce red door and no windows.

As primitive as the drawing was, Eden sensed a palpable aura of unhappiness about it. Black clouds of smoke poured from the chimney. No sun shone in the sky. No tree graced the flat landscape. No grass or flowers grew.

"There are more," Shannon said.

Owen turned the page. The same stark horizon. The same sunless sky. The same windowless house with the scarlet door and the same chimney pouring darkness into the air. This time the child stood alone beside the house.

Owen turned another page. Eden saw the familiar eyeless, boxy house with its door as red as a wound. This time the smoke rose not straight up, but in sharp zigs and zags that blackened the whole sky.

Three men with magenta hair stood in the barren yard. They held what seemed to be guns. A chill clutched Eden. "Who are these men?" she asked. "Did you ask her?"

"I tried," Shannon said. "She won't give me a straight answer."

"What do you mean?" Owen frowned.

"She says they're the mean soldiers," Shannon said. "And that she can't talk about them."

Eden stared at the drawing of the three men with their violently colored hair.

Mean soldiers, she thought apprehensively. She raised her eyes to meet Shannon's.

Shannon said, "Maybe she'll talk to you. She seems to like you. She was upset when she woke up, and you weren't there."

Eden looked dubiously at the child lying before the television. She was engrossed in drawing another stick figure.

"I think that's you," Shannon said with a nod toward the picture.

A shock of recognition ran through Eden. As crude as the drawing was, Peyton had somehow captured her, the triangular face, the way her bangs fell over her forehead. In the sky beamed a yellow sun.

"I've got to go," Shannon said. "I'll stay in touch— through Owen."

Eden nodded numbly but didn't want the woman to leave; she suddenly felt helpless, abandoned. Shannon gave her hand a last squeeze, then released it. "Good luck to you," she said. "And to your family."

"I'll get your suitcase," Owen said. His voice was gruff, and Eden thought he, too, seemed reluctant for his sister to leave.

Shannon knelt on the floor beside Peyton and told her good-bye and to be a good girl. Peyton yawned and did not look up. She flinched slightly when Shannon tried to kiss her on the cheek.

But she let the woman's lips graze her face, just barely. Shannon only smiled and touched her fingertips to Peyton's cheek. The child ignored her and gripped her crayon more tightly. She had drawn a black-haired child beside the Eden-figure.

Over their heads, she drew a floating man. Meticulously, she colored his hair turquoise-blue.

When Owen returned from walking Shannon to her car, Eden's skin prickled with uneasiness.

Even though Peyton lay on the floor between them, humming and coloring, Eden felt peculiarly alone with him. It was as if Shannon's leaving removed some protective wall from between them.

"I should pack up those things Jessie wants," she said.

"Yeah," he said, sounding bored. "I could drop them off now. I'm going back into town. I've got things to attend."

"Which is Jessie's room?"

"The first on the left, down the hall."

She excused herself and practically ransacked Jessie's drawers and closets, looking for the nightgown, robe, slippers, batteries. She packed everything haphazardly in a grocery bag, knowing Jessie would be displeased by the untidiness. Eden didn't care. Instinctively she wanted Owen gone from the house, the sooner the better.

But as she stuffed the slippers into the bag, she paused, staring in surprise at the top of Jessie's bureau. Ranged there, in inexpensive frames, were at least a dozen snapshots of herself and Mimi.

There was Mimi, little and grinning, all curly hair and with a gap in her smile, her front teeth claimed by the tooth fairy. There Eden was herself, a leggy twelve-year-old, looking proud and almost haughty in the cheap party dress she'd worn at her first singing recital. There were she and Mimi sitting in front of the trailer, their heads together, laughing at some now long-forgotten joke.

A pang stabbed her, heart-deep. Jessie still displayed their pictures? Kept them where she would see them the first thing in the morning and the last at night? After the pain they had both inflicted on her?

This skinny girl with the manic grin had really been Mimi, with her wild, pretty voice and her dreams of Nashville? And had this other girl, tall and seemingly so self-possessed, really been herself, hiding her fear from the world?

She could not think about it and would not think about it. She turned away and snatched up the bulging bag. She took it to the bathroom and stuffed Jessie's three vials of prescription drugs into it.

Her heart would not stop beating at too swift a pace. The knot lodged in her throat refused to diminish.

Damn! she thought. *Damn! I don't want to remember all this. I won't.*

She went back into the living room and thrust the

bulging bag at Owen. She was careful not to touch him. He seemed equally careful not to touch her.

"Yes," he said, looking her up and down. "Well. You're on your own now."

She managed a brittle smile. "Just us girls. We'll be fine. Fine."

He looked her up and down again. "I'll drop by when I get back. To check on the two of you."

"You don't have to do that," she said brightly, perhaps too brightly.

I know, his expression said. *I don't the hell want to. But I will.*

When he shut the door behind him, she was relieved. She hadn't realized she'd been holding her breath.

She exhaled between clenched teeth. *Find out about this child.*

She settled down beside Peyton, cross-legged. "You're a very good artist," Eden said in the same enthusiastic voice she used in commercials to sell children breakfast cereal and plastic toys.

"Umph," said Peyton, uninterested in flattery.

"So," said Eden companionably, "is that your house you draw? The house with the red door?"

"Umph," Peyton muttered. "You had a cat. I know."

"Yes," Eden agreed. "Except he was my friend's cat. Where is the house with the red door? Can you tell me?"

Peyton withdrew her thumb from her mouth and examined it solemnly. "The cat's name," she said, "is Po-lo-ni-us. Po-lo-ni-us the cat. Henry told me." She put her thumb back into her mouth.

Eden stared at the child, startled. "Who's Henry?"

"My friend."

Carefully, hoping for a clue, Eden said, "Where's Henry? Can you tell me?"

Peyton pointed her crayon at an empty chair. "There," she said. "He's watching you."

An imaginary friend, Eden thought. *Solace of the lonely child.* She sat back, drawing up her knees and locking her arms around them. "Oh. I see. Did Henry come all the way to Arkansas with you?"

Peyton gave Eden a shy glance and quickly looked away. She nodded. "His hair is blue. He can fly."

Eden tried another approach. "I'm from California. But I grew up here, with your mama. We were sisters. My last name is Storey, just like yours. Is hers still Storey, too?"

"I'm hungry," Peyton said. She gave Eden another shy look, this time hopeful. "Will you buy me some ice cream?"

"Later," Eden said craftily. "First I want you to tell me where you came from."

Peyton's face became apprehensive and she turned away again. "My mama told me not to." She bore down harder on the turquoise crayon. "My mama went away. She always goes away."

Eden leaned forward, putting her hand on the child's shoulder. "Peyton, listen. I'm trying to help you get your mother back. You can talk to me—I'm your mother's sister."

Peyton flinched at the touch, as if she'd expected to be hurt.

"If your mother was here," Eden persisted, "she'd say it's all right to talk to *me.* She'd want you to."

Peyton's lower lip quivered, her chin thrust out, and she clapped her hands over her ears. "See no evil, hear no evil, speak no evil."

Eden stared at the child in concern and frustration. The telephone jangled, startling her. She reached out to ruffle Peyton's hair but the girl dodged her hand, as if fearing to be touched.

The ring shrilled again, and Eden rose from the floor to answer it. It sat on a small table next to the statue of a dancing Hindu god with an elephant's head and six arms.

Eden picked up the receiver. "Hello?"

"I tried my psychic phone line," Jessie snapped. "It rang and rang with no answer. Ain't you hooked it up yet?"

Eden restrained a sigh of frustration. "I barely got here, Jessie. Shannon and Owen just left. And I'm trying to get acquainted with Peyton."

"Well, get acquainted while the phone's plugged in. Can't you walk and whistle at the same time?"

"I *forgot*, that's all. The child seemed more important."

"Of course she's important. I didn't say she wasn't."

"There are questions we need answered."

"Well, she don't answer them. She's like me. She can't be pushed. No sir."

"I'm not pushing. And in the meantime—"

"In the meantime, you've already missed Miz Eberhart's call. She calls every day, one o'clock, from Miami Beach, so's I can read her tarot cards."

"Every day?" Eden asked in disbelief.

"She's an old widow woman," Jessie said. "She likes to hear about herself. She'll be concerned about her arthritis. Tell her it'll get better."

"Will it get better?" Eden challenged. She hated lying.

"No, but what good would it do to say that?" Jessie retorted. "She might give up hope altogether."

Eden rolled her eyes heavenward. Jessie said, "Besides that, I want you to be there if that Constance calls. If she does, you play her, pump her. Be careful not to lose her. But first you need to plug in that phone line. Now."

"All right." Eden surrendered. "All right."

"Is Owen bringing me my apricot-colored rayon nightgown with the lace yoke?" Jessie demanded.

"Yes, he's on his way."

"My hearing-aid batteries? My best deck of tarot cards? My prescriptions?"

"Yes, yes, all of it," Eden said impatiently. "What's the story on you and this man, anyway? He certainly dances attendance on you above and beyond the call of duty."

"I didn't think," said Jessie, frost in her voice, "that you knew so all-fired much about the call of duty."

Irritation crackled through Eden's system. What did Jessie want from her? Heart's blood? She took a deep breath. "I came back, didn't I?" she said.

"It took you fifteen years," said Jessie in an accusatory tone.

Eden thought, *All right, Jessie, all right. Let's get it out in the open and have it over with.* She said, "You still haven't forgiven me for going to California, have you? And you're not going to."

"You ran off. You was the only one I could depend on, and you upped and ran off."

"I was eighteen," Eden countered. "I had the right to go, and I went. I *told* you I was going."

"You and me could have worked together," Jessie said. "I trained you up. I taught you everything I know. We could have had a good business."

Eden closed her eyes. Her temples pounded. "I had no gift for it. I'm not psychic."

"You thought fast. You could read people. You was creative. You say that's not a gift?"

"I felt like a fraud. It wasn't what I wanted."

Jessie snorted. "No. You wanted to be a *actress*. What kind of life is that? You got no security at all."

"Jessie, I make a good living—very good. I don't worry about money. And you don't have to, either. I'm doing fine, and I can help—"

"Pah," Jessie said in disgust. "For now, maybe. How about down the road? You're like the grasshopper in the story. You play your fiddle now, but when winter comes, what you got? Show business is fickle."

Everything Jessie knew about show business, Eden thought ruefully, was a cliché, and the old woman knew absolutely nothing about the voice-talent business and didn't want to learn. It was futile to argue with her.

"Jessie," she said, "this is the same argument we had fifteen years ago. Let's drop it, shall we?"

"You run off to Hollywood with nary a dime in your pocket and left me alone with your little sister. You was the one I'd always depended on."

"I don't want to talk about it," Eden said firmly. "There's a little girl here to take care of. That's all that matters."

"Finding Mimi also matters," Jessie shot back. "All you're thinking about is running back to California. You plug in that phone, hear me? You got *responsibilities*."

Click. Eden winced. Jessie had hung up on her, loudly and with vehemence.

Peyton sat in front of the television, crayons abandoned, legs crossed, thumb in her mouth. She stared at the animated animals on the screen, but did not seem to really see them; she looked drugged with sleepiness.

Wait. Now is not the time to push her, thought Eden.

But she was too tired herself to fight impulse. Against her better judgment, she said, "Peyton, do you know a woman named Constance? Does your mother know a woman named Constance?"

Peyton would not meet her eyes. She kept her thumb in her mouth, the angle of her arm rigid. "Henry and I have a secret song," she said. "It keeps us safe. La, la, la."

And then she would say no more.

FIVE

〜〜〜

GRUDGINGLY, EDEN WENT TO PLUG IN THE PSYCHIC phone line. The office was new to her, but, with a stab of remembrance, she saw objects familiar to her from childhood.

Jessie's desk was cluttered with statuettes and figurines and occult paraphernalia, including the crystal ball resting on the back of a bronze tortoise. The small kachina doll with a bear mask stood next to the aloof-faced Chinese goddess made of white porcelain.

Eden shook her head at the confusion of fetishes and talismans and charms. She reconnected the phone, then found she was trying to spank her hands clean, as if she'd handled something dirty.

But only seconds after the phone was connected, it rang. Eden flinched. It rang again. She sat at the big desk and glowered at the crystal ball, glared at the tarot cards. She picked up the receiver.

"Sister Jessie," she intoned in a voice as oracular as Jessie's. "God's gifted seer." *I feel like God's ungifted jackass,* she thought. *He ought to strike me dead.*

But she knew Jessie's routine. She set her jaw and reached for the box that held the file cards on clients. The box was carved with stars and suns and moons and comets.

"Have we talked before?" Eden asked.

"No," a woman said timorously. "I never made a call like this before. What do I do?"

"First, give me your birthday," Eden said in Jessie's deep voice. "Law says I can't talk to you 'less you're at least eighteen."

The woman seemed hesitant. "M-May second, 1956."

Eden wrote the date down on a fresh note card. "Ah, a Taurus," she said. "This is a year of change for Taureans. Tell me your name, and I'll tell you your lucky number. Tell me and spell it."

"Lily," the woman said with a swallow. "Lillian Marlowe." She spelled it.

Eden wrote the name on the note card, counted the letters, and did a simple calculation. "Your lucky number is four," she said with an air of pronouncement. "Use it wisely. Now, what's your first question for Sister Jessie?"

"I—I want a lottery number," said Lillian Marlowe. "I need a winning number. I need it bad."

Eden's heart sank. She hated questions about gambling in general and the lottery in particular. But she said, "All right. How many digits you got to have in that number?"

"Four," the woman said firmly. "I need four."

"Hmmm," Eden answered, making the sound vibrate like a mantra. "All right. But you got to help, or it won't work. I want you to concentrate on winning that money. You *visualize* winning it. See that money with your spiritual eye and touch it with your spiritual hand. Are you ready?"

"I—I've never done this before," the woman said.

"Squeeze shut your eyes and call forth a vision of that nice, green money," Eden ordered. "Can you see it?"

A moment of uncomfortable silence stretched between them. Then, with awe in her voice, the woman said, "Why, I can! I see it sitting all around me in pretty stacks . . ."

"Good. Now I'm going into a trance, and I'll read your numeric aura."

Eden took up a tiny mallet and struck a silvery set of Indian chimes that hung beside the phone. They jingled and jangled with a sweet, eerie otherworldliness. In the meantime, Eden racked her head for a number, any number.

As the fairylike resonance of the chimes died, she decided, rather desperately, to opt for the first four numbers of Jessie's zip code.

"I'm seeing it," she said importantly. "Seven-two-seven-six. I'm getting that very clearly. Write it down: seven-two-seven-six."

"Oh, thank you, Sister, thank you," the woman said excitedly. "You don't know how bad I got to have this money—my son needs an operation."

Eden's heart guiltily shriveled to the size of a raisin. She was helping this woman waste her money when medical help was needed? "An operation?" she echoed.

"He wants to be an Elvis Presley impersonator," the

woman said proudly. "But he's got to get his nose fixed. He got it broke bad in a bar fight."

Eden's guilt vanished, replaced by astonishment. "Oh."

"We go to Graceland twice a year. It's like a pilgrimage," said the woman. "I got all the T-shirts, the videos, everything, even the phone shaped like him."

"Umm," murmured Eden.

"Thank you, Sister. I'll say a prayer for you next time I'm at Graceland. Good-bye."

Eden replaced the receiver and put her face in her hands. "Ladies and gentlemen," she muttered. "Elvis has left the building."

She forced herself to scribble a quick note about Lily on the card. Then she rose from the desk to check on Peyton. The television set still blared, and the cartoon show was now *Fearless Fran*, which Eden had worked on, years ago.

Peyton lay in front of the set, her body a relaxed sprawl, the crayon fallen from her hand. She had fallen asleep. Eden leaned against the door frame, uncertain whether to wake her. The child needed sleep, but if she napped now, would she again be awake all night long?

The psychic line rang, and Eden was spared the decision. She moved back to the desk, lifted the receiver. She nudged her voice down an octave and prepared to imitate Jessie's grammar and phrasing.

"Sister Jessie," she said. "God's gifted seer."

It was a Lionel Bevans, phoning from New York. Hurriedly Eden located his card and was surprised to see that he was a stockbroker who regularly called for tips.

"Jessie—I couldn't get you this morning," Bevans said heartily. "I want to ask you about a few commodities."

"Ask away," said Eden, who knew no more about commodities than she knew about rings of Saturn.

From the other end of the line, she heard the rattle of papers. "I hope you've got that crystal ball polished up."

"To a high gloss," Eden lied with an admirable imitation of confidence.

"Good. Now tell me about Hammer Amalgamated."

Eden gritted her teeth. "What about it?"

"Should I hold it or sell it?"

Eden scribbled the words "Hold" and "Sell" on a scrap of paper, shut her eyes, and jabbed the paper with her pen point. She opened one eye warily. "Sell," she instructed.

"Absolutely?"

"Absolutely." *This is how the economy gets run?* Eden thought with horror.

"I love it when you're that certain," he chortled. "Always a good sign for me. Now, how about Amondale? Research company. Gene splicing. Buy it? Or pass?"

Eden scrawled "Buy" and "Pass" on the other side of the paper, squeezed her eyes shut and stabbed again. She examined her handiwork. "Pass," she ordered him.

He sounded disappointed. "You surprise me on that one. You sense something negative? Can you tell me what?"

"The stars is wrong for it," Eden said shortly. "And you don't argue with the stars."

"You're the psychic," he sighed. "Okay, this one's got me stymied. Pass or buy? Polar-Nilsen, Limited. They've got a new development in asynchronous communications protocol, maybe the biggest thing since duplexing."

Jesus, he's not even speaking English, Eden fretted, but she played her senseless game with the penpoint again.

She took a deep breath. "Buy it," she ordered with the authority of an empress.

"Jessie," he said with a smile in his voice, "you're a wonder. That one could be a real coup. If it works out I'll send you a box of those chocolates you like."

By the time he said good-bye, her hands were trembling at her own boldness. "What the hell," she muttered as she set down the phone. "It's only money. *His* money."

Almost immediately, the phone jangled again. It was a woman from Peoria, who wanted a horoscope cast for the newborn kittens of her cat.

Owen had been in Jessie's room only a few minutes, but he saw that she was growing tired. Her pale skin looked parchmentlike, and her spine, usually ramrod straight, was slumped into a curve.

But she toyed with the tarot deck, expertly shuffling and reshuffling. Autumn sunshine spilled through the window, twinkling on her myriad rings and bracelets.

"I'm sorry for all this trouble," she muttered. "You wanted to go hunting, I know."

Owen put his hand on her bare arm and was surprised by the coldness of her flesh. "It's no problem," he said. "You need rest."

"I'm fine," Jessie insisted, dealing the cards out in the form of a cross.

She frowned. "*Damn*, but I didn't want that moon card popping up. Ain't that a fine cup of tea?"

Owen knew better than to argue with her. "I should go," he said and patted her arm. He thought of bowhunting in the woods. He thought of Cosette's in Tulsa.

She looked up at him, fixing him with her extraordinary eyes. "No—wait. You said you'd watch out for Peyton. Can I hold you to that?"

His stomach knotted with distaste. But he said, "I'll keep looking in on her. You can hold me to it."

"I worry about Mimi. There's a man mixed up in it, I can feel it. I don't want him turning up *here*." She laid down another card and shook her head. "Speak of the devil, and here he is. Hello, goatface. Stay out of my grandbaby's life."

Owen suppressed a wry smile. It was Jessie's style to talk back, even to the devil.

She didn't smile in return. "There's something I ain't told you. I ain't told nobody."

A presentiment of trouble crept over him, and he said nothing, but waited for her to go on.

Her face somber, she said, "If something happens to Mimi," she said somberly, "and something happens to me, too—Eden's got to take that child. She's got to. It's her duty. You got to make her understand that."

Owen's muscles went taut. "Jessie, you're going to be fine. And we'll find Mimi."

She leaned against the pillows tiredly. "Tell Eden I said that. Please."

"That's between you and her, it's not my place to—"

"When has she ever listened to me?" Jessie said bitterly. "Please just tell her. Please."

Jesus Christ, what am I getting into? he rebuked himself. But Jessie suddenly looked so wan and weary that she frightened him. A muscle twitched in his jaw. "I'll mention it to her. Is that good enough?"

"It'll do," she said.

"Jessie, you're tired. I'll go. You can rest."

She waved her hand weakly, a gesture for him to stay.

"Not yet," she said. "There's one more thing. That woman yesterday, in that car. I told you I couldn't remember much about her. She was so *middling*—middling in her age, her size, everything."

"She had brown hair going gray, you said."

"Middling brown," said Jessie. "Going middling gray. But I remember one thing about her."

"Good. It may help."

"She was wearing a T-shirt," Jessie said. "It was faded and had a picture of a car or truck on it. It said 'Ness Ford,' or 'Ness Chevrolet.'"

"You're sure?"

"I remember because of the Loch Ness monster. Maybe it was 'Ness Hudson.'"

"Jessie, they don't make Hudsons anymore."

"Anyway," Jessie said, "it was Ness. Or it could have been Loch." Her eyes fluttered shut.

Shitfire, Jessie, he thought, *you're worn out. I never would have believed it. Life has worn you out.*

He swung the bed tray with its half-dealt cards out of her way. "Rest, it's an order," he said softly. He decided that while she was in the hospital, he'd call Alvin Swinnerton at GuardLok and have a security system put in her house, an improvement she'd always refused.

He turned and left the room. The hallway smelled of lotion and antiseptic and the stringent odor of well-scrubbed loneliness.

He didn't relish going back to Jessie's house. He felt repelled by the child and attracted by the woman, and disliked both reactions.

He decided to take the stairs rather than the elevator, then wished he hadn't. He had to pass the room in which Laurie had died.

Against his will, he glanced inside. In the room a

woman lay motionless upon the bed, her face lifeless. To
Owen, she looked as young and thin and wasted as Laurie had. He had to turn away.

Eden rose from the desk. She needed a cup of coffee,
strong and black, to send a jolt of energy through her
veins. The casting of horoscopes, even cat horoscopes,
was taxing. Just as she reached the door, the telephone
shrilled again.

Damn, she thought. But she steeled herself, turned
back, and picked up the receiver. "Sister Jessie," she said,
her voice deep and sonorous. "God's gifted seer."

For the space of three heartbeats, nothing but silence
answered her. Then a woman said, "Sister Jessie, it's me.
Connie. Constance. I got to talk to you."

My God, Eden thought with a chilling shock. *My
God.* She had almost forgotten about Constance. The
woman had a hoarse voice, whispery and breathy.

"Well, Constance," Eden said. "Hello, honey. How
are you?" She sorted swiftly through the files in the
carved box. She pulled a card covered with Jessie's spiky
handwriting.

NAME Constance (last name?)
FROM mixed acsent
BIRTHDAY Mar 21, 1965 (borned on a cusp)

CALLS:
9-11 Worry about a projeck she is supose do, want
to know when best sucess She says she got my
name from sombody that know me She wont say
who She is nerviss about somthing She askt about
a childs birthday 2-8-93.

9-17 She askt if she go somewhare else whare shood she go? I askt about whare she is but she say she CANT TALK ABOUT THIS I tell her cards say journy may be dangerous To be careful She askt about date in oct. is it good? I get no cleer answer I have strong feeling about Mimi

10-2 She askt if she'll be lucky and cards say a Strong No but I dont tell her that She is up to something I can tell She askts about dates and some other people's birthday One is Mimi's—I knowed I was rite!

10-12 She askt if she be lucky tonite Cards say strong yes She is very nerviss about somthing I get strong vision of Mimi that she needs help In my mind I get strong picture of snakes.

"I'm worried, Sister Jessie," Constance said. "I got . . . questions."

If the woman was worried, she sounded oddly calm, almost detached. There was a slight slur to her croaking voice. Either she was drinking, or the slur was part of her speech impairment.

"You want me to deal out the tarot, honey?" Eden asked.

"Yeah."

Eden sat down again at the desk and picked up the deck of cards. With nervous fingers she began to shuffle. "What's your question, child? You ask Sister Jessie."

"I want to ask about death," said the woman.

The words jolted Eden, and she tensed. "Yes?"

"When people die quickly, without—expectation— do they suffer much?"

"It depends on what you mean," Eden hedged.

"Like those people on that plane," the woman said. "All those people on that plane that exploded in Miami. They didn't suffer—not really, did they?"

Eden mentally rifled through Jessie's stock answers for dealing with tragedy. "Their suffering's over now. Everything happens for a purpose. Some souls are supposed to leave life quick. There's a lesson in it for them."

"I—don't understand." The voice rustled like dead leaves and broken sticks.

I don't, either, Eden thought. *I never did and I never will.* She tried not to think of her own mother, who had died without warning, hit by a car as she jaywalked across a dark and wintry street.

Instead she found herself echoing Jessie's weary truisms, in which she had no faith. "Death teaches you, just like life does. It ain't ours to question."

Again the caller hesitated before answering. "Most of the time anymore I'm not afraid to die," she said in her coarse, breathy voice. "But—but—sometimes I still am."

Just what is your problem, Constance? Are you sick, dying? Is that why you sound the way you do?

"There's nothing to fear," Eden recited. "You go into a tunnel of light. No suffering. No hurt, no fear."

I make Death sound like a painless dentist. That didn't hurt, did it? Now, rinse. Please floss between incarnations.

"You understand?" Eden asked.

There was a long pause that she found somehow ominous. "Yeah. Maybe. I don't know."

"You have other questions?"

"Yeah."

"About what?" Eden said uneasily.

"About a kid," the woman said in her hoarse, halting voice. "This kid went on a journey. Was it safe? Did she arrive okay?"

A child. Peyton. Eden stiffened as if she'd been struck. *Jessie's right,* she thought. *Oh, God, Jessie's right for once.*

"I—I," she stammered, "who is this child?"

"Just tell me," said the woman, her breathing ragged. "Did she get there okay?"

Eden's mind whirled giddily. She did not know how to answer. "This child," she said carefully, "does her name begin with a *p*?"

The woman made a broken little wheeze like a sob or a gasp. "Yes. Tell me—is she safe?"

Eden's grip tightened around the cards, and she bit her wounded lip. She did not even feel the pain.

"Sister Jessie?" the woman said. "Did you hear me?"

Eden took a long, shuddering breath. "The child is safe."

"Read her cards," the rasping voice said plaintively. "Tell me if she'll be lucky. I got to know."

Eden had a desperate, jittery feeling that the woman's mood was shifting and vulnerable, that she might hang up at any moment and that she shouldn't be pushed.

"If she'll be lucky?" Eden asked carefully. "Anything else? I'm dealing the cards now."

Constance hesitated. "That," she breathed, "and when should I leave here? I think I know. What do the cards say?"

Deftly Eden laid the cards into place until they formed the Celtic cross. She tried not to wince when the center card was a symbol of ill omen, the nine of swords.

"Ah," she said with false cheer, "the child's looking very lucky, indeed."

She turned over the first card. It was the hanged man, reversed, another inauspicious sign.

"You couldn't be luckier yourself," she lied. "Where

are you right now, honey? Where you thinking of leaving from?"

"Umm."

"Constance, where are you?"

"Umm. I can't say," she answered in her harsh, whispery way.

Eden gritted her teeth. Something—something almost indefinable in that ravaged voice nagged at her and made her nervous.

Gingerly, playing for time, she turned over the next card, the eight of swords, which augured the unforeseen.

"Why, your luck just goes stretching on and on," Eden said with a false air of confidence. "You're talking to the right person. In fact, I believe the spirits have led you to me, so I can be your friend."

She held her breath. The woman did not answer.

"You can trust me," Eden said. "Please. Trust me."

A long silence. Eden thought of the child sleeping in the living room, and her heartbeat rocked in her ribs.

Eden leaned her elbow on the table and cradled her brow in her hand. She closed her eyes against the evil little ache being born in her forehead. Still the woman did not answer.

"Are you in trouble?" Eden asked. "Tell me. I'll help you."

"You already have. Th-thank you." A soft click tickled Eden's ear. The woman had hung up.

Troubled, Eden stared at the file card and reread what Jessie had written. A suspicion was forming in her mind, but it was too terrible to utter, to put even into silent words.

Mechanically she started to add her own note to the bottom of the card, but the phone rang again. *Double damn!* Eden thought and threw down the pen in frustration.

She straightened her back, cleared her throat, and got into character again. She lifted the receiver and said, "Sister Jessie, God's gifted seer."

She stared at the crystal ball, which seemed to mock her, telling her she was not a seer at all.

The woman in the motel room took a drag from her cigarette and ran her hand through the dark tangle of her hair. She put the tattered scrap of newsprint on the night table beside her tickets, and her eyes blurred with tears.

I shouldn't have called, she thought, lowering her head. She wiped her wet eyes with the back of her hand. *I had to call. I shouldn't have called. Oh, shit.*

She exhaled and raised her eyes, watching the blue smoke rise upward, disperse, fade like a ghost.

Like me, she thought. *Like me.*

She was registered in the motel room as Constance Caine, a name she'd made up when she was a small girl. It was the name she'd meant to take when she grew up to be a famous country-and-western singer. The beautiful and talented Miss Constance Caine and her fabulous voice.

Now her voice was shot to hell, and Constance was just a name like any of the others she'd used over the years—Christ, she couldn't even remember them all. What did it matter, anyway? It was almost over.

She had the bottle of wine and a carton of cigarettes, and she'd bought cheap tickets to nearly every show in town. She was a real Rhinestone Cowgirl, all right. And this was it, her star-spangled rodeo.

She turned her gaze listlessly to the television screen.

Since yesterday the Cable News Network had been running the explosion of Nassau-Air Flight 217. Every hour they reran the story. It was starting again now.

The explosion was "mysterious," the news kept saying, its cause not yet known. All thirteen people aboard had died, including the pilot and copilot.

She sat hunched on the edge of the bed, watching the screen as if hypnotized. She was stunned and sickened, and she felt impaled by guilt, as if it were a great hook and she were a worm twisting on it.

Drace, the fucker, had succeeded. He'd really done it. The bombing had really happened, there was a body count, and it was thirteen, surely a terrible omen. She was done now, no way out.

The last report said the FBI had been called in to help investigate the explosion—my God, the FBI, my God, my God, my God.

She choked back a small, angry sob. Her eyes were red with weeping.

Numbly she rose and unscrewed the cap of the second bottle of cheap wine she had bought. She knew she was never supposed to drink again, but what the hell difference did it make? She'd sleep it off, then hit the bricks and take in a show, come back and get really blind, blackout drunk.

Half a dozen candy bars lay strewn along the top of the dresser. She hadn't touched them since she'd bought them, but now she picked up a Hershey's bar. She had not eaten since yesterday.

She went back to the bed and poured the wine into a plastic water glass, peeled the silver foil from the candy bar.

She took a long sip of the wine, then another. It did not help, it did not ease her. She thought of the thirteen people dead in Miami. *What have we gotten into? How did it happen? How?*

The fear had gnawed at her for weeks. It had eaten at her waking thoughts, it had diseased her dreams. *What have we gotten into? And how, in God's name, do we get out?*

It would take a miracle to free them, she had thought.

And the miracle had come, at least in part. It had been revealed to her through a humble and unexpected means—the small ad in the back of a supermarket tabloid.

She didn't even know who had bought the tabloid or why; Drace usually frowned on such trash. "The media," he was always saying, "is the new opiate of the masses."

She had been reading it, sitting alone in the kitchen of the farmhouse, and the men had been out playing in the quarry with their everlasting explosives. The sun had been shining through the small window. Dust motes had danced in the air.

Then she saw the ad. It said:

YOUR PERSONAL PSYCHIC! The real thing! Sister Jessie Buddress, God's Gifted Seer and Healer. Clairvoyant, Spiritualist, and GENUINE Medium. $3.99 a minute. 1-900-555-6631. Endor, AR.

She read these words, and it was as if the heavens had parted and instead of sending mere morning sunshine through the window, the light blazed down with a pure blue-white radiance. She had bent over the cheap newsprint page and wept.

Jessie was still alive. She was still in Endor.

It was a sign: Jessie would take in Peyton, she would have to—Peyton was blood.

So she'd waited, plotting, for the next time Drace granted her permission to take out the old Mercury, that rusting bucket of bolts. And when he had, she'd driven to the Nitehawk Diner out on the highway and phoned Jessie from the pay phone. She'd stolen one of the privacy toll cards of which Drace was so fond.

When the old woman answered, she sounded full of life and strong—indestructibly strong. At that moment, Mimi had known what to do. Somehow she had to get the child to Jessie.

She hadn't told Jessie who she really was. How could she? In her ruined voice she croaked out, "My name is Constance."

But Jessie's voice had hardly changed, and Mimi found the familiar sound of it so comforting, she'd let the old woman read the cards for her, foolish as it was, just to keep hearing her.

After that, she'd called again, on the flimsiest of pretexts, but only a few times. She'd wanted to listen only to the sound of the old woman's words, not the sense of them, just their resonance.

Once Mimi had hated Jessie's voice and rebelled against all that it had stood for. Now it seemed to her that same voice, full of mystery and solace, symbolized the only security she had ever known.

She could not go home to it again. That was impossible now. But she had sent Peyton.

And Peyton had arrived—hadn't she? Hadn't Jessie said so?

Peyton, Peyton, are you safe? Tell Jessie I loved her, I just didn't know. Tell her this time I'm going to do what's right.

SIX

---∽∽∽---

THE CALLER, A WIDOW FROM PEORIA, SAID SHE WAS corresponding with the loveliest gentleman and that he wanted to marry her.

The only problem was that he was unjustly behind bars in Joliet State Prison for fraud and embezzlement, although he was innocent as a newborn babe. What did the stars advise about such a union?

Firmly, but tactfully, Eden said that the stars not merely advised against it, they advised very strongly against it.

The widow, obviously displeased, began to argue. Eden sighed and tried to say good-bye. "If you don't believe me, call somebody else," she said.

It was at that moment that Peyton, in the living room, began to scream.

Eden banged the receiver back into place and sprinted down the hall toward Peyton's cries. Her heart hammered crazily in her throat.

Peyton sat before the television set, her head thrown back, howling like a little wolf. "Where are yo-o-ou?" she wailed. "Where are yo-o-ou? Help me! Bad dreams!"

Eden flung herself down on her knees beside the child and pulled her into her arms. "I'm here, I'm here," she said against the child's hair, hugging her tightly.

Peyton's little body was warm and damp, her curls tangled. She clung to Eden and dissolved into wracking sobs.

"There, there," Eden said ineffectually. "What's the matter? Nightmares?"

Peyton's tears were hot against Eden's shoulder. "Bad dreams," she said in a choked voice. "Bad dreams, bad dreams, bad dreams."

Eden patted the child's back, rocked her. "Dreams aren't real," she said in her most soothing voice. "Shh. Shh. The dream's all gone."

"Mama said they'd shoot me," Peyton wept. "I don't want to get shot."

Eden was struck momentarily speechless. She could not imagine Mimi telling the child such a terrible thing.

"I wouldn't let anybody hurt you—ever," Eden insisted. "And who would shoot you? Who?"

"I—can't—tell," Peyton gasped between sobs. "They'll—*get* me."

"No," Eden said fiercely, pressing her cheek to Peyton's round, wet one. "Nobody's going to get you. I'm here. You're safe."

She held the child and rocked her until the sobs dwindled to pained gulps and sniffles. She was shocked by her intense desire to comfort Peyton, by the tide of feeling that welled within her for this strange child.

Peyton sniffed and thrust her thumb into her mouth. "You left me," she accused.

Eden smoothed the tousled black curls. "No. I was right here. In Granny's room. I didn't leave you."

Peyton leaned moodily against Eden's shoulder, sucking her thumb. "Everybody leaves me. Where's Granny?"

Eden embraced the child still more tightly. "Your granny's in the hospital. The doctors are helping Granny."

"Nobody wants me."

Guilt twinged through Eden. She *didn't* want the girl, the thought of having a child repelled her, but she could not say so. She drew back, took the little girl by the shoulders. "I'm here right now. And I'll stay till Granny comes home from the hospital."

But no longer. I'll provide for you if I have to. But I can't be caught any deeper in this. I can't stay with you. I don't stay with anybody. It's not my style.

Louise Brodnik, a widow of fifty-two, lived in a small blue house on six hilly acres of dogwood and scrub pine, a dozen miles north of Sedonia, Missouri.

A woman of average height and weight, Louise had short mouse-brown hair that was dry and frizzled by a bad home permanent. Her broad-jawed face had once been pleasant, but was now coarsened and furrowed by care, and on bad days, she looked thoroughly harsh.

Today she looked harsh. She sat at the kitchen table, drinking black coffee and chain-smoking cigarettes, staring at the telephone on the counter. And wondering what she should do, or if it was too late now to do anything.

She had been back only a few hours, and had thought that being home would bring her peace. Instead she felt guilty for dumping the little girl, without warning or apology, onto the old woman—even though the old woman struck her as tough as nails.

Louise had driven the last long miles to Jessie Buddress's house with her nerves steeled, her resolve implacable, and her heart hardened. Something about the child—and her mother—had touched Louise from the first, but frightened her, too. She wanted it to be done, over, finished.

In Louise's front lawn was a hand-lettered sign: BABY-SITTING HOME CARE 4 YOUR CHILD, along with her phone number. She had similar signs up on bulletin boards all over town, at the Wal-Mart, the IGA grocery store, the Piggly-Wiggly supermarket, Harv's Stop'n'Shop, the Gas 'n' Go, and the three Baptist churches.

Louise had no trade. She sewed a bit and had a talent for growing vegetables in her big one-acre plot. She could sell quilts and vegetables and care for children. She had raised four of her own and baby-sat for her sister's three all the years her sister had worked at Tripmann's Restaurant.

Now all those children were grown and gone from Sedonia, and Louise's house was too far off the beaten track to draw customers. When Mimi Storey had appeared, proposing her strange bargain, Louise needed the money.

Last week, Mimi had wheeled into the dusty drive in a rusted-out Mercury hatchback. She wore dirty jeans, out at the knee, army boots, and a tight, sleeveless white T-shirt that had ketchup stains on it. Louise had recognized her and the child, too, for they had stopped at her house from time to time to buy summer vegetables.

Mimi was small and thin, but her bare arms were stringy with muscle, and she had an American flag, upside down, tattooed on one hard little bicep. Her dark brown hair was long, kinky, and untamed.

She'd had Peyton literally in tow, dragging her by the hand, and the child looked nothing like her. She was dark as a Gypsy, and her clothes were grimy, her knees filthy. She sat beside Mimi on the old orange sofa, and she wouldn't talk.

Mimi's high cheekbones jutted, and a long white scar threaded itself across the front of her throat like a crooked necklace. Her mouth had a nervous twist to it, and so did her voice, which was hoarse and wheezy. She said she needed help with Peyton.

"Look, the situation's complicated," Mimi had said, sitting on the edge of the sofa, a cigarette between her fingers. "This guy I live with and my kid don't get along. And I may have to go away for a while, but I can't leave her with him, you know?"

Peyton sucked her thumb and hugged a toy bear whose ragged fur was matted and filthy. She refused to look at Louise and stared at the bare wood of the floor instead.

Mimi tapped off the ash of her cigarette. "It's a long story. Basically, I gotta get her out of *here*."

Mimi put her lean, ropy arm around Peyton, but the child didn't respond. If anything, she seemed to withdraw further within herself.

"So," said Mimi, with a toss of her blowsy hair, "I've seen your sign, and I thought 'Why not?' I could pay you to take her to my grandma's for me. I know you got a car, I've seen it in the driveway. And nobody has to know—right?"

Louise had serious reservations, but stiffly, from between her teeth, she said, "Right."

"Just try not to be seen here with her," Mimi said. "Just get her out of town—fast."

Louise liked this less all the time. "You're one of the people at the old Wheaton place, aren't you?"

Mimi's face went coldly expressionless. She tossed her hair and said, "It's no big deal."

Apprehension swam in tingles through Louise. There were rumors about the people at the Wheaton place. That they were cultists or hippies or militants. She wanted to ask questions, but she said nothing.

Louise's old dog, Sweeney, came limping in from the kitchen. Sweeney was a mongrel terrier, graying, half-blind from cataracts, fat and bloated with gas. He seldom moved unless absolutely necessary to his own comfort.

"What's wrong with your dog?" asked the child, speaking for the first time.

"He's old," Louise murmured. She rose and opened the door for the dog to totter outside and do his business.

"Is he dying?" Peyton asked bluntly.

Louise sighed. "I suppose he is." She let the door ease shut and watched Sweeney hobble to the grass and squat to pee. He was too old and weak to lift his leg.

She turned to face Peyton, crossing her arms. "That doesn't frighten you, does it?" she asked as kindly as she could. She wondered if anyone had ever told the child about heaven and angels and Jesus.

Peyton only yawned, showing a badly chipped tooth.

Mimi shrugged one bare shoulder and looked Louise in the eye. "Look. I can pay you six hundred dollars to take her to Arkansas, drop her off. That's good money.

I'm not ready to send her yet. When I am, it'll be short notice. So I'm willing to pay that high."

Then she amazed Louise by digging into the rear pocket of her grubby jeans and drawing out a flattened wad of bills. "See?" she said. "I could pay you part in advance. Like a hundred dollars. I can put it in your hand now."

At the sight of the money, Louise's reservations had flown away like birds set free. *Six hundred dollars. What couldn't she do with six hundred dollars?*

Needs tumbled through Louise's head until she was half-drunk with them. The car needed a new tire; winter was coming and the furnace needed fixing; the bathroom window was cracked and held together by duct tape . . .

Mimi smiled and looked through her lashes. "It's good money, huh? See, when it comes to my kid, I'm willing to pay top dollar."

The little girl stared at the floor and clung to the filthy bear. *It would probably be a mercy for me to take that child,* Louise thought. *It's probably my Christian duty to take that poor child.*

"When would you want me to do this?" Louise asked.

"Soon," Mimi said vaguely. "Like I say, I'll have to give you short notice."

"How soon?" Louise asked apprehensively. "And how short a notice?"

"A couple days. Maybe sooner. I'll call you. You'll have to meet me somewhere and take her. What this guy doesn't know won't hurt him—right?"

Wrong, thought Louise. *This is all strange. This woman and her child are strange. The Wheaton place is strange.* But she thought, yearningly, poignantly, of the money Mimi had flashed so easily.

"Maybe," Louise said. "I'm not so sure."

"Look at her," Mimi cajoled, putting her arm around the child again. "She's an easy kid to take care of. Quiet. She's a little picky about her food is all."

The child frowned and stared even harder at the floor.

"I don't know," Louise said and thought of new glasses and seeing clearly again. "How far would I have to take her?"

"Down to Arkansas. Endor. It's only seven or eight hours," said Mimi.

Louise took a deep breath, thought hard. She could not drive seven or eight hours at a stretch. She would have to stop halfway, coming and going. That would entail a motel, which would cost even more money . . .

"I don't know," Louise repeated.

Mimi's toughness seemed to wither away, and naked pleading came into her eyes. "Please," she said. "You've got to help me. Things are getting out of control."

She lifted up Peyton's dark bangs, and Louise was shocked to see a purple bruise on the child's forehead.

"Please," Mimi said again. She lifted Peyton's arm and showed more bruise marks, like bluish fingerprints, above and behind the elbow. "I've got to figure out what to do. Please. For the love of God."

Louise's heart contracted in repulsion and fear. "You have money," she said. "You can run away."

"It's not that easy," Mimi said earnestly, her thin face suddenly seeming not only too thin, but vulnerable, as well. "I've got to have some time."

Against her better judgment, Louise had agreed, not knowing if pity or greed was the stronger of her motives.

Mimi pressed the first hundred dollars into Louise's hand. "This is our secret, right?" she said.

Louise nodded numbly, not sure the secret should be kept.

"Whatever you do, don't call me at the Wheaton place," Mimi warned her. "I'll get in touch with you, not the other way around."

A dozen worries danced a sickly dance through Louise's mind. "But what if I have the child, and—and there's an emergency?" she asked. "What do I do?"

Mimi brushed away the question. "Call my grandma. I'll give you her number. I don't have her address. You'll have to call when you get to town. I'll give you some papers to take her. Her name is Jessie Buddress. Don't tell her anything. Just give her my kid, all right? I'll—be along for her when I can."

"When you can?" Louise asked. "What do you mean?"

"Just that," Mimi assured her. "I'll be along when I can." She gave Peyton another squeeze. "See this nice lady? In a little while she's gonna take you to your granny. But it's a secret, see? You can't tell it. Or else."

The child looked frightened. *I want no part of this,* Louise wanted to say. But she said nothing.

"Your granny's gonna love you to pieces," Mimi told the child.

Peyton nodded listlessly.

"We gotta go," Mimi said, rising. "He doesn't like me to be gone too long."

"Let me give you some apples," Louise said on a sudden impulse to do something kind for the child. "They're not much, only windfalls, but you could make a pie."

Mimi did not look grateful or even interested, but Louise hurried into her kitchen and took up one of the small bags of bruised apples from her counter.

"There's a copy of my favorite pie recipe in there," Louise said. "Apple butter, too. And a Bible verse."

Mimi accepted the bag almost reluctantly, then took Peyton by the hand and led her outside. On the porch, the woman turned and looked at Louise again.

Mimi's eyes were hard, yet haunted, almost desperate. "You're going to help us?" she said in her rasping voice. "I'm counting on you. So's she."

Louise nodded silently and watched them go. She let the limping dog back in.

I'll call the child welfare people, she told herself. *I'll call the sheriff. I'll notify people.*

But she had done no such thing. Instead, she'd waited in apprehension for Mimi's call. It came on a Sunday night.

"Be at the NiteHawk Diner at one A.M." she'd told Louise. "Meet me in the ladies' can."

And Louise had done it. Mimi was dressed much as before, in dirty jeans and a T-shirt. This time she wore a faded denim jacket as well. But at least she'd cleaned up the little girl.

Peyton looked both exhausted and wide-eyed. "She's tired," Mimi said gruffly. "We had to walk here."

They came on foot? Louise thought. The woman and child must have walked over four miles through the country darkness.

Mimi handed Louise a sealed envelope. On the front was written "Peyton's grandmother, Jessie Buddress, Endor, Arkansas 1-900-555-6631."

"Her granny knows she's coming," Mimi told Louise. "I told her you'd probably make it tomorrow morning."

"Did you get her address?" Louise asked nervously.

"I forgot," Mimi said shortly. "Anyway, I'm going with you partway."

"What?" Louise asked, liking this less and less. "You didn't say anything about that before."

"What difference does it make?" Mimi demanded. "You gotta drive anyhow."

She reached into the pocket of her jeans and took out the wad of bills. She counted them into Louise's hand. "That makes six hundred dollars," she said. "Let's go. I want you to go through Branson."

Branson? thought Louise. *The town with all the music shows? Why?* But she said nothing.

Once in the car, Mimi did not talk, and the child, in the backseat, seemed restless, frightened. Mimi smoked and stared out the window with the air of someone stunned by grief.

When they reached the outskirts of Branson, Missouri, Mimi wanted to stop at a liquor store, but they couldn't find an open one.

"Screw it," Mimi had said petulantly. "The hell with it. In a little while, I'll tell you to stop. I'm getting out."

"But—but—" Louise said.

"Just *do* it," Mimi said so sharply that Louise clamped her mouth shut. Louise was tired and nervous and, in truth, frightened. She wanted this terrible adventure to be over.

A few miles later, Mimi told Louise to pull over at a motel that looked little better than a fleabag. In the parking lot in front of the seedy office, Mimi gave Louise a fierce stare.

"You take *good* care of this kid."

Then Mimi got out of the car and opened the back door. She leaned inside and put her hands on the little girl's shoulders. "Now you be good for Mrs. Brodnik," she said. "And be good for your granny. She'll take *fine* care of you, I promise. Mama's got to stay here awhile. I'll come for you when I can."

Peyton eyed her warily, as if she did not trust her.

"I love you a bunch and I'm proud of you," she said to Peyton. "I want you to know that. I love you a bunch." She gave the child a resounding kiss on the cheek.

Then she stood up, looked Louise up and down. "Get her to my grandmother's. Understand?"

"I understand," Louise said, her heart beating too hard and too fast.

"Bye, kid," Mimi said to Peyton. Then she turned sharply and walked away.

Peyton said nothing. She did not try to follow Mimi. She did not cry. She sucked her thumb and stared after her mother.

Louise, her heart beating hellishly, did not know what to say. She put the car in gear and headed once again toward Endor.

The child was uncommunicative to the point of unnerving Louise. She asked only one question. After twenty minutes, she tapped Louise on the shoulder and said, "Did your dog die?"

"Yes," Louise said nervously. The old dog had risen to go to his water dish one afternoon and fallen over dead. She didn't want to talk about it.

Louise forced herself to keep driving south, toward Endor. *I shouldn't have gotten involved in this,* she told herself uneasily. *Still, God knows someone's got to help this child.*

But she knew she had not done it out of pity or Christian duty. She had done it for money.

And she was punished for it. In the motel late that morning, the child wouldn't sleep, she wet the bed, she made Louise crazy. So Louise, exhausted, gave up, paid the bill, and drove on.

When she reached Endor, shortly before noon, and called the grandmother, she got an unpleasant surprise. "I'm here, like your daughter said. I've got the girl. Where do I come?"

The old woman said her only daughter had been dead for years and what the hell was going on?

This frightened Louise badly and now she was terrified she'd be stuck with this difficult child. At last, Mimi's name came up, and Louise wrangled the woman's address from her.

Fearing the old woman wouldn't accept the child, Louise had almost literally dumped the little girl on the front porch, thrust the envelope into Jessie Buddress's hand, and escaped.

She drove straight back to the Missouri border, her heart beating so erratically that she thought she was having an attack. Early in the afternoon she stopped at another motel, completely spent. *God help me, God help me,* she kept thinking. *And God forgive me for what I've done.*

She'd yearned, like a lost soul, for the comfort and safety of her own home. She'd been physically ill and thrown up twice.

Now she was home, had been home for half an hour, drinking coffee and smoking cigarettes. *It's over,* she kept telling herself. *It's over.* But her pulse wouldn't stop its hectic pounding.

Eden saw Owen's car pull into Jessie's drive. Her emotions clashed in unruly conflict. She didn't want to see him; she did. He made her uneasy, yet he was her only ally in this foreign land she had once called home.

She turned from the window and waited for his knock. When it came, she took a deep breath and swung open the door.

He stood on the small front porch, one hand propped against the door frame. He looked as tired and out of patience as she felt.

"How's Jessie?" she asked.

"Worried," he said shortly.

"*She's* worried?" Eden said. Jessie, lucky Jessie, was tucked into a nice, safe hospital.

He shot her an ice-blue look that told her he was in no mood to argue.

"All right, I'm sorry," Eden said, though she hardly felt repentent. "How's she otherwise?"

Owen didn't bother to answer. Instead, he entered the room without invitation, closing the front door behind him. "You and I have to talk."

Eden tossed her head. "I'd like to talk to somebody myself. I've had a very strange time here. And some strange calls. Including one from Jessie's friend Constance. It made me—uneasy."

The expression in his eyes didn't change, but one dark brow crooked and his jaw muscles grew rigid. Eden realized that he sometimes had a dangerous, almost predatory air.

He looked her up and down. "Where's Peyton?"

"Changing into a warmer shirt," Eden said, turning from him and staring out the window. "She's restless. I told her I'd take her out to play. I'm not letting her go out alone."

"Good," he said tonelessly. "I'll go with you."

Eden kept her back to him. "You didn't tell me how Jessie is."

"As well as can be expected," he answered.

Mr. Communication, Eden thought irasicibly. *His hair may be silver, but that tongue's pure gold.*

She turned when she heard Peyton coming down the hall. The child wore a faded blue sweatshirt that was wrong side out. Her dirty tennis shoes were untied, and she tripped over one dangling lace. She lurched down the hall sideways, trying to yank her twisted sweatshirt straight.

The child's hair hung in her eyes, and she looked like a ragamuffin. Eden's heart, reluctant and wanting to be hard, went out to her. "Oh, Peyton," she said, sighing in resignation, and knelt to help her.

She could feel Owen's eyes upon her as she tied and double-knotted Peyton's laces, and the knowledge made her fingers awkward. "Come here," she said to Peyton. "Your shirt's on inside out."

"I *want* it inside out," Peyton insisted, wriggling away from her. "It's lucky."

Eden blinked in surprised recognition. It was one of Jessie's crazy superstitions. "Did your mother tell you that?"

Peyton looked scared.

Eden was sorry she had alarmed the child, and tried to gloss it over by being matter-of-fact. "If you put it on wrong side out on purpose, it doesn't count. It has to be by accident. Come here."

Eden stripped off the little girl's shirt. Peyton looked resentful. "I want good luck *now.*"

"We'll look for four-leaf clovers," Eden said, turning the shirt right side out. "Put up your arms." She pulled the garment back over Peyton's head.

"Umph," grumped Peyton. "Ugh."

"Behave," Eden warned. "Or we won't go out. Go brush your hair."

"I *did* already."

"Go do it again."

As Peyton stalked off to the bathroom, Eden, still kneeling on the carpet, resisted the urge to bow her head and pray for strength. She rose, trying to hide her exasperating sense of inadequacy.

She turned and met Owen's cold eyes. "I know," she said. "I'm not very good at any of this. You don't need to point it out."

"Good or not," he said, "you're all she has."

"For now," she said defensively.

"Maybe for good. Jessie says she wants you to promise to take care of her if she can't."

Eden recoiled in shock. Her heart began to hammer crazily. She was not cut out for motherhood, even on this temporary basis. "Keep her? Me?"

Peyton strolled back into the room, her hair hardly touched by the brush.

Eden went silent. They could not discuss this subject in front of the child.

"I'll walk you to the park," Owen said. "Let her play. We can talk there." The way he looked at her stirred a shiver within her, deep and cold.

A narrow footpath ran through the woods behind the house and led to the edge of a small state park. Eden remembered the land from years ago when it had only been an overgrown wilderness, not a park.

It was wild no more. It had been "developed," tamed and domesticated. A network of paved roads and hiking paths had been gouged into the moutainside. Eden looked with distaste at the clearing where trees had been hacked down to make room for camper hookups and cement picnic tables.

At the far end of the clearing, a children's playground had been erected. The steel poles and chains of the swings glinted coldly in the afternoon sunshine.

Most jarring to the eye were four plastic animals mounted on thick metal springs, with plastic saddles and plastic handles through their heads. But Peyton seemed to think the animals were wonderful. She climbed onto the back of a bright pink fish and began to bounce cautiously, as if she were not used to having fun.

Eden thrust her hands deep into the pockets of her slacks and looked Owen in the eye. "All right," she said. "What exactly did Jessie say about keeping Peyton?"

"She said 'If something happens to Mimi and me, too, Eden's got to take that child. It's her duty.'"

Eden almost swore in despair. She raised her chin high. "Me? How? I don't know anything about children. I don't want to know."

His voice held no sympathy. "Somebody has to take her. And Jessie's over seventy. Frankly, she's got no business taking on a child."

Eden turned from him, shaking her head. "Neither do I."

"She's concerned. She wants you to promise."

Eden kept her back to him, a stubborn, futile gesture, but she didn't care. She was overwhelmed—*keep* Peyton? It was impossible.

She was startled to feel his hand on her elbow, more startled when he wheeled her about to face him.

"Lie, if that's what you have to do," he said. "Words—that's all she wants from you at this point. Just words. In the meantime, I'll try to find Mimi."

Eden's breath congealed in her chest. She stared up into his blue eyes. "You? How can you find her?"

"Jessie said she thought the woman who left Peyton wore a T-shirt that said 'Ness Chevrolet.' She also thought the car had Missouri plates. When I left the hospital, I went to the local PD, had them run a computer check."

His hand still rested on her arm, and she was as conscious of it as if it were a burning brand. She could say nothing.

He said, "I got lucky. There's a Ness Chevrolet dealership in Sedonia, Missouri. I'm going up there, ask some questions."

"When?" She breathed the question.

"Now," he said. "I can make it before midnight, start checking things out in the morning. In the meantime, tell Jessie what she wants to hear."

Eden looked at Peyton, who was now earnestly riding the blue plastic elephant. The child's eyes met hers, and numbly Eden held her gaze. Gamely, hypocritically, she smiled.

"Give Jessie your promise for now," Owen said in a low voice. "Break it later. I don't give a damn what you do down the road. I'm worried about her now."

Eden felt as if she were slowly plunging into a nightmarish, limitless pit. *You've known from the start it would come to this,* she told herself. *Jessie's too old to be responsible for a child. That leaves me. Oh, God. Me, of all people.*

"She's an old woman," he said. "Promise her. That's all she wants."

I can't do this, she thought, but she looked at his relentless face and found herself saying the words: "All right. I—I promise."

He bent nearer, spoke in her ear. "Don't look so lost. If we find Mimi, your problems are over."

"No," she said, shaking her head and keeping her eyes trained on Peyton. "When it comes to Mimi, problems are never over. Never."

His hand clamped her elbow more tightly, and he drew her a fraction of an inch closer. "You said the woman named Constance called," he prompted. "What did she say? Do you think Jessie's right? Does this woman know Mimi?"

"Yes," Eden said miserably. "She asked right out if a child had arrived. She knew that Peyton was coming here. And she had such bizarre questions—"

"What sort of questions?" Owen demanded.

"Mysterious questions. Morbid. She asked—let me get things straight in my head—she asked where she should go."

He frowned. "Where was she calling from?"

"She wouldn't say. And she asked about death."

"Death?" His hand tautened against her flesh.

"She asked if people who died suddenly suffered much. She mentioned the people who died in that plane crash."

"The one in Miami? It wasn't a crash," he said, his brow moody. "It was a bomb. I heard it on the news."

"Either way, it was a strange thing to ask. And she was tense about it. I could hear it in her voice. And it's a strange voice, damaged. Like something's happened to her larynx. But there's another thing. I—I—"

"You're shaking," he said quietly. His tone was neither kind nor unkind.

"I am not," she replied.

"Yes, you are," he said. "I can feel it. What's wrong?"

"I had this crazy feeling," Eden said, "that maybe she didn't just know Mimi. That maybe she *was* Mimi."

He stared at her, his face expressionless. "Wouldn't Jessie have known?"

She said, "Jessie's hearing isn't what it used to be. And like I said, the voice is damaged. Even the speech rhythm's different from Mimi's. But there's something familiar about it. I don't know. Maybe I only imagined—"

"You're shaking," he repeated. He led her to a cement bench, made her sit, then sat beside her. He took his hand from her arm, and she was surprised that she wished he hadn't. His body was strong and surprisingly comforting.

He said, "Do you really think it could be Mimi?"

"I don't know. I just don't."

"If it's her, and she keeps calling, we'll find her."

Eden shook her head. "But what if she doesn't want Peyton? Or can't keep her?"

"Then maybe we can find the kid's father."

"Mimi doesn't know the father."

"That's what it says on the birth certificate. But what if there is a father somewhere? And a raft of other relatives—grandparents, aunts, uncles? There may be people out there who miss her, worry about her—want her."

Eden didn't answer. His argument offered a tempting new possibility of escape.

"Don't tell me it never occurred to you," Owen said, "that this kid could have other family besides you and Jessie."

"No, it didn't occur to me," Eden said tightly. "There's been no time. And I'm so used to thinking of all of us as loners—"

She paused, not wanting to finish the sentence.

"All of us?" he asked.

"Yes. Jessie. Mimi. Me—loners," she said unhappily. "I don't think in terms of—of families."

He gave her a fraction of a smile with no mirth. "Mimi didn't produce this child by Immaculate Conception. There had to be a man somewhere."

"Knowing Mimi, it was the wrong man."

"He could still love his daughter."

Eden said nothing. Peyton's father might not know she existed. He might not want to know. He might not care.

And maybe, she thought tiredly, the caller wasn't even Mimi at all. The whole situation had become surreal to her.

"Jessie hasn't got caller ID on that phone," Owen said. "I'll get it. And put a recording device on it. In the hope that Mimi—if it's her—calls again. I've already called about a security system."

"I don't need your help," she countered. "I can take care of myself—I always have."

"I promised your grandmother," he repeated.

Then he startled her by reaching out and gently straightening the collar of her blouse, his fingers lingering as if he were reluctant to do such a thing, and even more reluctant not to.

Eden's breath stopped, seemingly stuck in her throat, and warning rippled through her nerves. But she did not tell him not to touch her, and she did not move away from him.

She gazed up into his unwavering blue eyes and realized, *Damn, he wants me. And I want him. This is a complication I don't need. Damn. Damn. Damn.*

SEVEN

━━━∞∞∞━━━

EDEN SAT ON A PLAYGROUND SWING, LETTING IT SWAY
gently. Since the unexpectedly charged moment between her and Owen, neither of them had spoken.

Peyton played on the jungle gym, but not as tirelessly
as before. At last she climbed to its top and sat, staring off
into the distance, a small, lonely figure.

Eden forced herself not to look at her niece. Instead
she gazed down at the four-leafed clover Peyton had
given her. She twirled it between her thumb and forefinger.

I understand how she feels, she thought. *I know what
it's like to have a mother you can't depend on, who goes off
and leaves you. I know what it's like to be trundled off to
relatives you've never seen before.*

Owen stood leaning against one of the swing's metal

supports, arms crossed, watching the little girl atop the jungle gym. Without turning to Eden, he said, "She seems to be wearing down. Are you ready to go back?"

Eden kicked the swing into action. "I'll *never* be ready to go back."

"It can't be that bad," he said.

"You're not the one answering that phone. Or trying to watch a child all day. I don't belong here. I belong in California."

He gave an unsympathetic shrug. But to her surprise, he said, "I can help. Or try."

Eden's heart took a little lurch that was half wary, and, to her dismay, half excited. "You must have more important things to do."

"I'd just be hunting," he said. "I can arrange my time how I want."

"Lucky you," Eden said, pumping the swing so it would go faster. "Don't you work?"

"My family's got property. Since my father died, I manage it."

" 'My family's got property,' " she said, gently mocking him. "I like the sound of that. We were never able to say it. What property? Castles? Racehorses? Diamond mines?"

"Real estate," he muttered. "That's all. I manage my sisters' shares, too. They like the income, but not the math involved."

"Real estate's a nice, genteel business," she said. "So why'd you become a policeman—of all things?"

"Genteel's the last thing I wanted," he said. "I've got no talent for it."

"But you quit the police?" she asked, arching her body to the swing's motion. "And became genteel?"

"I quit," he said, stepping behind her. "I didn't become genteel." He caught the chains and brought her to a stop. His lean hands nearly touched hers. "Come on," he said. "Let's go back."

Raylene had picked up her car at the Dallas airport and spent the night in a Holiday Inn on the outskirts of the city. It had taken another eight tablets of Xanax to get her to sleep. This morning she'd risen early and driven straight through to Sedonia.

By the time she pulled into the farmyard that afternoon, she was half-ill from nerves and exhaustion. She got out of the car feeling used up and old.

But then Drace appeared on the porch of the farmhouse. It was as if a young god had manifested himself, and her fatigue fell away as if by magic. He descended the stairs of the farmhouse to meet her, the late afternoon sunlight gleaming on his golden hair.

Drace came to her and looked deeply into her eyes and smiled down at her, and she smiled back, tremulous and happy. They had done it. Flight 217 was ashes.

Wordlessly, he embraced Raylene, holding her close for a long, intense moment. Tears of joy and weariness welled in her eyes, and she clung to him.

"Soldier," Drace said against her hair, hugging her more tightly still. "My beautiful soldier girl."

Raylene closed her eyes in pleased surrender, her heart beating fast. But slowly she realized that there was tension in Drace's trim body, and that the arms that held her were rigid.

"Come to the creek," Drace said in her ear. "We need to talk."

He drew back but kept his arm around Raylene's shoulders. Together they walked toward the field that separated the farmyard from the creek. She was home again, she thought. Home at last.

Drace was a tall young man with sinuous, graceful movements. He wore his blond hair rather long and parted so that it fell forward in two waves that framed his brow. He was fair and blue-eyed and proud that he had one hundred percent Aryan blood.

His skin was flawless, and he much resembled Raylene, who was his cousin. She thought he had the most winning, most heart-stopping smile she had ever seen, a movie star's smile.

Raylene was smaller and seemingly more delicate than he, but she was strong for her size, well muscled without being muscular. She could go on many maneuvers with the best of men, including Drace himself.

Drace ruffled her hair with affection, but he seemed distracted somehow, not altogether happy.

"How's Yount?" Raylene asked, circling her arm around Drace's waist. She had seen no sign of the others.

"Better. He's healing."

"Is Stanek back yet?"

Stanek had traveled separately to meet Raylene in Florida. It was he who had assembled the bomb. Such things were his specialty. Yount had originally been selected to place the bomb, but the day before, he had badly cut his foot with an ax. Drace was going to plant the bomb himself, but Raylene had insisted she could do it.

Now the two cousins walked in silence, Drace's arm still draped around Raylene's shoulders. She did not ask about Mimi, she did not like her. She hated it that Drace wanted other women, even that he wanted other followers, though he said such thoughts weren't worthy of her.

She rubbed her cheek lightly against his bare, muscular arm. "Where's the next bomb?" she asked. "Have you decided?"

"Not yet," Drace said, his expression remote. He raised his eyes to the sky, which was gilding with twilight. "Maybe New Orleans. Maybe not."

"Who'll take it this time? Yount? Me?"

Me, she thought almost prayerfully. *Let it be me again.*

"Yount, if he's well enough."

Raylene's heart sank, but she kept her face stoically blank. She said nothing.

At last they reached the creek's high dirt bank. Drace dropped his arm from her shoulders, stooped, and picked up a handful of pebbles.

He stood watching the brown water swirl beneath him. He skipped a pebble along the water's surface. Then he turned and gave Raylene a measuring look.

"Mimi's gone," he said in his quiet voice. "She took the kid and split."

At first Raylene felt a surge of joy. But then the true import of what he said struck, and a shocked dread surged through her.

Mimi, she thought, stunned—that trashy guttersnipe. The bitch was gone, run away? She could undo them all, utterly.

Oh, Raylene had despised it when Drace had brought Mimi and her brat among them—but what could *she* say? She had resented both intruders, Mimi and that strange child of hers, with her black eyes always watching, her ears with the big, ugly earrings always listening.

She stared at Drace, too stricken to speak.

Drace shook his head sadly, so that his golden hair stirred around his face. "When you left for Miami?"

"Yes?"

His gaze locked with hers. "That same night, Mimi took the kid and left. Just walked away in the middle of the night."

Raylene's knees felt weak, the trees around her seemed to turn gray and dance drunkenly, and she wondered if she was going to faint. "Walked away?" she repeated. "But how far could she get walking?"

"I had all the car keys locked up," Drace said. "Of course."

Raylene nodded numbly. Of course. Drace was the keeper of the keys and the weapons, this was a given. And Mimi had never been allowed access to any of the vehicles except the old Mercury. Even if she'd secretly had another key made for it, the Mercury's gears were so faulty she could not count on it to get her far.

Yet it was fourteen miles to Sedonia, the only town of any size. She and her bastard brat might have caught a bus from there—but how could they have walked fourteen miles?

"She had help," Drace said, his jaw hardening.

"Help?" Raylene's voice rose. "Who in God's name would help her?"

"I gave that some thought," Drace said dryly. He let his fingers open slightly, let the pebbles sift through and fall.

"She's got no friends here." Raylene frowned, sincerely baffled. "She only knows us. She never went anywhere."

Drace leaned toward her, tenderly clasped the back of her neck. "She took money. A couple hundred dollars or more. She paid somebody to help her. I know who."

His breath was fragrant and she could feel it, warm, against her face. She looked into his beautiful eyes helplessly.

Drace seldom allowed Mimi to leave the farm; it was Stanek and Yount who usually went out. Mimi bitched and complained, but Drace let her go only a few places, none of them in town.

Sometimes, just to get her and Peyton out of the way, he would send them on minor errands. Mimi was allowed, for instance, to go to the NiteHawk Diner and convenience store to buy things like bread or milk or cheese.

"The diner," Raylene said accusingly. "She picked up some trucker or something."

Drace gave a silent laugh and shook his head. "I figured she must have contacted somebody last time she had the car. So I looked inside. I found a bag of spilled apples."

"Apples?" Raylene repeated, uncomprehending.

"Rotting," he said, his smile dying. "Stinking. Full of worms. And there was this with them."

From the pocket of his jeans he drew a folded square of paper and handed it to Raylene. She unfolded it and saw it was a badly photostated copy of two recipes and a Bible verse. Beneath the verse was written, in a shaky scrawl, "From Your Freind Louise Brodnik."

The page seemed familiar to Raylene, for she had seen others like it, in bags of raspberries and beans and tomatoes. She had a sudden mental image of the woman's tacky little blue house, the signs in the yard for vegetables and baby-sitting.

"The Garden Lady?" she breathed.

Drace caressed her cheek with the back of his hand, then turned from her to stare out over the creek. "I looked up her number, phoned her. I called her. No answer. Finally, last night I drove over there. No lights on. No car in the garage. She was gone."

Raylene was bewildered. "Then it wasn't her?"

"I had this feeling," Drace said almost dreamily. "So today I had Stanek keep an eye on her place. Drive past it once every hour or so. She got back this afternoon."

Raylene's heart pounded hard. She nodded, waiting for him to go on.

"So I called, told her I'm looking for them. That I have reason to believe she'd seen Mimi and the kid. I say 'You better tell me, lady, because I'm that kid's father, and I'm looking for her. I don't want to bring the law up against you.'"

Raylene's heart beat more wildly. The lie about the father was good, she told herself, very good.

"I scared her, I could tell," Drace said with a soft laugh. "But she's spunky. She said 'Don't ask me about her whereabouts. Ask her *people*.'"

"Her people?" Raylene said, bewildered. "What did she mean?"

"That's what I said. 'What do you mean, her people?' She says 'Her family. Her blood kin.' And she hung up on me. Rude. Extremely rude."

"Then she knows where they are," Raylene said, awed by Drace's powers of detection.

Drace turned to face her again. The fading sun made his face look golden. "We need to get to them. I want them. She's burned us. And they know too much. Both of them."

It was true, Raylene thought, her fear rising again. Mimi knew almost everything about the bombing, and the damned kid had always been underfoot, listening and watching like a dark and evil imp.

"But how do we find them?" she asked.

"I'm having Stanek keep watch on the old woman's

place," Drace said and stared up at the sky. It was slowly starting to darken.

"B-but," Raylene stammered, "what's this about Mimi's 'people'? About 'blood kin'? She always said she had no family."

Drace kissed her lightly on the lips. He smiled his beguiling smile. "We'll have to have a talk with the Garden Lady about that," he said. "Won't we?"

Owen came into the office to hook up the recorder and caller ID, and Peyton followed him. She stood in the doorway of Jessie's office, a truculent expression on her face. "Are you going home soon?" she asked Owen.

"Peyton!" Eden exclaimed. "That's not polite. Say you're sorry."

Owen bent over Jessie's desk, attaching his own caller identification device to her unplugged phone.

"You shouldn't touch my granny's phone," Peyton said accusingly.

"I *want* him to do this," Eden said, warning in her voice. "Now say you're sorry. I mean it."

"I'm sorry," Peyton said with no sincerity whatever.

Eden put her hand on the child's shoulder and drew her from the doorway and into the hall. "Go watch television. Draw pictures. Leave Mr. Charteris alone."

Peyton shrugged and skipped off down the hall.

"Oh, God," Eden said, raking her hand through her bangs.

"Forget it," he said shortly. "You ever used a caller ID before?"

"Yes," she said, "but will it do any good? A lot of Jessie's calls are long distance. Most won't register."

He shook his head. "It's a long shot. Anybody who

wants to block his name and number from showing can do it. But we cover as many bases as we can."

He reached into the worn leather satchel he'd brought from his house and took out a sophisticated-looking black device with buttons and cords.

"This is a recorder," he said. "It'll tape all your calls, incoming, outgoing. You can get eight hours on a tape." He took off the cord that attached the phone to the receiver and plugged in the one that fed into the recording machine.

Eden watched, feeling dubious. "It looks complicated."

"It's not. Once I set it up, it's voice-activated. You don't have to do anything but change the tape when the red light comes on. You take out the cassette, put another one in. It's simple."

"But is this legal?" she asked. "To tape someone without telling them?"

"It varies from state to state," he said. "You can do it here."

She was hesitant. "Some of the people who call say—well—pretty intimate things."

"We'll erase those. It's only this 'Constance' we want."

Eden shook her head uncertainly. "But even if she phones again, what good will it do to record her?"

He slipped in a cassette, punched a button, then straightened and met her eyes. "It's surveillance. If she identifies herself, lets anything slip, we have a record."

"And if she doesn't identify herself? What then?"

"I want Jessie to hear her. To see if she thinks it could be Mimi."

Eden wasn't certain Jessie should be told of her suspicion, but she said nothing.

"And," Owen said, "if she calls again, keep her talking as long as you can. Draw her out. Play her. You're smart. You can do it."

"Right," she said sardonically. "Eden Storey, junior G-girl."

"Are you ready for me to plug this phone back in?"

"Of course not."

"Tough," he said and plugged it in.

She gritted her teeth and looked at the carved box of file cards on the desk. "I should ask Jessie about these repeat callers today, the steady customers. I'm flying almost blind."

"She'll call," he said. "Right now let's order the kid's pizza."

Eden squared her shoulders stoically. "I suppose we should use the other phone."

He nodded.

She moved to the doorway, wishing she did not so strongly sense his presence behind her.

"I don't know what to do about Peyton," she said, glancing up at him. "Her manners are terrible. But I hate to discipline her when her mother's disappeared and her whole world's topsy-turvy. I don't know the right thing—"

From Jessie's office the telephone rang shrilly. Eden stopped, her body tensing. "No," she said in utter disgust. "Not yet. Not so soon."

The ring summoned her again. Owen's angular face was almost sympathetic. "Go on," he said.

She sighed and crossed the room to the desk. Owen stayed in the doorway. She picked up the receiver as gingerly as if she were taking up a snake that might be poisonous.

She reached deep within herself to find the right personality, the right voice, the right cadence. "Sister Jessie, God's gifted seer," she said.

"Jessie, this is Floyd S. Copley in Las Vegas. Remember me? Somebody in Phoenix offered me a sweet little real-estate deal that sounds too good to be true. Lay down those cards for me, will you? Tell me yes or no."

Eden put her fingertips to her head, which had started to ache again. "How much money we talking here, Floyd?"

"Couple million, Jessie, honey. Come on. You always been lucky for me. Lay those babies down."

Eden's sense of inadequacy pinched her like an evil elf. *Floyd,* she thought bleakly, *you're asking the blind to lead the blind.* But she took a deep breath and began to deal out the cards.

Twenty minutes later, Owen heard Jessie's phone ring again—yet another call coming in—and walked down the hall to check on Eden. He knocked, opened the door, and leaned against the door frame, one eyebrow cocked in question.

She darted him a brief look and shook her head to say no. None of her callers had been out of the ordinary.

She turned back to the receiver and unleashed a line of occult chatter, sounding more like Jessie than Jessie herself. He found it eerie to hear the old woman's deep and ominous voice coming from Eden's pretty lips.

He stood in the doorway, watching her. Intense concentration marked her smooth brow, and she held her body rigidly, but nothing in the voice sounded forced or false. Still, he could see she was not merely uncomfortable doing Jessie's job, she hated it.

But she was good. Owen allowed himself a small,

cynical smile. As she expertly shuffled the cards, she threw him a short, eloquent look that said, *Go away. I don't like being watched.*

Mirthless smile still in place, he turned from her, but her image lingered, haunting him. For the first time he allowed himself to imagine undressing her, of undoing her buttons, sliding away her clothing, piece by whispering piece. He envisioned her body beneath his own, bare and opening to him.

No, he told himself in cold common sense. No. She was too different from him, and she was his friend's granddaughter. All he wanted was a lay. That he could always find.

In the living room, Peyton lay, as usual, before the television, her crayons scattered around her. The news was on, the serious-faced anchorman droning about the explosion of the Naussau-Air plane in Miami.

The child stared at the screen, her crayon motionless against the paper and, for once, her thumb not in her mouth. Her expression was dazed, almost drugged, and her face pallid. Did Owen see tears rising in her eyes, or did he only imagine it?

In concern he gazed down at her. "Hey," he said gruffly, "are you all right?"

She did not answer. Her gaze, unblinking, remained fastened on the screen as if she were hypnotized by it. Her breathing had become shallow and somewhat raspy.

The anchorman spoke in the solemn tones of a funeral director. "Several terrorist groups have claimed credit for the explosion, but FBI officials say the investigation is still open. The bomb may have been in the luggage hold—"

Peyton squeezed her eyes shut and covered her ears with her hands.

Owen's concern turned to alarm. Was the kid having a fit, a tantrum—what? He knelt beside her, gripping her by her shoulders. "Peyton?" he said. "Peyton?"

"The plane burned up," she said in a quavering voice. "They burned it all up."

Owen's hands tightened on her shoulders, and he drew her up to a sitting position. She was limp as a kitten, but she sat, her eyes still shut, tears streaking her cheeks. She grimaced, showing her broken tooth.

"Peyton," he said earnestly, "it's all right. What happened to the plane happened a long way off."

She tried to struggle from his grasp. "I want Eden."

"Eden's right down the hall," he said. "She'll be here in a minute, I promise."

"I want Eden *now*," Peyton said, her voice a small wail.

Owen wondered if he should try to take the child into his arms, but he could not bring himself to do it.

He tried to take her by the hand. Peyton's eyes flew open, and although they still had a glazed, otherworldly look, she wrenched away from him with surprising strength. "Don't!" she cried.

"I'm not trying to hurt you," he said, holding his hand toward her, but she wouldn't touch it.

What should he do? Owen wondered bleakly. Call a doctor, an ambulance, a psychiatrist, an exorcist?

The doorbell buzzed, a harsh, unexpected sound that made the child jump. Owen, startled, turned toward the front door.

He heard Peyton take a large, gasping breath, like someone preparing to dive into an enormous deep. He hoped she wasn't going to scream.

"It's okay," he said, not looking at her. "It's probably just the pizza delivery man."

He went to the door, glanced through the spyhole. A skinny kid in a yellow shirt stood holding a large, flat box with a grease stain on it.

"It's just the pizza man," Owen reassured her. "I'm opening the door, okay?"

She was blessedly silent as he took the pizza, paid for it, and gave the skinny kid a tip. If the boy noticed anything strange about Peyton, if he saw her at all, he gave no indication.

Owen turned, shutting the door. The living room was empty. The back door to the kitchen stood open, swaying in the cool evening breeze.

Peyton was gone. She had run away, vanished into the thickening dark.

EIGHT

—◦◦◦—

THEY FOUND HER IN THE WOODS, HIDING AMONG AN outcropping of huge stone ledges. She lay in the dirt, huddled under a shelf of limestone that was mottled with moss and lichen.

She had knotted herself into the smallest size possible, like an animal that hides because it fears for its life. It was Owen who discovered her, the beam of his flashlight illuminating her terrified, staring face.

The child had been missing almost twenty minutes, an interminable time, an eternity. Eden wept in relief. She managed to half draw, half haul Peyton out of the shallow crevice. Then she buried her face in the girl's neck and sat weakly on the shelf, unable to stand.

Peyton sobbed against her chest, a crying that Eden found rending because the child fought so hard to keep it silent. "It's all right," she kept repeating to the trembling girl. "It's all right."

Below them, the wooded hill fell gently away, and the forest thinned into the tamed lawn of the park's playground clearing. The moon glittered silver on the chains of the swings, and the plastic animals on their springs seemed to sleep, enchanted, under the stars.

At last Peyton fell into an uneasy sleep, from exhaustion, perhaps. Owen took her from Eden's arms and hoisted her to his shoulder. He held her easily in place with one arm, and with his free hand used his flashlight to find their way back to the path.

Eden's bones ached with fatigue, her hands and face and clothing were dirty, and she felt bedraggled and emotionally spent. She trudged at Owen's side, the leaves crackling beneath their feet. Somewhere a mockingbird sang ecstatically at the moon. Eden barely noticed.

She shook her head in weary wonder. "How'd she ever find such a place? Off the beaten path?"

"It's not that far off," Owen said in a low voice. "The rock's pale—it stands out in the moonlight. Instinct must have told her not to go for the clearing."

She glanced up at him, the stern angles of his face shifting in the changing light and shadow. "How'd *you* ever find it? How'd you know where to look?"

"My nephews found it. My sister Rita's kids. They pretended it was a fort."

"But how did you guess?" she demanded. She gestured at the forest surrounding them, trees like dark pillars.

He shrugged his free shoulder. "She couldn't run forever. It's a good place to lie low. I guessed lucky, that's all."

You guessed smart, Eden thought, but she said nothing.

"The doorbell threw her into a panic," he said, his voice moody. "Like she thought somebody'd come after her. But she was scared before that. I went into the living room, and she was staring at the TV screen like it was a snake. It was a news story. Then she freaked out."

Eden frowned helplessly. "A news story?"

He nodded curtly. "About the plane burning in Miami. Didn't want to look at it, didn't want to hear it."

"The plane in Miami?" Eden asked. "That woman—Constance—mentioned that same plane. Do you think it means something?"

"I don't know," he said. "It's in the news. Maybe it's a coincidence."

Peyton stirred restlessly in his arms. He thrust his flashlight toward Eden. "Here. Take this, will you?"

She did and watched uneasily as he shifted the girl in his arms, cradled the back of her head with his lean hand. Peyton sighed and nestled limply against his shoulder. The child looked safe in his arms, taken care of.

It occurred to Eden that Owen Charteris's arms might be a very wonderful place, indeed, in which to rest, to renew her own strength. Shamed, she pushed away the thought with almost savage force.

"What do you think?" he asked quietly. "We put her straight to bed? Clean her up, feed her first? What do you do in a case like this?"

"I have no idea," Eden said.

They rounded one of the path's many twisting curves. Through the dark, autumnal forest, she could see the first sign of light from Jessie's house.

Almost home, she thought, then her mind recoiled from the word.

This was not home and never would be again, never. They would find Mimi and give back her child, and then Eden could truly go home, a place as distant from this one as possible.

In the house, Owen carried Peyton into the bedroom, then transferred her to Eden's arms. Gingerly she lowered the girl to the bed. She unlaced her muddy shoes and drew them off. Leaving the bedroom light on, she carried the shoes into the kitchen and set them down beside the back door to dry. Owen followed her.

As she rose, he gave her a meaningful look. "Listen. We need to talk about that kid."

Eden's muscles were taut, and her ears buzzed as if phantom phone voices still teased them. The pizza, cold and still unopened on the table, smelled vile to her. All she wanted was coffee, hot and black and bracing.

She said, "We've been a lot of trouble to you. I'm sorry. You've been very kind."

A deep line appeared between his brows. "Frankly, right before she ran away, it was like she had some kind of—spell or something. I think there's something wrong with her."

Eden's heart lurched sickly. "A spell?"

"She shook, her eyes were a million miles off—you should probably take her to a psychologist. And a doctor. Whatever's happening to her, this kid is *not* normal."

Not normal, not normal, not normal. The words rang like an evil knell in Eden's head. It was what she had always feared. Given the family history, if she or Mimi ever had a child, it would, in all likelihood, not be *normal.*

"Don't look so stricken," he said. "It's not your fault."

But somehow it did seem like her fault, or at least her inevitable heritage, some unclean thing that she, like Mimi, carried in her genes.

"She's such a pretty little girl in her way," she said softly. "She seems smart and creative. It's such a shame—" She could not finish the sentence. "It's such a shame," she whispered.

She set about making coffee simply to have something to do. She didn't want to meet Owen's ice-blue eyes.

He moved to her side. "What I said, I didn't mean it the way it probably sounded. I meant her situation isn't normal, that's all. And it's affecting her."

"Yes, well. It'd affect anyone, wouldn't it?" she said briskly. "And my family has its little peculiarities, I'll be the first to admit."

"I said it wrong," he returned. "I don't know about things like this, and I said it wrong."

She busied herself with measuring out the coffee. She wondered, in a dim, harried way, if he was actually apologizing.

He leaned his hip against the counter, crossed his arms. In the small kitchen, he seemed too near for comfort.

For the first time she noticed how bedraggled she was. Dirt and pieces of leaves clung to her white sweater, and the knees of her slacks were filthy from kneeling in the dirt, struggling to budge Peyton from her hiding place.

Suddenly all the night's emotions came swarming back so thickly they seemed to smother her: concern for Mimi, shock and despair at Peyton's disappearance, the panic of the hunt, the wave of relief so strong she'd been faint with it.

Her knees weakened, and she turned from Owen so he wouldn't see her tears. She put her hands to her eyes to hide them. "Oh, God," she said in a strangled voice. "What am I going to *do* with her?"

Immediately she despised herself for being so weak. She clamped her lips together, but her shoulders shook with repressed sobs.

She was surprised to feel his hands on her, warm and strong. "Oh, come here," he said gruffly and put his arms around her, turning her to him and drawing her close.

She tried to resist both tears and his effort to comfort her. "Crying's not a felony," he said. "Just do it."

Her body felt stiff and awkward in his embrace, and she knew she should pull away from him, but didn't even know if her legs could support her. She gave in to the overwhelming clamor of her emotions and sank against him. She wept until she was exhausted.

He held her tightly, almost rigorously, his hands not moving. Her cheek rested against the hardness of his chest, and she could feel the steady, powerful beat of his heart. Her own hands, she realized, gripped his upper arms almost convulsively.

She forced herself to untighten her fingers, to draw back slightly. "I'm sorry," she said shakily. "I shouldn't have done that. I don't even know you."

Slowly he raised his hand and with his thumb stroked at a tear streak drying on her cheek.

She drew in her breath, held it. Hesitantly, as if against his wish, his thumb traced itself down her cheek again.

"You've known me for years," he said in a low voice.

Her heart rapped crazily at her ribs. "I never really knew you. I don't even know what you are to Jessie. Or why you're helping us like this."

His hand went still. Although he did not move, a distance seemed to insinuate itself between them, to grow and widen. At last he said, "When my wife was dying, Jessie—helped her."

"Oh," she said and thought, *Of course he had a wife. A man like this would have had a lovely wife. A man like this would have had a perfect wife.*

"Oh," she said again. "I'm sorry."

"Not as sorry as I am," he said, his face hardening oddly.

They looked at each other. He drew back. In confusion, she tried to gather her thoughts, her dignity, her usual coolness. She turned toward the counter.

"Coffee?" she asked, making her tone brisk and businesslike.

"No, thanks," he said. "If I'm going to Sedonia, I need to start. I've got a cell phone. I'll leave you the number."

She watched as he moved to a notepad Jessie had on the far counter. He picked up the pen beside it and quickly scrawled the number. He looked up at her, his blue eyes unreadable.

"If Peyton says anything that might help, call me."

She nodded, trying again to be brisk and businesslike.

"I'll be in touch with you, too," he said. They eyed each other almost as if they were opponents taking the other's measure.

He said, "You'll be all right alone?"

She looked away. "Of course." She was used to being

alone, taking care of herself. She had grown to *like* being alone.

"Right," he said. "Well. I'll let the dog out, then go. I'll leave a key under the mat. If you'd let him out in the morning, I'd appreciate it."

"Certainly," she answered, still not looking at him. "I'll be glad to."

"Thanks," he said. "Tell Jessie hello."

She nodded. She heard him move to the kitchen door, let himself out. She heard the sound of his boot heels cross the cement porch, descend the steps, fade away.

Her heart still hammered drunkenly in her chest.

Fifteen minutes later, she heard his car pull out of the drive. *There,* she thought, with a strange surge of relief, *he's gone.*

But she felt lonely, in a way she'd never felt in Los Angeles. The house seemed small and vulnerable and lost in the midst of nowhere. Without him, it felt as fragile as an eggshell. She was glad that he'd said he'd ordered a security system for it.

She rinsed out her coffee cup, just to keep busy, and realized that she hadn't gone to see Jessie tonight, hadn't even called her. "Damn," she muttered.

She moved into the living room and picked up the receiver of Jessie's home phone and dialed the hospital. When Jessie answered, she sounded in a combative mood. "Good of you to call—at last," she said. "Nice of you to take time—finally."

Eden fought back a sigh of exasperation. "I'm sorry," she said. "There's been a lot to take care of."

"Indeed?" Jessie said. "I hoped you'd bring my little

Peyton to see me. How is she? How's my little honeyduck?"

Eden knew she could not tell Jessie the truth, that Peyton had run away. She settled for the half-truth. "Peyton's exhausted. She fell asleep half an hour ago."

Jessie made a sound suspiciously like *hmmph*. "Have you heard anything from Mimi?" she demanded.

Eden blinked hard, gritted her teeth. Had she heard from Mimi? Or was she only imagining wild and impossible things? "Jessie, if I knew anything, I'd tell you right away."

"I dreamed about her," Jessie said in her sibyl's voice. "I dreamed she was standing by the river. She was standing by the flowing river, ready to follow it home."

"Owen's gone to Missouri to look for her. He's got a lead." Eden explained about the Chevrolet dealer in Sedonia.

"Sedonia," Jessie said thoughtfully. "I get vibrations from that name. Sedonia. What's Peyton say about it?"

"Peyton's not talking. She's scared to. I don't want to push her too hard. She gets—emotional."

"How's my phone line? Did Constance call?"

Eden made her voice cool and confident. "Yes. I couldn't get much out of her. She was vague. And odd. She started by asking some strange questions."

"About what?"

"About that plane wreck in Florida, for one thing. She wanted to know if the people suffered."

Jessie was silent for a long moment. "I dreamed about that plane," she said at last. "I saw a woman. She was standing with her hand full of fire. It danced in her hand like a live thing."

Eden frowned. "A woman?"

"Indeed," Jessie asserted. "She's got yeller hair. Pretty as a picture on the outside, but inside she's a burning flag."

"A burning flag?" Eden repeated, puzzled.

"I don't know why that come to me, it just did," Jessie said. "I seen her hand was full of burning, and her heart was, too."

"But a flag?" Eden questioned. "Why a flag?"

"I don't *know* why," Jessie retorted. "It's what the spirits showed me. That, and the letter *d*. Somebody important in her life, their name's got a *d* in it."

"Jessie, millions of people have a *d* in their name," Eden objected. "*Your* name has a *d*. So does mine."

"I don't care to argue," Jessie said rather grandly.

"All right," Eden said, "but there's more. This—this Constance. She said she was worried about a child who took a journey. She wanted to know if she'd arrived safely. She had to mean Peyton. And almost as soon as I said the child was safe, she hung up on me."

"Ha," said Jessie. "I knowed it. You wouldn't believe me. Well, now you see."

Eden shook her head in bewilderment. Jessie didn't sound upset or even surprised. Only triumphant.

"Jessie . . ." Eden paused uneasily, "Did this woman, this Constance sound familiar to you? At all?"

"Ha," said Jessie. "I'd remember that voice. She croaks like a raven."

"You don't think you might know her from somewhere?"

Jessie ignored the question. "Tomorrow you bring Peyton to see me," she said. "In the meantime, you mind that phone. Hear?"

"I hear, I hear. But—"

"Here comes the nurse with my sleeping pill," Jessie grumbled. "They push pills down your gullet and poke you and prod you all day. You give Peyton a hug for me. I got to hang up now."

Jessie's receiver banged down so aggressively that Eden winced.

She turned and saw Peyton's tablet and scattered crayons on the floor in front of the television. She bent to pick them up, but when she saw the child's drawing, her hand stopped in midair, and her blood chilled.

The crude picture again showed the house with the angry red door. Beside it stood a woman with yellow hair and one arm stretched out before her. In her upturned hand danced a bright orange fire.

Bright orange fire flared from the match. Mimi inhaled.

It was almost midnight. Tonight, for a while, the music had made her feel almost healed, but now the music had faded, so she killed the pain with wine.

Drace hadn't let anybody drink or smoke—except himself. And only Raylene was allowed to take pills of any kind. Mimi wished she'd stolen about a hundred of those pills.

But she had the wine, at least, and cigarettes again. Now, by the dim glow of the bedside lamp, she wrote. She sat cross-legged in her underwear on the unmade bed, hunched over the tablet, her pen moving laboriously.

The words danced and weaved in her vision. The more she'd drunk, the more erratically she'd written and spelled, but she didn't care. One thing had become of the utmost importance to her.

Tell the truth to everybody.

To Whom it May Concern:

I did not mean to become involved with the bombing of the flight to the Bahamas. I thought the plan was just talk nothing more until it was too late. By then I was frigten frihgten frighten for my life and the life of my child. I had objected to bombing and made them angry and we were littel better than prisnors there with them I was not even really sure they would really do it until it was too late, it was done.

My first concern was to get my child to safety but I feared that I could not go with her as I would bring danger down onto her and my famly. At first I thougt I would send her away and return to my former companions and let them do what they would to me, what did it matter, I have ruined my life.

But I was frihten what they would do to me, they would make me say where I had sent her. So when time came to send away my child I knew I could not go back to them, they would make me tell and kill me but I could not go with her, they could follow and kill us all

I am writeing this now so that authoritis will know who is responsabel reposnible for the bombing but I do not want to go to prison again, I can't stand to go to prison again, but I want my famly to be safe and happy and I want to do the rite thing.

Here are the peopl involve in bombing
Drace Johansen
Raylene Johansen

Wm Stanek

Jame Yount

They claim to be agains a corupt goverment, I was misled, I thought I was among freind, Drace befreind me and recrute me and I thought he love me but he did not There is only one person he ever love beside himself and they are both

Since childhood they have been

He olny wanted me because of

When I protested he and she

When I start to understand he and she

When I understand he and she her and I

Mimi frowned harder and tried to cross out the last lines. Her pen wavered, missed its stroke, made a senseless scrawl across the page.

Oh, Christ, she thought in anger and disgust. *All I'm doing is incriminating myself. Peyton and Jessie are better off never knowing any of it. Eden, too.*

She was a fucking fool to try to explain it, there was no way to explain it, none. Suddenly she realized what was really of the utmost importance:

Don't tell the truth to anyone.

She rose with a lurch, stumbled into the bathroom and tore the piece of paper to bits. She flushed it down the toilet and stood, leaning against the counter.

Another drink or two, she told herself. Then she'd be able to sleep. She made her way back to the bed, refilled her wineglass, took one long draft, then another.

The drink made her eyes heavy. She closed them and sagged against the pillow. Dizzily she remembered the music and thought, *Once I had a beautiful voice and could have been somebody. I hate my voice. I hate it.*

She slept and dreamed of her childhood, of her and

Eden playing behind the trailer. They were singing together in their strong, young voices. It was a pleasant
dream.

Beside her, on the nightstand, lay her show tickets
and cigarettes and matches. The wine bottle was nearly
empty.

The other bottle, the one that did not contain wine,
still stood unopened on the bathroom counter, waiting
for her.

Owen didn't reach Sedonia until after midnight. He
checked into a drab room in a humdrum motel on the
edge of town. The mattress felt as if it had been stuffed
with shot puts and anvils.

He slept restlessly, and toward dawn he had an unsettling dream about Laurie. She was alive, healthy, and
whole again, and she was impossibly young, eighteen
perhaps.

It was twilight, and she faced him across the clearing
in the park, which was slightly misty. Between them
stood the foolish plastic animals on their thick springs,
looking empty and forlorn.

"I want children," she said, her young face sad. "I
want children."

"I know," he said and swallowed hard. He wanted to
go to her, but he could not move. He was rooted, like the
artificial animals, to the earth.

"Why can't I have them?" she asked.

"It isn't meant to be," he told her. "It doesn't matter
to me. I don't need them. All I want is you."

Her beautiful hazel eyes filled with tears. "Why can't
I have them?"

"I don't want them," he told her. "I just want you."

Then she stretched out her hands as if reaching them to children who were running through the mist toward her. But instead, his mother materialized, and it was she who took Laurie's hands.

His mother looked very old, at least a hundred, although she was only sixty-five. She wore a hospital dressing gown and had an oxygen tube clamped on her face, feeding her nostrils. She looked at him without recognition.

"Who are you?" his mother demanded, looking frightened of him. "Who are you, and what do you want?"

He woke with a start, because he knew where the dream went next: the hospital, with Laurie dying in childbirth. She died in horrible pain in the dream, and what she labored to bring forth was a tiny, fragile skeleton, with empty eyes and an emptier grin, lying motionless in a pool of blood.

He sat up in bed with his heart galloping painfully and his temples banging. He ran his hand over his face, not knowing at first where he was. Sweat filmed his upper lip.

Swiftly, in vivid pieces, it came back to him: the strange, abandoned little girl whose mother had disappeared, Jessie's accident, the arrival of Eden Storey. All this had led him to the shithole town of Sedonia, Missouri, on the outside chance he could scare up a trace of Mimi.

He rubbed his hand over his face again and forced himself to get out of the lumpy bed. He knew he would not sleep again.

He showered, shaved, and dressed. He got into his Blazer and realized he still had his bow-hunting equipment in the hatch. How simple his plans had seemed a few days ago, how elemental.

He drove to an all-night convenience store, the Gas 'n' Go. He bought a large container of black coffee, drove to the edge of the Gasconade River, and parked. Drinking the bitter coffee, he watched the sun come up, tinting the haze over the river. He found himself thinking of Eden Storey.

Last night, he'd taken her into his arms too easily; it had disturbed him and, against his will, excited him. But he didn't want that excitement; it seemed too much akin to caring. He never wanted to care for a woman that way again.

As Owen watched the rising of the red sun over the river, Drace, Raylene, and Stanek made their way through the misty wood. The wood bordered Louise Brodnik's land.

Raylene was proud that Drace had let her come, and she felt a certain feminine righteousness as well; she was a better shot than Stanek, better in general with firearms than either he or Yount. She and Drace had grown up with hunting rifles and target pistols; they had known how to shoot from childhood.

Now she and the men moved through the thinly lit forest with its wisps of low-lying fog. They moved with eerie silence over the carpet of damp cedar needles and fallen leaves, their heavy boots falling soundlessly.

Their trousers were the dull, splotched colors of woodland camouflage. Raylene had taken tucks in hers, so they fit more becomingly. They all wore ski masks, black thermal sweaters, and gloves of black leather.

They emerged noiselessly at the edge of the woods and stopped, looking at the back of Louise Brodnik's small blue house. The sky was growing lighter but the sun was not yet visible, and the mist weaved about them like ghosts dancing to slow, unheard music.

Drace made a gesture for them to advance on the house, and they did so, Drace behind the other two, covering the rear. Stanek drew a pair of sharp-edged pliers from his belt and snipped the phone wire that fed into the house. It fell, like a long toy snake to the dewy ground.

Then he used a glass cutter to etch a circle in the window of the back door, and with a suction cup he pulled the disk away and kept the glass from falling or shattering. He reached inside the door and unlocked it.

The door creaked open, and Stanek edged his way into the kitchen, and Raylene and Drace followed. The room was small and shadowy, the blinds of its single window drawn. Raylene took her flashlight from its holster and flicked it on. She saw a dog's small, empty bed in the corner, but no dog.

She went to the door that led to the living room. Stanek was behind her now, and so was Drace. The living room was quiet, somnolent, the only sound the ticking of a small cuckoo clock over the television.

Drace took the lead and moved silently down the hallway, softly opening doors that revealed first a linen closet, then a bathroom, and then a bedroom. A huddled figure lay on a bed in the darkness, snoring quietly. It was the woman.

Beside Drace, Raylene gripped her rifle more tightly and felt a swell of excited power that was triumphant and unexpectedly sensual.

NINE

❦

THE SUN HAD RISEN, HIDDEN BY GRAY CLOUDS. FOR AN hour it had climbed, its pallid light veiled.

Although the bedroom was still dark, Peyton clambered into Eden's bed and shook her shoulder to wake her. Kneeling, she bounced, making the mattress buck.

"Eden, get up. It's morning. I'm hungry."

Eden groaned and covered her eyes with her arm. Memories crowded back in a jumble as she realized where she was and who was caroming about her bed.

Peyton stood up, then fell backward onto her rump so that the bed shuddered as if in an earthquake. "Get up!" Peyton urged.

"Oh, Jeez," Eden said, sitting up sleepily. "We've got to work on your etiquette."

She rose and stumbled into the kitchen, the child at

her heels. Although Peyton wanted pizza, Eden cajoled her into eating Froot Loops in milk and drinking orange juice.

The child was still dressed in the muddy clothes she'd worn last night, and there was still a fragment of leaf clinging to her dark hair. She ate noisily and far too fast, like a person who does not know when the next meal will be. Eden itched to correct her but did not.

Time, she told herself, watching the child gulp down a second bowl of cereal. It was going to take time to win Peyton's trust and civilize her ways. It was like trying to tame a little wild creature.

After a fourth helping, Peyton pushed the bowl away and wiped her mouth with the back of her hand. She turned to Eden, a look of apprehension suddenly coming into her eyes.

"Are you staying today? Henry says you should stay."

Sympathy, mixed with remorse, pinched Eden's heart. "I'll stay today," she said. *I don't want you, kid, but for now we're stuck with each other.*

"Will you stay tomorrow?" Peyton asked uneasily.

"Yes. Go brush your teeth. We'll go to Mr. Charteris's house and walk his dog. Then we'll come back and give you a bath and wash your hair."

Peyton's face went sulky, but she obeyed. Eden dressed hurriedly in jeans and an aqua-blue T-shirt. She put on her shoes and helped Peyton with hers.

She held the girl's hand as they crossed the hundred yards that separated Jessie's small house from Owen's large one. Eden found the key under the mat and unlocked the door, swinging it open.

She stepped inside, drawing the suddenly reluctant Peyton with her. "I don't like this house," Peyton said, wrinkling her nose in distaste. "It's not happy."

The child's words struck her with unexpected accuracy and force. The house, empty, looming, shadowed, smelling of sawdust, was *not* happy.

It did not seem possible to her that someone lived here. The living room and dining room were empty, torn apart, with exposed beams and wires hanging like raw ganglia from the ceiling. The only furnishings were a pair of scarred sawhorses and a paint-spattered stepladder.

Plaster dust lay across the raw wood floors like frost, and the only sound was that of a thin scuttling, as if a small rodent or large insect were fleeing from the human intruders.

In the kitchen, an elderly refrigerator hummed in one corner. The stove had been torn out, but a small microwave, incongruously new, stood on the remains of a counter. The back door was boarded shut.

There was a brand-new sink, a dilapidated table with one folding chair, and in the far corner, a dish for dog food, a dish for water, and a faded pet bed.

In the bed lay an elderly dog, truly an ancient dog, staring toward them with eyes clouded with cataracts. He sniffed the air. His tail gave a hesitant thump.

Instinctively Eden knew this animal must have belonged to Owen's wife; it was not a man's dog, it was the sort of animal bred to lie in a lap and have ribbons in its hair.

A worn leather leash hung from a nail on the wall over the water dish. Eden took it down, then knelt by the dog. She spoke to it, and it wagged again, more enthusiastically. When she stretched out her hand for its inspection, it sniffed, wagged, and licked her fingers, delicately at first, then with something akin to ecstasy.

An eerie realization seized her. The dog was happy to see a woman. *I will not be sentimental about this miserable dog,* she told herself sternly. *I will not.* She snapped the leash to its collar with a businesslike click, scooped the animal up, and started toward the front door.

Peyton hung back. "That dog's going to die."

"Come on," Eden said, purposely ignoring the statement.

Peyton trudged behind her, scowling. "I know what a dying dog looks like. I seen one."

Eden's instincts prickled. "You have?" she asked casually. "Where?"

Peyton looked suddenly wary. "Somewhere," she said.

They passed a hallway that Eden hadn't noticed before. She looked down it and saw a door standing ajar. Peyton saw it, too, and went to peek in. "That's where *he* sleeps," the child said with distaste. "That man."

Curiosity overcame Eden, and she stepped down the hall and peered inside the room. Immediately she regretted it. She, who fiercely guarded her own privacy, had invaded someone else's. But Peyton was right. The room was his.

A narrow mattress lay on the floor, covered by rumpled, mismatched sheets. A rickety desk stood against one corner, along with a wooden chair.

On the desk were small tools and a strange metal clamplike device that held what seemed to be an arrow that was only partly feathered.

"See?" demanded Peyton, standing behind her.

My God, he lives like a monk, she thought. The dog twisted in her arms, whined, and tried to lick her face. "Come on," she ordered Peyton. "We've got to walk a dog."

Eden went out the front door and carried the animal down the stairs. Peyton hopped down them, one by one.

"This is a farmhouse," the girl said, frowning. "I don't like farmhouses."

Again Eden's nerve ends tingled. "Really?" she asked carefully. "Why not?"

"I just don't," Peyton answered. "Will we have pizza for lunch?"

Eden put the dog down and let it lead them toward the path through the woods. Peyton half walked, half skipped beside her. "La, la, la," she sang.

Get your act together, Eden scolded herself. *There are questions you need answered.*

She chose her words carefully. "Peyton, you drew a picture last night. It's a very good picture. A blond lady holding fire in her hand. Who is she?"

Peyton's gait slowed, her skipping stopped. She looked at Eden almost fearfully.

Eden said, "Mr. Charteris went to Sedonia, Missouri, to look for your mother. Have you ever heard of Sedonia?"

Peyton gave a tiny, pained gasp. Tears rose in her dark eyes, and Eden knew she could not ask the child about Sedonia, the plane, or anything else that might upset her further.

"But none of that matters," Eden said smoothly, stretching her hand to Peyton. "You don't have to talk about it unless you want to. I have just one more question."

Peyton cringed as if she expected to be hit. Eden fought not to wince at the child's fear.

"Did you say you wanted pizza for lunch?" she asked with a smile and took Peyton's hand in hers.

The child's face went carefully blank. "I don't know," she said tightly. "Maybe Henry does."

"Fine," Eden said and squeezed her hand. "That's

the most important question of all: what Henry wants for lunch."

But her heart pounded, fast and giddy with small triumph. Peyton had recognized the name Sedonia. Eden knew it. She was certain to her very marrow.

The late morning sun beat down.

Raylene sat on the back porch, watching as Drace stored the weapons beneath the false floor of the van. She'd changed her clothes and wore autumnal brown slacks and a yellow angora sweater. Drace liked her in angora.

He tossed a pair of handcuffs in among the rifles and covered them with the false panel, the strip of carpeting. He set a stack of newspapers atop the panel, weighted them with the cell phone.

He straightened, turned, and gave Raylene a disgusted look. "A heart attack," he said, his lip curled. "A fucking heart attack."

Raylene tried not to flinch at his unhappiness. She herself had at first been upset and frightened by what happened.

The Brodnik woman had died, writhing and twisting on the floor in front of their incredulous eyes. They'd hardly touched her, only bruised her a bit, broken her finger.

Raylene knew Drace needed her to show her faith and affection. She rose and went to him. She wound her arms around his waist, laid her head against his chest. "It's going to be all right," she soothed. "You'll make it all better again."

He wrapped his arms around her, rested his chin

atop her head moodily. "She didn't answer half our questions."

"She answered some," Raylene consoled him.

Before she had died, Louise Brodnik had stammered that she'd let Mimi out alone in Branson at a motel with a name she was too frightened to remember, maybe it had the word "inn" in it. Mimi had wanted something to drink but couldn't find it. She'd told the child she had to stay in Branson for a while. Then the Brodnik woman had taken Peyton on, she'd said.

Drace had slapped her and shaken her roughly, demanding to know where the child was. The woman had babbled out something barely comprehensible about somebody named Jessie in Endor, Arkansas.

Then, suddenly, Louise Brodnik had lurched in Drace's grasp like a dog having a fit. She'd vomited something curdled all over herself and him, too.

He had let her go, and she sank to the floor like a broken puppet tottering into a puddle of filth. For a moment Raylene had stared down at her, flooded by distaste and something like terrified doubt.

They had planned for this woman to die—but only after they interrogated her. The death was to be a clean military strike, a bold act of guerrilla warfare. How could their operation fail, be aborted in such a messy, muddled way?

Then, as they stood over the body and the vomit, enlightenment came washing over Raylene in a radiant wave. They'd intended for Louise Brodnik to die, and a higher power had carried out the execution. It was as if destiny itself exalted Drace's judgment, bowed to it and served it. It had not given them all the answers, but it had given them enough. They would find Mimi and Peyton. It was decreed.

They burned the Brodnik woman's house, although Stanek, foolishly, had dared to object. Raylene had no doubt whatever about Drace's orders, and she was certain that the death was not a botch or a slovenly accident; it was a sign, a message, a lesson.

Now Raylene closed her eyes and kissed Drace on the chest, over his heart. She felt its steady beat beneath her mouth, felt his warmth. "You think Mimi's still in Branson?" she murmured.

"If she started drinking, she is," he said. "I'll find her—one way or another."

"I know you will," Raylene said, kissing him again in the same place, letting her lips linger.

"I want you to go with me," he said, surprising her.

She drew back, her joy mingling with disbelief. She stared up at him, smiling tremulously. "Me? Really?"

"You." He nodded, putting his hands on her shoulders.

"I thought—I thought you'd take Stanek."

"I may need a woman," he said.

"To help you ask about her?"

"Yes." He gave her a boyish half-smile, squeezed her shoulders. "Besides, you're a better shot. Let Stanek stay and play nursemaid to Yount."

She clasped her hands behind his neck, kissed him on his chin. "Thank you," she whispered with fervor. "Thank you."

His face grew serious again. "Will it bother you? Killing her?"

She looked at his perfect face. Drace was freedom's chosen instrument—she was growing more certain of this each day, and she loved him all the more for it. She had once thought it not possible, that she could love him more.

Mimi had been a rival and Mimi had tried to betray him and, with him, the divine force of freedom. For this last, she had to die, and so, of course, must her daughter. And Raylene would be glad to kill them both.

"No," she said honestly. "It won't. I never liked her."

"You were jealous," he said. "You didn't have to be."

"But I was," she said, clinging more tightly to him.

"What about the kid?" he asked. "That won't bother you, either?"

She did not hesitate. "Not at all. I'd love to do it. For you."

He searched her eyes. "You're sure?"

"Oh, Drace," she said breathlessly, "for a minute in Miami, after the explosion, I thought the old-fashioned way. I thought 'I'm damned.' But I'm not. I wasn't. With you I'm saved."

He touched her face tenderly. "What a girl you are," he said.

Peyton, clean and smelling of Jessie's lavender bath salts, had gone shy.

She stood in Jessie's hospital room, dressed in her freshest clothes, her hair brushed and gleaming. She shifted her weight from one foot to another. She sucked her thumb. She tried to hide behind Eden.

"Aren't you the prettiest little thing?" gushed Jessie. "Don't you hide from me. You come out where I can see how pretty you are."

Peyton hung back even more. She tugged at the back of Eden's aqua-blue shirt. "I got to go pee-pee," she said.

"Then go," Eden said, pointing to the bathroom. "And wash your hands afterward."

Peyton slipped away and off into the bathroom, closing the door behind her.

"Little darling," chuckled Jessie.

"The little darling needs a million things," Eden said. "After we leave here, I've got to take her shopping. Her clothes are rags."

"Don't you go running all over creation. You need to get home and tend that phone."

"I need to get home and *use* that phone. I have to make a dentist's appointment for her. And a doctor. And a psychologist."

"A psychologist?" Jessie bristled. "I *beg* your pardon."

"There's no shame in seeing a psychologist," Eden said. "This child's been traumatized. She won't talk about the past."

She paused, wondering how much to tell Jessie. "And she draws odd pictures," she said, "extremely odd."

"Like what?" challenged Jessie.

Again Eden hesitated before she spoke. "Jessie, did you tell Peyton about your dream? About the blond woman with her hand full of fire?"

"Of course not," Jessie said with a snort. "I only had it yesterday afternoon. I never talked to her at all yesterday. Thanks to somebody here I won't name."

A worried frown line etched itself between Eden's brows. "Well, somehow she drew the same thing—a picture of a blond woman with fire in her hand. How could she do such a thing?"

"Oh," Jessie said and shrugged. "That's easy."

"Easy?"

"Well, can't you figure it out?" Jessie demanded. "She's flesh of my flesh and bone of my bone. My powers saw inside her head. It's simple as that."

Eden was extremely skeptical, but she forced herself to say nothing. She pressed her lips together in a tight line.

Jessie shook her head. "As for that blond-headed gal, she won't get out of my dreams. She come again last night. She's got a pocketbook full of faces, and she wears a blue ring."

"What?" Eden asked, putting a hand on her hip. "What's that supposed to mean?"

"It means she can change how she looks. Like one of them lizards. And a blue ring means a blue ring. A blue stone in it. Like your shirt."

Eden glanced down at her T-shirt. "Turquoise?" she asked dubiously.

"Yes," Jessie said and folded her arms. "That's a true fact, or I'll eat my own head."

Peyton pushed open the bathroom door and eased out. She tried to slip into the far corner, but Jessie pointed at her. "You—Miss Peyton Honeyduck. You come here, honey, sit on Granny's bed."

Peyton stopped, the expression on her face both guilty and reluctant.

"She shouldn't sit up there. You've got a broken leg."

"Pish, poot, and tush," said Jessie. "You set my little lamb right here beside me."

Eden sighed, swept up the hapless Peyton, and set her on the edge of Jessie's bed. "Don't bounce," she warned. "Don't even wiggle."

Peyton wiggled her shoulders and screwed up her face, but then sat still, not looking at Jessie, but staring instead at the tarot deck on Jessie's beside tray.

"I want to know about Owen Charteris," Eden said. "We went over to his place this morning to take out his

dog. He lives like some sort of hermit. Why? And why's
he so protective of you?"

"He don't have much truck with worldly things,"
Jessie said with an air of pronouncement. "Because what
meant most to him in the world, he lost."

Eden felt an odd sense of inadequacy that she didn't
understand, almost a sense of loss. "His wife, you mean."

"His wife. A sweeter woman never lived, and that's
God's truth. She loved everybody, it was her nature to
love, and you couldn't help but love her back. Everybody
did. And he protects. Because it's his karma."

Eden tried to look cool, disinterested. "His karma?"

"Yes, ma'am. He thought life'd take him one way. It
took him the other. That's karma for you."

"How so?"

"He went off to Texas, on one of them athletic schol-
arships," Jessie said. "Basketball. He was going to be big
time, he was. But in a game, he got knocked down, broke
his shoulder. Couldn't throw overhand no more. Most
folks, that'd make no difference. For him, it changed all.
Karma."

Eden watched as Peyton picked up Jessie's deck of
tarot cards. "And then?" Eden asked casually. "He came
back here?"

"Indeed. He went to the police work. He got married. And he was happy for a time. But things went
wrong all to once. His father died, his wife took sick. His
mother, she started to fail—"

Jessie tapped her temple significantly. "The Allsim-
mer's," she said.

"Alzheimer's," Eden said.

Jessie shrugged. "His two sisters, they're nice
enough, but when it came to choosing men, them girls
was behind the door when they passed out the brains.

They's both single again, both got children. They live on the family money. He sees to it. He sees to all of them."

Eden lifted an eyebrow. Self-sacrifice hadn't made him happy. Far from it. "That's all very noble, I suppose. But it doesn't explain why he's so concerned about you."

Jessie had begun laying the tarot cards out on her sheet in the form of a cross. Peyton, sitting still as a little statue, watched her.

"Shall we see what the cards say, honeyduck?" asked Jessie.

She turned over the center card. It was a card of the major arcana, the thirteenth. On a pale horse rode a knight in black armor, his face a grinning skull.

The death card, Eden thought with a chill.

Jessie stared at it, obviously shaken by the sight. "My God," she whispered. "All of a sudden, I sense a fire. A little blue house turned to ashes. I sense a woman undone—dead—everything gone."

Peyton looked up, her face pale, her eyes suddenly brimming with tears.

"Jessie, don't," Eden cautioned. "You're scaring her."

"I can't help it," Jessie said, putting her hands to her temples. "Blue house and woman, all done gone by fire."

Peyton hid her face in her hands. "The house, the lady?" she said in a tiny voice. "They burned it up? They burned her, too?"

Eden seized the child by the shoulders. "Granny didn't mean to scare you. Talk to me. Tell me what you mean."

But Peyton wouldn't answer. She wept into her hands in silence and a despair that seemed far too old for her years.

Eden was alarmed. She scooped up Peyton and cradled her against her shoulder. "Jessie, be careful," she warned. "You shouldn't say such things in front of her."

Jessie's face paled. "I couldn't help it," she said. "I had me a vision. A strong one." A forked vein leaped in her temple. She reached toward the child, but her ringed hand was unsteady.

"And you—you need to calm down," Eden told her. "I'm buzzing for a nurse."

"I don't want a nurse," Jessie said stubbornly, but Eden had already pressed the button to summon one. She hugged Peyton closer. The child burrowed her face against Eden's neck and cried silently.

The tarot cards lay scattered across the bed and on the floor now. "Give me my cards," Jessie ordered. "I want to see what they tell me."

Eden couldn't, she was holding Peyton in both arms. Besides, she didn't want to touch the cards, didn't want even to look at them. She pressed her lips together and shook her head.

A small brunette nurse appeared, her expression annoyingly perky. Eden hastily said her good-byes and made her escape. Stepping over the fallen cards, she carried Peyton away, holding her tight.

TEN

MIMI HAD GONE TO A BREAKFAST SHOW CALLED "JEMMA in the Morning." The singer, Jemma, had a good voice, almost as good as Mimi's had once been, and the comedian was funny. Breakfast was coffee and a sausage roll and a pear that wasn't quite ripe.

For almost ninety minutes, Mimi was close to happy, but when the blue velvet curtain finally came down on the stage, her happiness dissipated. There wasn't another show until two o'clock.

She walked back to her motel room, stopping at a liquor store to buy another bottle of wine. She sat in the room, smoking and thinking of Peyton.

She thought of Jessie and of Eden. She'd been jealous of Eden all these years. But now she missed her, deeply so.

She drank wine from the plastic glass. When the glass was empty, she poured it full again.

Owen's score was exactly zero.

He'd spent the morning asking questions, but getting no satisfactory answers.

He'd gone to Ness Chevrolet Sales and Service, but they were the biggest dealership in three counties. They had hundreds of customers, and dozens of those customers could fit Jessie's description of the woman who'd left Peyton.

Ronald Ness, the owner of the dealership, said the T-shirts had been used as an advertising promotion five years ago, but were handed out not only to buyers, but to staff and their families, as well. The shirts had been given away as prizes on the radio and at the county fair and during the townwide Midsummer Madness Sales.

In all, five hundred Ness Chevrolet T-shirts had been distributed, said Ronald Ness, and sometimes people didn't want them and gave them away to somebody else. They turned up in the local Salvation Army store, where anyone could buy one for twenty-five cents.

Owen had brought an old photograph of Mimi and a Polaroid he'd taken of Peyton. The pictures didn't jog Ness's memory in the least.

Owen visited every child-care service listed in the Sedonia Yellow Pages. Nobody recognized either Peyton or Mimi. He was given the names of several women who did baby-sitting. Those he tracked down only shook their heads when he showed them the photos. No, they'd never seen them.

He went to the three elementary schools in Sedonia,

figuring Peyton was old enough to be either in kindergarten or first grade. But no teacher knew her.

He went to the police department and talked to a detective who grumped, yes, Endor police had contacted them about the woman, but there was not enough information to go on. He clearly did not want to be bothered.

It was almost the same story at the county sheriff's office, where the fat deputy that Owen talked to kept yawning, displaying a fine collection of silvery fillings in his molars.

The deputy, Carl Biddemeyer, explained he was in the Freedonia Hills Volunteer Fire Department and had been routed from bed just after dawn.

"Bad fire," Biddemeyer said, shaking his head so that his big jowls wobbled. "Ragin' by time we got there. Couldn't do nothing but contain it. Burnt to the ground. Woman died. You hate it when that happens. You sure the shit do."

Biddemeyer looked troubled at the memory. Owen nodded with a counterfeit of sympathy and steered the conversation back to Peyton and Mimi. He showed Biddemeyer the pictures.

The fat man frowned. "I could have seen that woman somewhere before. Maybe. Maybe not."

"You remember where?"

Biddemeyer shrugged massively. "Nope. So many newcomers moving in. It used to be nice here, peaceful. It's getting too crowded. It's the chicken business did it. Chicken business gonna be the ruin of this town. That's why I moved out to the country. Four months ago. Bought me a little farm. Got a pond with catfish *that* long in it."

Owen kept his face impassive. If the detective had

been stingy with his time, Biddemeyer seemed to have too much of it. He was ready for a nice free-form chat.

Owen thanked him and took his leave. He'd been putting off calling Eden, but he supposed it was time. He drove to the Gas 'n' Go, bought another cup of coffee, then parked near the river again.

As he dialed Jessie's home number, he realized his pulse had begun to beat harder and faster. For no reason, he felt as edgy as a bumpkinish boy calling up to ask for his first date. It annoyed him, and he gritted his teeth.

She answered on the fifth ring, sounding slightly breathless. "Buddress residence. Jessie isn't here right now. This is her granddaughter Eden. May I take a message?"

For the first time he noticed how low and supple her voice was, and it sent unwanted vibrations through his blood.

"It's Owen. I'm in Sedonia. You sound out of breath."

"I was in Jessie's room, plugging in the psychic line. Have you found out anything? About Peyton or Mimi?"

She sounded both hopeful and anxious. He could not feed the hope, only the anxiety.

"Nothing," he said. "I keep hitting brick walls. Sorry."

"Oh," she said. Then, after a pause, "Thanks for trying. Will you come back now?"

"No. There are paths I haven't tried. Which means, in all probability, there are more brick walls to hit. If I have to hit them all, I'll hit them all."

He told himself that cop habits died hard. He told himself it was the least he could do for Jessie. He told himself he was doing it to get Eden and Peyton out of his life, that was all.

Slowly, clearly, in her unfaltering voice Eden told him of last night, of Jessie's cryptic description of the blond woman with her hand full of fire, and how Peyton's drawing had shown the same inexplicable image.

Owen scowled as Eden recounted how the card of death had triggered an unbidden vision in the old woman. "Wait a minute," he interrupted. "She said what? Exactly what?"

He heard Eden draw a deep breath and then she repeated what Jessie had said. "Then Peyton put her hands up to her face and cried, and she said, 'The house, the lady, it's all gone? They burned it? They burned it up, too?'"

"Hold on," he said. "'The house and lady'? 'They burned it?' What house? What lady? And Jessie said a fire? What fire? And who's 'they'? You're sure Peyton said 'they'?"

"I don't know. She wouldn't say anything else. But yes, she said 'they,' I'm sure of that. Why?"

"I don't know," he said. But a memory that had seemed small and inconsequential stirred in his head like a tiny snake coming out of hibernation.

"Jessie shouldn't have said such a thing in front of her," Eden said, and he could hear the disapproval in her voice.

"But what about this vision?" he asked quietly. "Do you believe it?"

"All I know is the poor kid's traumatized, and Jessie frightened her. I called my friend Sandy in L.A. I asked her to find me the best child psychologist in this area. She's got connections. I don't care if I have to drive clear to Little Rock or Tulsa. Jessie won't like it, but—"

"Yeah," he said, but he wasn't thinking about a psychologist. When Peyton had been frightened about the explosion in Miami, she'd said, "The plane burned up. *They* burned it all up."

Who was this mysterious "they" she spoke of, and why had she twice mentioned them in connection with fires?

I hate Alexander Graham Bell and the horse he rode in on, Eden thought uncharitably.

She would no sooner set down the receiver of Jessie's phone than it would ring again. Everyone, it seemed, wanted a hot line to the mysteries of the past, present, and especially the future.

Peyton sat in the living room, watching television and playing with a box of buttons Eden had found in the closet, stringing them into long necklaces. She seemed used to amusing herself and was absorbed in her private game.

Today Jessie's callers were as diverse as they were unrelenting. There was the grief-stricken woman searching for her lost dog, the man wanting advice on a sex-change operation, the real-estate developer agonizing over land that he itched to purchase.

Using numerology, she assured a harried hostess in Memphis that the omens for chicken Kiev as a main course tonight were excellent. She read the cards for a banker from Ohio who wanted to know what was to happen to the Japanese yen, and she cast a horoscope for a lonely farmer in Iowa.

When the farmer hung up, she leaned her elbows on Jessie's desk and put her head in her hands. The phone rang. She raised her head and stared at it. "Damn," she muttered. It rang again.

With an exasperated sigh, she reached for it. "Sister Jessie," she intoned. "God's gifted seer."

A voice, hoarse, slurred, and breathless, greeted her. "Hello, Jessie. It's me, it's Constance."

A giant hand seemed to clutch Eden's heart, making her breathless herself. Her mouth was suddenly dry. She checked the small green on light of the tape recorder, looked at the caller ID. The readout said, "Unavailable."

The woman spoke in a rush. "I want to talk to you. I got questions, important ones. I want you to read the cards."

Eden tried to make her voice sound as old and wise as the earth itself. "Constance—I been thinking of you, honey."

The space of three heartbeats passed before the woman spoke. "Thinking of me? How?"

That voice, Eden thought in dismay. It did not sound like Mimi's voice at all. Yet once again, she sensed an eerie familiarity, an elusive quality that she could not name.

"You asked about a child," Eden said carefully. "I had me a vision about that child. She needs her mother."

"No," said the woman with surprising force. "She doesn't. Her mother's no good for her. No damn good."

She's been drinking, Eden thought, certain of it. "This mother," she said carefully, "could she be in trouble of some kind?"

There was a strange little sound—a sob or a laugh? "Yeah. You could say that."

Mimi? Is this you? What's the matter?

"How bad is this trouble?" Eden asked, her heart hammering.

"About as bad as it gets."

Eden felt sick with apprehension. "Maybe—she should go to the police."

"No. She can't."

"Then," Eden took a deep breath, "maybe she should go home to her people. They'd take her in."

"She can't. She"—the woman hesitated—"it wouldn't be safe."

"For her?"

"Oh, God," the woman said miserably. "Just lay out the cards. Just talk to me, okay? Let me hear you."

Eden ran taut fingers through her hair. The voice sounded weary, desperate, irrational. It sounded like Mimi, yet it didn't sound at all like Mimi.

"I'm dealing the cards," Eden answered. "Sister's here to help you any way she can. I mean that. Any way she can."

The woman made a small, mysterious sound, like a tired gasp.

"This woman," Eden said, "I know if she'd come home, she would be cared for. That's a fact. I know that."

"No. No. Read the cards."

Eden thought of Jessie's words and Peyton's drawing. She tried another tack. "Do you know a blond-headed gal?"

There was no answer, only husky breathing.

"She carries fire in her hand."

"Oh, God," the woman rasped.

Go for it, Eden told herself. She said, "She's pretty, mighty pretty. But she can change how she looks, just like a chameleon. She's got a whole pocketbook full of faces."

"Oh, God—oh, my God," she moaned.

Pull back a litle, this is scaring her.

"Now, I don't know what that means," Eden soothed. "It's something the cards say, that's all. Now what questions you got for me, honey? I'm here to help."

"What else do you know about this woman? Tell me."

"Who is she, honey? You sound scared. Are you scared of her?"

"What else do you know about her?" The voice trembled.

Eden took a deep breath and made a tactical decision to go with Jessie's dream. "Has she got a ring with a blue stone in it? Like a turquoise maybe?"

The woman drew in her breath, a cracking, sucking sound.

"I see this gal and a flag is burning inside her and her hand is full of fire."

"Miami," the woman said shakily. "You know about Miami?"

What is this about? Eden wondered, tense with anxiety. *What in the name of all that's holy is she talking about?* "Miami?" she echoed.

"What else do you know?"

Eden bit her lip and winced. "These cards say, don't you do nothing rash, be careful. Oh, yes, I just turned another card, I see it plain, you got to be mighty careful—"

"Oh, God, somebody's at the door. I got to go."

"Honey, the spirits are speaking very strong to me. They say they want to help you. But you got to talk—"

"I have to go."

An abrupt click cut off the conversation, and the line went dead.

•   •   •

In Branson, Mimi rose numbly from her seat on the bed, her legs weak and unsteady. Who was at the door? Had they found her? Had Stanek somehow traced her here? Or had Drace himself hunted her down and come to punish her?

Or was it the police, the FBI, the ATF? Either way she was dead. Why hadn't she made sure she was beyond their power, the whole lot of them?

The knock rapped smartly at the door again.

"Yes?" asked Mimi. Her heart galloped in fright.

"Housekeeping," said the voice of an older woman. "You want clean towels? Or not?"

Half-faint with relief, Mimi leaned her forehead against the door. "No," she said. "No. Go away. Just go away."

She sat down on the edge of the unmade bed. She put her head in her hands. Her money was running out. Her time was running out. And her luck, it seemed, had run out, an eternity ago.

She wept.

Owen finally tracked down John Mulcahy of the Missouri State Police, the investigative officer who'd been called to the scene of the fire. Mulcahy was a beanpole of a man with a jutting chin, a beak of a nose, and cold sea-green eyes.

He was at home, on his hands and knees in a well-spaded plot of front yard, planting tulip and crocus bulbs. The call to the scene of the fire had been the last of his shift.

"It was good of you to see me," Owen said. "I thought you'd be asleep."

"I got a sleeping disorder," Mulcahy said rather

sourly. "When I can't sleep I get up, work around the house. Might as well."

The white house shone in the afternoon sun, the green shutters gleamed. The porch and walk were immaculately swept, the lawn mown and raked. Behind the tulip bed, yellow mums stood in military precision. Even the birdfeeder looked waxed. Mulcahy must get very little sleep, Owen thought.

"I wouldn't be talking to you if it didn't involve a kid," Mulcahy said, not looking up. "A kid makes it different."

Yeah, Owen thought. *It does.* He said, "This Louise Brodnik, the woman in the fire, you said on the phone that sometimes she took care of kids."

Mulcahy nodded as he patted a tulip into its winter grave. "Her mail carrier, Gordon Freefoot, contacted us. He'd been worried. Brodnik hadn't taken in her mail the last couple days. Either she was sick or gone. But she hardly ever went away. He said she wasn't much on driving."

A woman who didn't like to drive might not drive straight through to Endor, Owen thought. *She might be gone for a couple of days.* He drew Peyton's picture from his shirt pocket and knelt, showing it to Mulcahy. "Ever see this kid?"

Mulcahy gave it an austere glance, then Owen one that was even more severe. "You should take that to headquarters, buddy."

"I will. Look at this one, will you? It's the mother. Do you recognize her?"

The gaunt man scrutinized the photo and shook his head. He grunted and went back to geometrically perfecting the hole in the soil.

Owen thrust the pictures back into his shirt pocket. "This mail carrier, Freefoot, did he know Brodnik well?"

"No. She was on his route, that's all."

"Who did know her, then?"

"Nobody much. Her kids are all grown and gone. She had a sister, dead two years now."

"Neighbors?"

"None close. Brodnik wasn't sociable. She didn't mix with people."

"When did she stop picking up her mail?"

"The thirteenth. She'd left no notice to stop it. She must have got back sometime yesterday."

"Where'd she gone? Have you checked?"

Mulcahy gave another negative grunt, interred another tulip bulb.

Owen set his jaw. "Her death. Your department thinks it was accidental?"

Mulcahy slipped him a cold sea-green squint. "Until we have reason to think otherwise."

"Her body's at the medical examiner's?"

Mulcahy slid him another glance that said, *Of course, you asshole.*

Owen nodded. "When do you expect the report?"

Mulcahy shrugged. "It could be a day or so. The office is shorthanded right now." He paused and smiled bitterly to himself. "The medical examiner died. Found him on the floor of his garage, maybe a heart attack. Got to autopsy him."

A nice graveyard joke, that, thought Owen. But he wasn't interested in the late medical examiner. "Did Louise Brodnik have any enemies, anyone who would want her dead?"

"No enemies, no friends," Mulcahy said. "She was a family person whose family all left. She kept to herself. I told you that."

Owen ignored the rebuke. "What caused the fire?"

"We don't know. The ashes have hardly cooled down."

"What's the likeliest explanation at this point?"

Mulcahy evened the sides of another hole. "Fire department *says* the water heater exploded. They shouldn't say anything. Investigation's still in progress."

"Who are Louise Brodnik's closest survivors? Who might she have talked to about this kid?"

"Two daughters and two sons, all out of state. Couple of nieces and nephews, nobody near. Talk to the undertaker who'll handle her—Hastings."

Mulcahy sat back, his bony rear resting on his heels. He stared at Owen almost hostilely. "Wherever she was, she shouldn't have come back. That place blazed. It was an inferno."

"Yeah," Owen said. "Too bad."

"You got kids?" Mulcahy asked. He asked it like a challenge.

"No," said Owen. "I don't."

"You should," Mulcahy snapped. "I got three. They live with their mother. Nothing more important than kids."

"Yeah," Owen said, rising. "Well, thanks."

"You go to the department, tell them what you told me," the man said, standing. He peeled off his dirty gloves and offered Owen his hand. "We'll find that kid's mother for you. Women—such bitches. They can break you in two, can't they?"

Owen nodded wordlessly. He shook the skeletal hand, then released it.

He walked back to his car, the old, familiar emptiness stirring inside him, bitter and sickening. *Yeah,* he thought. *They can break you right in two.*

ELEVEN

〜◦〜

WHEN THE WOMAN HUNG UP, EDEN HAD BEEN SWEPT BY a dismal sense of failure. *God, God, I screwed it up. I scared her. She'll never call back.*

She put her face in her hands. With all her heart she did not want to believe the desperate caller with the slurred speech and ruined voice was her sister. But she feared that it was.

She sensed Peyton in the doorway behind her and straightened. She turned to her, forcing herself to smile, worried the girl was still upset by Jessie's vision of fire. But Peyton didn't seem distressed, only restless with boredom.

"Can we go to the park? Henry wants to ride the fish. I want to ride the elephant."

Tell me what you know, Eden thought, studying the

child. *What sort of trouble is your mother in? How can I help her?*

Yet she dared not push Peyton, not after seeing how upset she could become. She wondered about the best way to win the girl's confidence. Then she unplugged the psychic line, stood, and offered Peyton her hand. "To the park," she said and smiled again.

Shyly Peyton smiled back, and trustingly she took Eden's hand, adoration shining out of her dark eyes.

They went to Owen's house for the dog, but the creature grew tired halfway down the path and had to be carried. Now it slept in the sun-warmed leaves, curled up into a fragile, ratty knot.

Eden turned on the swing so that the chains twisted, and her heart twisted with them guiltily. She didn't want the child's love. She wanted only her information.

Peyton dismounted the bobbing elephant and ran to Eden. She put her hands on Eden's thighs and looked up at her entreatingly. "Can we really go shopping? Can we have pizza again for supper? Will you really buy me an ice-cream sundae?"

"Yes," Eden said, cupping the child's chin in her hand. "We'll do all those things."

Peyton's chin was not rounded like Mimi's, but pointed like her own. The set of the girl's eyes, the angle of her brows, the way her hair waved instead of curled, all were more like Eden than Mimi. Once again Eden had the unsettling sensation that she was gazing at an exotic alternate self.

Peyton gave her a hesitant grin that showed her chipped tooth. Eden touched one of Peyton's big earrings. "We'll buy you different earrings, too. These are too big for you."

Peyton climbed, wriggling, onto her lap. She reached

up and touched the diamond stud in Eden's ear. "I want earrings like you got. I want to be just like you. Swing me, Eden?"

An unwanted frisson trembled through Eden's insides, making her feel slightly sick. *You already are like me, too much,* she thought. *You can't count on your mother, you don't know your father, and nobody wants you but Jessie. You're different, you don't fit in, you're not like other people.*

But holding Peyton tightly, she kicked the dirt beneath them and, with skill long forgotten, launched the swing into its first high arc. Peyton squealed with delight.

The old dog did not seem to hear; he lay in the leaves, dozing in the beautiful light that was starting to die.

Eden took Peyton to Little Caesar's for supper, to Wal-Mart to shop, to the Dairy Queen for an ice-cream sundae.

I have wooed this child with franchises and discounts, she thought. *I am a cheap and shoddy cheeseball.*

Now Peyton lay asleep in their room, her thumb in her mouth. Her hair had been washed and trimmed and styled. She wore fresh, clean pajamas, and her big earrings had been replaced with small ones with studs of cubic zirconia.

Half of Eden's mind said, *Cubic zirconia: I am indeed a cheap and shoddy cheeseball.* The other half said, *Grow up to buy your own diamonds, Peyton—they're the only ones worth having.*

Eden had talked to Jessie, but she still hadn't told her about her suspicion that the woman calling herself Constance might be Mimi. She didn't even want to think about it.

She'd walked the dog, straightened the house. Her friend Sandy Fogleman had phoned from California with the names of two highly recommended psychologists, one in Little Rock, one in Tulsa. The quickest appointment Eden could get was in Little Rock and not for five days.

If Owen had phoned, she'd missed him, and she would not let herself call him. Her refusal was partly from simple stiff-necked pride, but partly from emotional exhaustion.

The exhaustion had been whipped nearly to the breaking point when she'd discovered that among Peyton's few possessions was a book that had once belonged to herself and Mimi. It was a volume of fairy tales by Hans Christian Andersen.

Years ago, Jessie had given them the book for Christmas. The longest and most complex story was "The Snow Queen," and Eden had forgotten how strange and disturbing the illustrations were.

The fat, naked devils of "The Snow Queen" sat in almost mastubatory positions as they propped up their cold and mocking mirror of humanity. *Love, love, love,* said the sentimental story, *love is what matters.*

Nothing matters, leered the devils. *Nothing.*

She heard a car pull up in the drive and stop. Owen, she thought. A moment of silence pulsed, then a knock rapped at the door. She rose and answered it.

His jaw was shadowed and his silver hair rumpled. The ice-blue eyes seemed to pierce through her. "I tried to call. Nobody answered."

She felt awkward and almost schoolgirlish under that steady gaze. She turned from him and set the book on the arm of the couch. "We were out a lot. We had to eat and shop and do—girl things."

"Girl things," he said without expression.

"Get her hair fixed, get some decent clothes, replace those awful earrings."

"Did she tell you anything?"

Eden shook her head and made a helpless gesture. "No. I'm sorry. Can—can I make you some coffee?"

"No, thanks. Jessie's got a bottle of brandy in the kitchen. I'll take a shot of that."

"Certainly," she said. She let him lead the way. He opened a cupboard door, took down the bottle and a small glass.

"What about the woman who says she's Constance?" he asked. "Did you hear from her?"

Reluctantly she told him of her conversation. "I don't know what to think. Yet part of me seems to *know* it's Mimi, though there's no logical reason."

"Life's not always logical," he said.

"Anyway I think I blew it," she said in self-disgust. "She won't call back."

"I think she will," he said. "She's getting addicted to the sound of Jessie's voice."

She shook her head in doubt. "How about you? What did you find out in Sedonia? Anything?"

"Not enough," he said with an unhappy frown. He leaned against the counter, nursed his drink, and told her about Louise Brodnik.

"Her house burned early this morning," he finished. "She was in it."

A cold, empty sickness hovered in her stomach. She turned away. "Oh, my God. How horrible."

"And it's just like Jessie said." He took a sip of brandy. "About the fire and the woman and the house."

She could feel him looking at her, his cool, steady gaze. He said, "That bothers you, doesn't it?"

She raised her chin defiantly. "I never much believed in the paranormal."

"You don't think she has any special power?"

Eden shrugged. "Sometimes she gets lucky, that's all." Slowly she turned and looked at him again, her expression dubious. "But you think she does?"

His gaze held hers. "Yeah. I do."

She gave a small, nervous laugh. "But you were with the police. You're supposed to be cynical."

"I am cynical. But I think your grandmother does have some kind of—power. She's not a hundred percent accurate. But she knows things other people can't."

Eden crossed her arms and shook her head. "She's wrong more often than she's right. A lot more."

"You're bitter," he said.

"I'm a realist." She took a deep breath. "I know she helps some people. I'm glad she helped your—your wife."

He leaned nearer. "It was more than that. Jessie had a soft spot for me because I was the one who pulled Mimi out of that wreck all those years ago."

For a moment, her expression softened. "That was you? You're the one? It was you who stopped the bleeding till the ambulance came?"

"That was me, that was my job. And I was the one who came to tell Jessie. I drove her to the hospital. She was too shaken to do it herself. I stayed with her till we knew Mimi was out of the woods."

Regret and perhaps shame shadowed Eden's eyes. "I didn't know it was you. I—I wasn't here then. I'd left for California, and Jessie hadn't wanted me to go. She was hardly talking to me."

"I know," he said. "But there's more to this story. Four years later, Jessie called me up, out of the blue. She told me she had a powerful feeling that I needed to be careful that night, that something could happen."

"And?" asked Eden.

"And I thought she was crazy. I laughed it off. But that night we were called to a trailer court between Endor and Fort Smith. We'd been tipped that a guy who'd kidnapped his two kids was holed up there. We had a warrant. We didn't expect too much trouble."

He paused, as if trying to find the right words. His dark brows knit together in a frown. "Another pair of detectives went around to the back door. My partner and I took the front. I was in the lead, just at the top stair. Then I heard—I swore I heard a voice. My wife's voice."

He spread his empty hands in incomprehension. "I heard her say 'Take care. Take care.' Her voice was so clear I turned, expecting to see her. And just then, a rifle blast came through the window."

Eden stared at him as if she did not believe him. He unbuttoned the top two buttons of his shirt.

"The bullet creased me here," he said, showing her the flat white scar across his sternum. "If I hadn't stopped and turned just then, I would have walked right into it. It would have hit me square in the chest, probably the heart."

She gazed at the scar with a horrified fascination. He tapped his forefinger against it. "This made me a believer. How it happened, why it happened, I can't explain."

She raised her eyes to his. "You said you quit the police. Is that why?"

He rebuttoned the shirt. "My wife asked me to quit. And not go back. It scared her. I promised."

She stared at him in bewilderment. She could not imagine giving up her career because someone asked her. She simply could not imagine loving someone that much.

He shrugged. "Jessie said it hadn't been my time to die. That I had work to do. A year later, I found out what the work was. Taking care of my wife. She was dying."

"I'm sorry," Eden said so softly it was almost a whisper.

Owen felt he'd said too much, but it was as if he were impelled by a force he couldn't understand, and the words kept coming. "Laurie felt close to Jessie after the shooting, like Jessie was a fairy godmother or something. When Laurie was sick, she'd talk to Jessie about death and dying. Like I told you, Jessie gave her comfort."

"I—I see," Eden repeated. "I can see why you feel protective toward her."

"Then," he said, a bitter twist to his mouth, "I moved out here. To remodel that farmhouse. Jessie was already renting this one. She and I were sort of thrown together. So I tried to watch out for her. She's getting old."

Eden made a helpless gesture. "I never meant to abandon her. Truly, I'm grateful to her. When my mother was killed, Jessie took us in. But she never could handle Mimi, and she tried to mold me into something I wasn't. We're both strong-willed, and we clashed. It was inevitable."

"She loves you, you know."

Eden shook her head. "She's never forgiven me. Not really. She knows we can't get along."

"You don't know her as well as you think," Owen said. "You've seen this house. Haven't you noticed anything strange about it?"

"It's a fine house," Eden said. "I'm delighted she finally got out of that ratty old trailer. This seems downright luxurious compared to where we grew up."

"There were other places available, closer to town, more convenient, smaller, easier to keep. No. She wanted three bedrooms. Why does one woman want three bedrooms?"

She looked at him questioningly. "It—it never crossed my mind."

Owen found himself wanting to touch her, a troubling urge. Restless, he rose, jamming his hands into the back pockets of his jeans and pacing away from the couch. He said, "One bedroom for her office, one for her to sleep in."

He turned to face Eden. "And one for you. And Mimi. Two beds for her two girls. She's always wanted you to come back, at least for a visit. She's always dreamed that Mimi would get her life straightened out and come home. She doesn't talk about it. But it's what she wants. I know."

Eden's lower lip quivered dangerously. "That's hard to believe," she said. "It's like nothing I can do can ever please her."

"You've pleased her a lot by just being here. She can't tell you, that's all. And she thinks Peyton hung the moon."

"Peyton," Eden said with a note of despair. "What am I supposed to do about Peyton? I've got to get back to California. Rehearsal starts soon."

A sudden coldness gripped him, and he felt a wave of self-disgust. *Why'd I say all that to her? Spilling my guts. Why didn't I shut the hell up?*

"Ah, your career," he said out of the side of his mouth. "Excuse me. I forgot your career."

Eden stood and moved to where he stood, his hands still jammed in the back pockets of his jeans. Fire sparked deep in her blue-green eyes. She said, "I have a job to do and a living to earn. Some women are happy to clean babies' bottoms and wipe runny noses and bake cupcakes. I'm *not* one of those women."

He looked her up and down coolly. "No. You're not."

He thought of Laurie, who had wanted desperately to be one of those women. She had died wanting to be one, betrayed by her own infertile and diseased womb.

Then Eden turned her face, shame written on her features. He thought he saw the glint of tears in her eyes. "I'm sorry," she said. "I didn't mean to snap at you. I had no right."

Against his better judgment, almost against his will, he put his hand on her shoulder. "You're tired. Go to bed."

Her body tensed beneath his touch. He had meant for his gesture to be merely conciliatory, comradely even, but the feel of her was as powerful as a blaze, and a fiery shiver ran through his veins.

His hand tightened. "Get some sleep," he said.

He remembered the tailored-looking sleep shirt she wore. He thought of her breasts free and unconfined beneath the shirt, her long legs bare. He thought of her body naked, warm and fragrant and opening to him.

He told himself to stop thinking that way. He could not stop. He bent, his face poised over hers, and the only thing stronger than his reluctance was desire.

Eden thought, *And now he's going to kiss me, and I'm going to let him. And it can lead to nothing but trouble. All hell will break loose.*

She felt him bend nearer, and his hand slid from her

neck to her shoulder. Her nape suddenly felt cold, naked, and vulnerable. He pressed his warm mouth against the flesh where his hand had been, and she could not repress a shudder of response. God, but he had a nice mouth. A wonderful mouth. Oh, God. Oh, God.

Slowly she opened her eyes and turned her face toward his. Then both his hands were on her shoulders, and his lips moved to her jawline, then to her mouth.

Her body felt both weak and energized. Slowly, reluctantly, she let her hands rise to touch the sides of his face. It was firm and angular and vital beneath her fingers.

This time it was he who shivered, as if encountering some force too great to resist. His hands tightened possessively on her shoulders, and he kissed her so deeply she felt faint. Suddenly, she was frightened.

She tried to draw away and succeeded only in putting a few inches between them; it was as though some strange power held her in a field of magnetism. She stared up at him, feeling dazzled, yet resentful of her own dazzlement.

"We can't do this," she said, her heart beating too hard. "There's a little girl in there."

"I know," he said and bent to kiss her again.

She turned her face away, closing her eyes to shut out her awareness of him. It only intensified that awareness.

In a terse whisper she said, "This is wrong. If she wakes up—I can't do this. Everything is wrong."

"I know," he said and kissed her ear. "We hardly know each other. Not really."

He kissed the tender skin beneath her ear. "Stop," she insisted, her breath shallow.

"I thought about you all day," he said in a low voice.

His lips trailed down the side of her throat, lingered over her hammering pulse.

Realization of her own desire flooded through her, feared, dizzying, and unwelcome. *I thought about you, too. I didn't want to. But I did.*

Desire felt too much like weakness, so she could not admit to it. "I don't have—flings. You and I have no future. None."

"I don't want a future. Do you? I just want now." He gathered her to him more hungrily, but she went cold and stiff in his arms, turned her face farther away.

If she let him kiss her again, there would be no turning back, she knew. Her body thrummed and burned and hungered with the knowledge, but her mind recoiled. She did not easily yield intimacy.

"I have no 'now' to give you," she said. "My 'now' is overcrowded, thank you. You and I would just be using each other—that's all. That's not how I operate."

For a moment, she thought he would ignore her protest and kiss her again; she half hoped he would. But he drew back. She saw something odd, a mixture of anger and sorrow cross his face. It seemed to briefly mix with disgust—for her? Or for himself?—then disappear.

He gave her a cynical little smile. "I do," he said. "Operate that way, I mean. Sorry. For a minute there you didn't seem to mind."

She took a deep, shaky breath. "I'm grateful for everything you've done for us. But I think you'd better go."

"Yes. But don't bother being grateful. I did it for Jessie."

She hesitated, torn between wanting him and fearing her own want.

His hands dropped away from her, he stepped away from her, his expression almost bored.

She stood. *This is the right thing to do,* she told her-self. *This is the only thing to do.*

"Good night," she said. He made no reply. He gave her the small, ironic smile again. He left her standing alone, her heart beating too wildly, her mind full of con-fusion, and her body vibrating with too much loneliness and need.

TWELVE

—◦◦◦—

Mimi came out of the Prestons' Family Theater in a dreamy haze, almost happy.

The five Preston Brothers had appeared on television since they were children, and Mimi had had a girlish crush on the youngest, Marlowe Preston, who had always been the most handsome. He was still the most handsome, for the other brothers had gotten middle-aged and stout, and their gleaming black hair looked suspiciously as if it were dyed.

But they could still sing, and their tunes echoed, ghostly and sweet, in her head. She tried to hum their theme song, but her ruined throat would not hum; it made only a cracked, feeble growling noise, and she hated it.

Her frail euphoria died, and her mood plummeted.

The starless night suddenly seemed chill to her, and she drew her denim jacket more tightly around her.

I miss my voice, she thought.

But her voice had been only one more thing given to her that she'd wasted. She'd had talent—but not the drive or the single-mindedness to use it. She'd sneered at Eden's lessons and hours of practice, mocked her dedication. And now whatever talent she herself had once had was ravaged and gone.

She touched the scar on her throat, hating it, hating the coarse, wracked ruin that was left of her voice, wanting to punish it, destroy it.

She thought of Peyton, and worry shadowed her mind like a cloud. She rubbed at the scar as if she could scour it away. Peyton must be talking to Jessie about things she should not—how else would Jessie know about Raylene? A woman with fire in her hand and a flag burning in her heart?

And Mimi herself, in shock, had carelessly blurted out the word "Miami." How much more did Jessie know about Drace, Raylene, Miami?

Nothing, Mimi tried to tell herself, yet she was profoundly uneasy. She must call Jessie one more time, tell her she mustn't listen to anything Peyton might let slip.

One more time, thought Mimi. *It's all right to call her one last time. I'll be careful what I say. I'll say exactly the right thing.*

She had tickets for two more days' worth of shows, and then it was over. It was like that movie she'd seen once, *Leaving Las Vegas.* Only Mimi was leaving Branson.

Her steps quickened. She wanted to be back in the safety of her room. And she wanted a drink. She wanted a lot of drinks.

She hurried across a street, ignoring the red light. A

car turned the corner and screeched to a stop to avoid hitting her. The driver struck his horn, and leaned out the window. "Watch where you're going, you dumb bitch!"

Mimi glared at him. She clenched her hand into a fist and brought it down with all her force on the hood of his car.

"Hey!" he cried in surprised outrage. "Hey!"

She hit the hood again.

"Hey!" He stared at her as if she were crazy.

"Fuck you," she snarled. Then she gave him the finger, tossed her hair, and walked on, defiant, into the darkness.

The night turned cold, and Owen could have used a blanket; there was an old quilt in the closet, but he went without it, a penance, a voluntary mortification of the flesh.

He rose early, put the leash on the arthritic old dog, and walked it twice around the yard. The morning was gray and misty, edged with an autumnal chill. The old spaniel moved more slowly than usual, his limp more pronounced. Owen took a deep breath of the cold air. *Your dog is dying.*

He went back in the house, took a shower so cold it was icy. He shaved and dressed in clean jeans, a blue work shirt, his black cowboy boots. He told himself that he didn't need to be encumbered by a woman, especially one with a kid on her hands. He should be out in the woods with the bow, hunting.

You don't need her, he thought. *She just looked good because she was close. A week or so of really fine screwing, and then good-bye, that's all you wanted.*

The phone rang, and he glanced at his watch. It wasn't yet eight o'clock. He frowned when the caller identified himself; it was Mulcahy, the dour state policeman from Sedonia.

"Charteris," he said, "I may have something for you. About the kid. Louise Brodnik's younger daughter got in early this morning from Maine. She talked to her mother by phone last week. Brodnik said she had a strange job coming up—baby-sitting."

Owen's nerve ends prickled. "Strange how?"

"She wasn't supposed to actually keep the kid. She was supposed to transport her to her grandmother's."

Bingo, thought Owen. *A bull's-eye at last.* "Did she say anything about the kid's mother?"

"The daughter said Brodnik felt 'kind of sorry' for the mother. But she can't remember anything else. She's not too coherent, she's still in shock," Mulcahy said. "We haven't found anybody else yet who knows anything. We'll keep checking it out at this end, but it may not lead anywhere. Wanted to let you know, that's all."

"Thanks. I appreciate it."

He hung up, surprised that Mulcahy had been kind enough to call. The information wasn't great, it was only a confirmation of what he'd believed, but he should tell Eden. He looked out the window. Jessie's kitchen light was on. Eden must be awake.

His mood grim, he crossed the yard to Jessie's house and knocked at the door. He heard someone moving about in the kitchen, and he smelled the scent of coffee.

She swung open the back door, hardly looking up from a piece of toast she held on a saucer. She was dressed in jeans and a pale green sweater. The color made her eyes, with their catlike tilt, look green.

Her hair was wet and brushed simply into place. She

wore no makeup and no ornament other than her earrings. She managed to look remarkably untouchable and
desirable at the same time.

"I saw you walking your dog," she said. "Peyton's
still asleep. Do you want some coffee?"

Her voice was neutral, impersonal. He went to the
cupboard, took out a mug, and poured it full. Her coffee
looked dark and strong enough to float a horseshoe.

He said, "I just got a call from Sedonia. From an
officer with the state police. Louise Brodnik's daughter's
arrived there. From Maine."

Her eyes met his again. They looked full of wariness.
"Yes?" she breathed.

He told her Mulcahy's news as briefly as the man
himself had conveyed it.

"So she *was* the one," Eden said, putting aside the
saucer, the toast untouched.

She paused and shook her head. "Peyton had another bad dream early this morning. About fire. Fire
seems to be a recurrent fear."

She crossed her arms and stared out the window, her
back straight. "Whatever she's gone through, I know it's
not—normal. It's probably going to affect her for the rest
of her life. When I think about her, the present and the
future get all caught up with the past. I thought I'd left
the past behind."

"I don't think anybody leaves it behind," he said
quietly. "The dead maybe." *If they're lucky,* he thought.

She shook her head. "I need the name of a pediatrician. I don't even know if she's ever had a physical. And I
have to find a dentist who's good with children. She's got
that chipped tooth."

"I'll ask around. I'll find the best for you."

She did not look at him. She moved one shoulder

restlessly. "I called the hospital. Jessie's the same. I called the police, too. Nobody knows any more than they did before. Why, for God's sake, can't they do something as simple as find out about a six-year-old child?"

"They need time. And luck."

"Luck," she said, "is something this family seems fresh out of."

"Luck can be like that."

She said nothing. She didn't seem to want to meet his eyes.

"About last night," he began, "I'm sorry. I was kind of an—" The word he'd intended to say was "asshole," but he realized he'd make a bigger asshole of himself by saying it.

She acted as if she hadn't heard him. "Peyton crawled in bed with me again last night. She's a restless sleeper."

You're saying it's a good thing you weren't in bed with me, he thought. *And you'll keep it that way, won't you?*

He turned and saw Peyton standing barefoot in the doorway. She sucked her thumb and stared at Owen with her usual hostility. Her hair had been cut like Eden's, and her big earrings had been replaced by small, sparkling ones. For the first time he saw the resemblance between the adult woman and the girl.

"Good morning!" Eden said brightly. "Want some Froot Loops?"

Peyton nodded and climbed up onto a kitchen chair. She tossed Owen an aloof glance. "You should go away," she said. "We don't want you. And we don't need you."

Eden looked horrified, but Owen crossed his arms and regarded the child coolly. "Tell me something I don't know," he said.

•   •   •

Owen went to the hospital to see Jessie, but Eden stayed behind with Peyton. She watched as the girl colored a picture of the Little Mermaid in her new coloring book. Quiet, her head bowed, Peyton looked so normal, so pretty and well-behaved, that it twisted at Eden's heart.

She profoundly wished that she could exorcise whatever possessed Peyton so that the child could take her place in the world like a normal human being. It hurt deeply to be different. Eden knew.

Other children had been cruel to her and Mimi.

Hey, Eden, your mother was a drunk!

Hey, Mimi, I know why your father ran off—he took one look at your face!

Yah, yah! Your grandma's a witch! You belong to the devil! You belong to the devil!

Your grandma dances naked and fucks Satan! She sucks the devil's dick! So do you!

Eden always pretended to ignore such gibes; she'd sealed herself up in an aura of cool privacy. As if addicted, she watched old movies on television and pretended she too was an actress, a beautiful being in a beautiful world full of happy endings.

In town, in school, she perfected a role of her own: she held herself aloof from people. If she cared for none of them, none of them could hurt her, no matter what they said or thought. Someday she meant to leave them all behind, and she would never look back. Never.

But Mimi, of course, took things harder. Mimi always did. As a child, Mimi would pitch into anyone who tormented her, hitting and kicking and scratching. As an adolescent, she specialized in rebellion and escape: she drank, she took drugs, she discovered the power of sex.

Eden survived by becoming a model of discipline. Mimi survived, or tried to, by throwing all discipline aside. Now here was Peyton, another child carrying the burden of difference and a difficult past, and the old cycle was starting over again, like a wheel doomed to turn forever yet go nowhere.

Suddenly Jessie's psychic line rang from the office, a shrill summons. Eden, startled, rose from the couch, grateful for anything that drew her away from her thoughts.

She sprinted down the hall and snatched up the receiver on the third ring. "Sister Jessie, God's gifted seer," she said in a voice that tolled like a bell.

"Jessie, it's Constance," came the whispery, damaged voice.

Mimi? Is it you? Eden's heart ratcheted faster and harder, her breath caught in her lungs.

"I need to talk to you again," the woman said. "I—I shouldn't, but I—got to."

Eden was determined, this time, to keep her on the line. "Honey, what do you mean 'shouldn't'? The spirits *want* you to talk to me. They want to help you. Indeed they do."

The other woman paused and laughed ironically. "Help me? Why? And how?"

Eden marshaled all her concentration. "They want to reach out to you. But I only see them as through a glass darkly. Help me. Help me understand what it is they want to say."

The caller was silent for a long moment. At last she said, "You talked about a blond woman with her hand full of fire."

"That vision came to me, yes," Eden said as mysteriously as she could. "Her with her blond hair and flames dancing in her hand."

"Somebody told you that, didn't they? What else do you know about her?"

"Nobody told me nothing," Eden lied. "You got reason to fear fire, honeyduck? You can tell me. Help me see what I'm supposed to see."

"Don't talk about it," the woman said, sounding fatalistic. "There're things that shouldn't be talked about. Not by me. Not by anybody."

Eden's elbow was on the desk, and she clenched at her bangs in nervous frustration. "You can talk to me. Let me help you."

"Then read the cards to me, that's all."

"You want to know about that child again? That child that needs her mother?"

"She's better off without her. She shouldn't even talk about her. If she talks, people shouldn't listen. You understand me? The cards?"

Eden swore under her breath, but picked up the tarot cards and dealt the cards. "Do you have a question for them?"

Eden took a deep breath and waited.

"Yes." The voice was tremulous. "I'm thinking it. I don't want to say it."

"Hmm," Eden said, pretending to study the first card, the eight of staves. As bait, she offered its traditional meaning. "I see things in motion. I see the arrows of desire. Love? Hate? Dispute? Discord? Does this mean anything to you?"

Again the caller paused. "Yeah," she said hesitantly. "Yeah. It might mean something. I guess."

Eden turned over the next card. "The two of swords," she breathed. "Reversed. Oh, me. Oh, dear."

"What—wha's that mean?"

Eden studied the card and decided to follow the lead

of its symbolism. "I see a young woman blindfolded. Two swords frame her face, and the rocky sea stretches out behind her. But her world is upside down. Oh, me. Oh, dear. It's a good thing you called me. A good thing, indeed."

"What's that supposed to mean?"

Eden pondered what it meant. Today the caller sounded even less like Mimi than before, the voice more ragged and scratchy, but more truculent, too, and on edge.

Eden squared her shoulders. "You must do nothing reckless, nothing that will hurt you."

Another long silence. Then, in a bitter whisper, "It's a little late for that."

"You must take care, protect yourself," Eden insisted. "Now listen to me. I'm turning over the next card."

The five of pentacles revealed itself.

"I see a child, needy in the snow," she improvised. "A black-haired child, a girl. This child's mother must do the right thing—"

"The right thing is going to be done," the caller said. "The wrong things were a mistake. Mistakes, that's all."

"Don't hang up," Eden said urgently. "The spirits have something important to tell you. It's on the edge of coming to me. It's vital. I'm here to help you. You must tell me—"

"No," the voice said sharply.

"What do you need? Ask your kin. They'll help you—"

"No. They can't."

"You'd be surprised, you—"

But the click of a disconnecting phone cut her off. The woman had hung up.

"Damn!" muttered Eden. She slammed the phone

down, and tears of exasperation welled in her eyes. She'd lost her again. Once again, she'd pushed too hard and too far.

She gnawed at her injured lip. The caller seemed to be in deep trouble—but was it Mimi? Eden still was not certain of it. She was no longer certain of anything.

Drace and Raylene had been in Branson almost twenty-four hours, but had found no trace of Mimi Storey.

This put Drace in a foul mood, as did Branson itself. He hated the town, he hated the godawful traffic, he hated the gaudy-looking country-western theaters and the cheap souvenir stores, and all the hillbilly and hick humor the signs tried to convey.

"I'd like to come back here someday and destroy this fucking place," he said. "And all its fucking flag-waving tourists."

He sat on the edge of the bed in the motel, eating a tuna-salad sandwich from a grocery-store deli and drinking a glass of milk.

Raylene sat at his feet, daintily picking baked corn chips from a bag. A desultory rain tapped at the window.

They ate in their room rather than at a restaurant because Drace hated restaurants, suspecting their kitchens were filthy and roach-ridden and that the cooks spit in the food and did other disgusting things.

"Shit," he said. "She's here somewhere. I know it."

"We'll find her," Raylene said soothingly. She leaned against his knee, rubbing her cheek against the denim of his jeans. "She can't have gone far."

Raylene figured that Mimi had stolen one thousand and ninety-eight dollars from the general fund. Before

Louise Brodnik died, she'd confessed that Mimi had given her six hundred dollars.

That left Mimi with almost five hundred dollars herself, and Drace believed what the Brodnik woman had said about Mimi, that she was going to stay around Branson and she was going to drink. It sounded exactly like the sort of stupid, low-rent thing Mimi would do, her and her stupid country music.

But Raylene was worried about Peyton. Where was the child and who had her? Mimi had always claimed she'd had no family, and she'd had few friends; that was one reason it had been easy for Drace to convert her to their communal life.

"She's holed up drinking someplace, I know it," Drace said. "Christ, I tried to save her from all that. She was headed for a life in the gutter."

"I know that, sweety," Raylene said, and ate the last of her chips. Personally, she would have preferred that Drace had let Mimi fall into the gutter in the first place, but she didn't say so, his disposition was dark enough already.

She opened the telephone book to the Yellow Pages again, the section on motels.

"We just have to be persistent," she told him, "that's all."

"Persistent," he said contemptuously. He finished his sandwich, drained his milk, and flopped back on the bed to glower at the ceiling. "She's probably spending all our money on booze and that goddamn bourgeois hillbilly shit music. Christ. I never should have took her in."

Raylene suppressed a sigh and studied the Yellow Pages. Motels had sprouted all over Branson, covering the place like mold, and half of them, it seemed, had the word "Inn" in their names.

She had underlined each neatly, and she and Drace had spent all yesterday evening and this morning checking them, asking about Mimi, showing her snapshot.

If the person at the motel office was male, Raylene talked to him. Drace handled the women. They painted a picture of Mimi as a family member, a disturbed runaway, and they charmed most people into cooperating with them.

But there were so *many* motels—and most had to be visited more than once because different people worked in the offices on different shifts.

There was the Alpine Rose Inn, Americana Inn, Armitage Inn, Branson Inn, Clarion Inn, Country Inn, Dew Drop Inn, Economy Inn, Elvis Inn, Fiddler's Inn, Good Shepherd Inn, Guesthouse Inn, Hillbilly Inn, Island Fun Inn, Jamboree Inn, Jeeter's Inn, Kleen Klassy Inn, Lovebird Inn, Lucky Seven Inn, Mountain Inn, Music Inn, Ozark Inn—the list seemed to go on forever. And there were the chains as well, the Ramada Inn, Holiday Inn, Executive Inn, Comfort Inn, Days Inn, and Best Western Inn. These would have to be checked, too, even if they seemed too expensive for Mimi.

"I hope she isn't shacked up with somebody," Drace grumbled. "I want her to be alone when we find her."

"Absolutely," Raylene agreed.

"Then I have to shake out of her where that goddamn kid is. Or cut it out of her. The kid's got to go, too."

"Absolutely," Raylene said with feeling. "Amen."

She sighed, stretched luxuriously, and stood, laying the phone book on the nightstand beside the empty milk carton.

Then she climbed onto the king-sized bed and knelt over Drace, looking down at his face. His expression was brooding, almost sulky. She smoothed his blond hair from his brow.

"Ready to start again?" she asked softly.

"Give me a few minutes," he said, not looking at her.

"You've got a milk mustache," she said fondly, leaning nearer. The milky upper lip made him look almost like a little boy, a beautiful, pouty little boy.

He turned his blue eyes to hers, put his hand on her thigh.

She smiled. At last he smiled back.

She stroked his hair.

"A milk mustache?" he asked.

She nodded and kept looking into his eyes.

"Lick it off," he said.

She bent over him and began to do so, slowly, sensually, and delicately.

THIRTEEN

———◦◦◦◦———

SHORTLY AFTER NOON, CALLS ON THE PSYCHIC LINE slowed. Eden unplugged the phone and warmed up the leftover pizza for Peyton. She could eat nothing herself. She sat at the table with the girl, drinking black coffee.

Thoughts of Mimi ran almost obsessively through her mind; the last call from "Constance" had disturbed her deeply. Did Peyton know where Mimi was? And if she did, how could Eden induce her to tell?

Eden's gaze drifted to the kitchen window, and through the sheer curtains, she could see Owen's house, stark and handsome and empty-seeming like Owen himself.

Owen, she thought, and sucked almost angrily at her

sore lower lip. He hadn't phoned, and she hated herself for wanting to talk to him.

She, who hadn't depended on anyone in years, had somehow in a ridiculously short time come to depend on him. *Run away,* her survivor's instinct said.

"I like cartoons," Peyton announced solemnly. Eden's eyes returned reluctantly to her. The child sat with her elbows on the table, one hand twiddling with a new earring. With the forefinger of the other hand, she traced the outline of the figure on the pizza box, a skinny caricature of a man in a Roman toga and a laurel wreath.

"I like cartoons, too," Eden answered with manufactured cheer. "Sometimes I work in the cartoons. Did you know that?"

Peyton looked up at her, the small dark brows drawn into a suspicious frown. "How do you work in cartoons?" she challenged. "Cartoons are *pictures.* You're a person."

Eden shrugged philosophically. "Somebody has to draw the pictures—just the way you draw yours. And then, for movies and TV, somebody has to talk for them. Because pictures don't talk by themselves."

Peyton's mouth took on a stubborn I-don't-believe-you slant.

"It's true," Eden assured her. "Did you ever see the Peter Pan Fruit Punch commercial on TV?"

Peyton nodded dubiously. "Well, I used to be the voice of Peter Pan."

"Peter Pan's a *boy,*" Peyton countered.

"I can sound like a boy," Eden said. She gave Peyton a knowing smile, then assumed a spunky, prepubescent male voice. "Hey, kids! Get all your vitamin C in one great drink! It's head-over-heels good!"

Peyton gaped at her with surprised delight. "Do that again."

Eden repeated the slogan, and Peyton laughed aloud. She demanded another encore, and Eden complied.

"Part of you goes away," Peyton said in wonder.

Eden nodded, pleased at the child's astuteness. *Yes,* she thought, *that was as good a description of acting as any: Part of you went away, and somebody else came.*

"Can you do more?" Peyton asked, clearly smitten.

"I can do lots more," Eden said. "I can be a singing sunflower, the Jumping Jiminy cereal kangaroo, or a duck. I can be a baby or an old lady or an elf. What do you want?"

"The kangaroo," Peyton said without hesitation. Eden assumed the kangaroo voice with its Australian accent and sang the Jumping Jiminy cereal jingle.

Peyton wriggled in her chair with excitement. "I can do that, too," she said and took a deep breath. "Listen!"

She astonished Eden by mimicking the song in a lilting voice that, despite its childishness, was startlingly like Eden's. She even had the accent nailed.

"Why, Peyton," Eden said, pleased, "that's *very* good."

"Show me another one," Peyton said.

"Did you ever see *The Fearless Fran and Milton Mutt Show?*"

Peyton nodded enthusiastically. Eden adopted a confident yet spritely girl's voice. "Uh-oh, Milton. Someone's in trouble—this sounds like a job for Fearless Fran."

Fearless Fran had been a Saturday-morning cartoon series, one of Eden's first leading roles. She had liked the premise: a bookish little girl named Frances Anne lives in a house next to Dismal Bog. One day she discovers both she and the family dog, Milton, have superpowers. But although Fearless Fran had been designed as a feminist heroine, the show's writing was derivative, its animation mediocre. It was lucky enough to hang on for barely two years, but it was still alive and well in reruns.

But Peyton seemed delighted. She echoed Eden with uncanny accuracy. "This sounds like a job for Fearless Fran."

"That's *excellent,* Peyton."

"I know her song," Peyton said excitedly. "I can sing it."

She pitched her voice low and gravelly and sang:

Here I come, I'm out of sight—I'm Fearless Fran
'Cause I don't know fright.

"Don't know what?" Eden cued her.

"Don't know *fright,*" Peyton sang emphatically. She slipped from her chair and seized one of Jessie's tea towels from the rack, tucking one end of it under the collar of her shirt so that it hung down her back like a cape. She struck the Fearless Fran pose, back straight, chin held high, fists clenched, one arm extended skyward.

Eden smiled. She'd never seen the girl so playful. "Why, Fearless," she said with admiration. "I'd know you anywhere."

Peyton put her fists on her hips, puffed out her chest heroically, and recited, "Fearless Fran at your service. Always brave. Never nervous."

She's got talent, Eden thought with a pang. *A natural. She'd be wonderful with training.* At the same moment, an idea, small but full of radiant possibility, struck her.

She said, "Would you sit down and talk to me, Fearless?"

For a second the child seemed to hesitate, but then she strode back to the chair and sat down with her arms crossed.

"Tell me, Fearless," Eden said. "Aren't you afraid of anything?"

"Nope," said Peyton.

"A shark?" Eden asked.

"No."

"Outlaws?"

"No."

"The dark?"

"No."

"You're completely brave?"

"Yes."

Eden leaned her elbow on the table and rested her chin in her hand, studying the child.

"You're not afraid of anything in the whole, wide world?"

"No."

"Why not?"

"I'm Fearless."

"Hm," Eden said casually. "Do you know a little girl named Peyton?"

"Yes. I know Henry, too."

Eden chose her words carefully. "Sometimes Peyton's scared. She can't even tell me why."

An uneasy expression came into Peyton's eyes. She suddenly looked on guard.

"If I knew what she was afraid of," Eden said, "I could help her. But she won't tell things. But you could. I mean, you're Fearless—right?"

Peyton said nothing. She put her thumb in her mouth.

"Peyton's staying with me now," Eden said. "At her grandma's house. Did you know that?"

The child stared at her, wordlessly, then slowly nodded.

Go slowly, Eden warned herself. "A woman brought her here. The woman's name was Louise Brodnik. She brought Peyton here from Sedonia, Missouri."

Peyton did not contradict her, only watched her as a small animal might watch a larger one that offered potential danger.

"Oh, Fearless—" Eden said, as if suddenly remembering her manners. "I didn't offer you any supermolecule tea. Would you like a cup?"

The answer was silence, but Eden pretended to pour a cup of tea and set it in front of the child. Then she glanced about the room as if searching for someone. "I don't see your friend, Milton Mutt. Maybe he went to the bog. I wonder if he's with Mister Swampgas."

The corner of Peyton's mouth twitched nervously, as if she wanted to smile but did not dare.

"I remember when Mister Swampgas got kidnapped by the cosmic carp people from Carpathia. But you saved him," Eden said solemnly.

"Now where were we? Oh, yes. Peyton's mother asked Mrs. Brodnik to bring her here. Peyton's mother's name is Mimi. She had to go away. Do you know where she went, Fearless?"

Peyton swallowed hard. "No," she said in a tiny voice.

"Oh," Eden said, as if it hardly mattered. "I'll tell you something else. Peyton's mother knows a lot of people. Me and Mrs. Brodnik and Granny." Eden took a deep breath. "Peyton must miss some of those people her mother knew."

Peyton stiffened in her chair and looked distressed.

Eden hurried on. "Peyton and Mimi used to live in Michigan," she said. "I wonder if Peyton ever misses Michigan. Do you think so?"

The child nodded warily but said nothing. "Who does she miss the most? Who do *you* think she misses, Fearless?"

Peyton twisted uncomfortably in her chair. "Mrs. Stangblood," she said so softly it was barely audible. "In Detroit."

Eden's skin prickled. "Mrs. Stangblood? Detroit?"

Peyton made no reply. Eden smiled encouragingly. "Why, thank you, Fearless. You really are very brave. You're quite a good friend to Peyton."

Peyton fidgeted and looked away. "Anytime you want to come talk to me, Fearless, you do it," Eden said warmly. "Because you can say things that Peyton can't. You can help her that way. Will you do that?"

The child shrugged, an uneasy movement.

"I'm Peyton's friend, and so are you. Just like Mrs. Stangblood."

Eden put her arm on the child's shoulder. "Can you tell me about Peyton's mother, Fearless? We need to find her, to help her."

Peyton tugged the ends of the makeshift cape from her collar. She sat clutching the tea towel and staring down at it almost guiltily. She was tired of the game or frightened by it or both.

Eden said, "Is Fearless going away?"

"Yes," Peyton said in her own voice.

"Is she going back to the house by Dismal Bog?"

Peyton nodded and let the tea towel fall to the floor.

"Fearless can come back to talk anytime she wants. You know that, don't you?"

But Peyton said nothing in reply, only stared down at the poor, makeshift, abandoned cape.

Eden thought, *Thank you. Thank you for telling me about Mrs. Stangblood.*

She rose from her chair and went to the little girl, bent and hugged her.

Peyton clung to her. "Eden," she said, her tone pleading, "do you love me?"

Eden's heart felt as if it had been jerked from her chest. She did not want to love anyone, especially this mysterious and needy child.

But she hugged her more tightly. "Of course," she lied. "Of course I do."

She knelt before the child, holding her by the upper arms, and looked her in the eyes, feigning the utmost sincerity. "And, Peyton? The more I know about you, the more I can love you. So you must send Fearless to talk to me again. Understand?"

Peyton nodded dumbly, tears rising in her dark eyes.

After lunch, Eden and Peyton took the old dog and walked down the path that led through the woods to the playground by the lake. When they returned, Owen's black Blazer was parked in the drive beside Jessie's house.

Owen himself was in the side yard, facing away from them, toward the thick woods that fringed the houses. He stood with a crossbow cocked and aimed at a torn target pinned to a bale of hay. A small cluster of arrows already bristled from the circles.

At the sight of him, Eden's hand tightened around Peyton's, and her heart took an unsettling leap. Owen's back was straight, his face tense with concentration, and the October sun glinted on his silver-gray hair.

She saw him release the trigger, and the arrow flew to pierce the edge of the bull's-eye, burying itself to the hilt. He loaded another arrow, raised it, and aimed again. The crossbow, Eden thought, had a cruel, medieval look.

"What's he doing?" Peyton asked uneasily.

"Target practice," Eden answered, watching him loose the arrow again. It embedded itself in the target with remarkable accuracy and force.

"But he doesn't have a gun," Peyton said, with something like disapproval. "For target practice you got to have a *gun*."

Eden looked at her. "How do you know that, sweety?"

Peyton shifted uncomfortably. She got a furtive, shuttered look, and Eden could tell she wasn't going to answer.

Owen retrieved his arrows and thrust them into the bow's built-in quiver. When he turned, he saw Eden and Peyton standing at the edge of the drive. He gave them a curt nod, walked back to the Blazer, and put the bow back in its case and stowed it in the hatchback.

He came up to Eden, giving Peyton a cursory glance and something that might have been a tight smile that failed. He looked at Eden, and his eyes seemed as blue as the flawless October sky.

She was suddenly self-conscious. "Hi," she said as brightly, as casually, as she could. "Did you find my note—that we'd be right back?"

"Yes."

"Did you see Jessie?"

"Yes. She's fine, but tired."

He gazed down at the old dog, which Eden held in her arms. A frown line appeared between his dark brows. He said, "I need to talk to you. Alone."

Eden swallowed in apprehension, but released the child's hand and gave her an encouraging pat on the shoulder. "Go run and play a minute, Peyton. But stay in the yard."

Peyton, her head cocked curiously, went off to examine the target.

"She's interested in that," Eden said, looking after her. "She talked as if she knew something about guns and target practice, but she wouldn't say what. Owen, I hate to admit it, but I'm getting scared."

She told him of the disturbing call and how she could not stop fearing the woman was Mimi. She told him, as well, what Peyton had said of Mrs. Stangblood in Detroit.

Owen nodded. "Stangblood? I'll check her out."

"Owen—you said we had to talk. About what?"

He gazed up at the sky, his eyes narrowing. "After I saw Jessie, I got a call. Some information you won't like."

A frisson of foreboding ran through her. "What's wrong?"

He took her arm, drew her closer to him. His voice was low. "Louise Brodnik's house didn't burn by accident. Somebody torched it. And she was dead before it burned."

Stunned, Eden stared up at him in bewilderment. "What?" she breathed.

"Right after I left the hospital, I got a call from John Mulcahy, a detective in Missouri. The fire at Louise Brodnik's house was set."

She felt as if all the air had been knocked from her body. "But—but why?" she asked.

"We don't know why," he said. "But the autopsy report shows no smoke in Louise Brodnik's lungs. Whatever she died of, it wasn't the fire."

"Then what killed her?"

"They're not sure. It may have been her heart. But if she died of natural causes before the fire was set, who set the fire? And how? And why?"

Eden stared up at him without comprehension. "What's this got to do with us? With Peyton?"

"I don't know," he said. "But maybe somebody was looking for Peyton. Maybe they still are."

Eden touched her fingertips to her mouth, unable to breathe, to speak.

"Think about it," he said. "Peyton's afraid of something, deathly afraid. She's been coached not to talk, told it's dangerous. What does she know? And is it important enough for somebody to shut her up?"

Eden glanced automatically at Peyton to make sure she was safe. The child poked her finger at the holes in the paper target, peered at them warily. Eden thought of the nameless blond woman with her hand full of fire. She thought of the plane in Miami. She was afraid to say what she was beginning to fear.

She turned back to Owen and knew that he could see the alarm in her eyes. His grip on her arm softened.

"I'm sorry," he said. "I didn't mean to scare you. I think I'd better stay with you until we know what's going on."

Eden sucked in her breath sharply. "No. I can't let you do that."

"We'll argue later. Come on," he said. "Let's take this thing back to the house." He took the dog from her arms, set it on the ground, held its leash.

She nodded numbly. But she kept looking over her shoulder, to assure herself that Peyton was all right.

Even with the sunshine flooding down, Eden felt cold. A minute shudder trembled through her.

Owen noticed. His arm slipped around her shoulders, and she didn't object. The old dog hobbled behind them, and at last Owen had to scoop it up and carry it in his free arm.

Peyton played alone, by the riddled target.

Tomorrow's the last day, Mimi told herself. *Tomorrow it's over.*

She had tickets for tonight and for tomorrow morning, for another breakfast show. She had tickets for tomorrow afternoon and night.

She took the money out of her jeans, unwadded and counted it. She had exactly sixty-eight dollars and seventy-one cents. It was enough to keep her in wine and cigarettes until tomorrow and pay for the room one more day.

She sipped at the wine, and felt a stab of grief that she could not go home to Jessie with Peyton. She was not only an embarrassment to them, but a danger. There was only one gift she could now give her child—her absence.

She sat on the edge of her bed, crossed her arms on her knees, and buried her face. She was weary to the marrow of her bones, and she felt old, thousands of years old, but as if age had never brought her wisdom.

At first, stupidly, she had thought that Drace and the others were simply talking big, playing games, that they didn't *actually* mean to strike out in violence against the government. It was posturing and blustering, she thought, just a kind of theater to them. She hadn't minded. Like them she was full of anger and suspicion, and like them, she was wont to posture and bluster and blow off steam herself.

And, at first, she had been a perfect fool for Drace.

She hadn't understood what he wanted from her. He liked having two women, of course, and he would have liked to have had more. But Raylene was jealous as hell, even if she couldn't say anything, and Raylene had hated her guts and Peyton's, too.

By the end, Mimi had belonged to all the men, not just Drace, who seldom wanted her anymore, and Raylene treated her little better than a slave. When Mimi objected, she was "disciplined." It kept growing worse, it kept growing crazier, it kept spinning more wildly out of control.

She realized now that she had not thought clearly during any of it. And when she finally understood what was happening, it was too late. She had trapped herself, and for her there was no exit.

But when she'd discovered Jessie's ad in the back of a tabloid, she'd thought she'd found a way for Peyton, at least, to escape. At first, that had seemed enough.

But she'd known that night she'd walked away from the farmhouse with Peyton and the stolen money that she didn't dare go back.

So, this was the only plan she could come up with for herself. She had run this far, and it was futile to run farther. She knew the one best thing she could do for Peyton.

She raised her head and scrubbed her palms across her wet, burning eyes.

She got up from the bed and took her wallet from her scuffed purse. She went into the bathroom, and one by one, she tore up her false identity cards. She had no real ones left.

She looked a long time at the one photograph she carried of Peyton. Although it hurt, she tore that up, too.

She flushed away the scraps of paper that had validated her life. She kept only the piece of newsprint with Jessie's ad and phone number. She would keep that until tomorrow night. Perhaps she would allow herself one last call. Just one.

She looked at her mottled face in the mirror, at the hated scar across her throat. She looked at the bottle on the sink.

She heard Jessie's voice in her ears, strong and vital: *Don't do anything rash. Take care. Don't be reckless.*

"Don't worry, Jessie," she croaked in her broken whisper. "It won't be rash. It won't be reckless. I'll get it right."

She washed her face, brushed her tangled hair, changed into a clean T-shirt. She stuffed her ticket into the pocket of her jeans and set off walking for the Moon River Theater.

It was nearing showtime.

FOURTEEN

---·•◦•·---

"YES, YES, YES," EDEN TOLD JESSIE AT THE HOSPITAL THAT evening. "He's staying with us. Stop fussing about it."

"I'm not fussing," Jessie contradicted. "I'm looking out for Peyton's welfare. I don't know why you didn't bring her. I was counting on seeing her."

"I told you, she got as far as the hospital door, then didn't want to come in. I think the place scares her. Owen's taken her over to the ice-cream parlor."

"Make sure he stays close to her," Jessie ordered. "That child needs protection. That fire in Sedonia wasn't no accident. I know it."

Eden allowed herself to show no reaction, not an iota. She and Owen had decided not to tell Jessie yet that her vision about the fire had proved true.

"That fire's bad news," Jessie said, "but I got good news, too. Mimi's coming home soon. I seen it clear as day. She'll walk in the front door and say, 'Hi, Granny, I come home to stay this time.' "

Eden frowned. "Home to stay—Mimi?"

Jessie gave a thin smile of satisfaction. "Indeed. It'll be soon. Before the year is out."

"She'll stay with *you*?" Eden said dubiously.

"Till she finds a place of her own for her and Peyton," Jessie said. "Why not? This last trouble's made her grow up. She wants to settle down. I got a very strong feeling about that, so wipe that skeptical look off your face."

Eden was deeply worried about Mimi, but she kept her expression as blank as possible.

"Let's hope you're right," she said. "But I have something to ask you. This person—Constance—called again. She sounded disturbed, very disturbed, and she hung up on me. If she calls back, I need something to hold her, to keep her on the line. What can I say?"

Jessie shrugged, almost irritably. "I don't know."

"You've been doing this most of your life," Eden said, putting her hand on her hip. "I tell you, this woman worries me. How do I get through to her?"

"No thought of Constance has crossed my mind today," Jessie said. "I been concerned with Mimi. My own flesh and blood, thank you very much."

Eden sighed. "All right, Jessie. I'm begging. Please give me your expert advice."

"You should have brought my crystal ball," Jessie complained. "I'm too tired to lay out the cards. Let me see what I can get."

Jessie leaned back against the pillow and closed her eyes. For a long moment she stroked the largest of the rings on her left hand, a moonstone set in silver. Then her fingers went still, her breathing became deep and even, and her eyelids twitched slightly.

A full minute passed. Then two.

"Jessie?" Eden asked in a cautious whisper.

Her only answer was the most delicate of snores. Jessie slept.

Peyton, sated with ice cream, went to bed at nine o'clock without argument. She slept, her small, limp body curling in on itself, her thumb in her mouth.

Eden left the night-light on in the bedroom and padded barefoot into the living room. Owen stood by the little phone table, studying a handwritten list. The lamplight gleamed on his pewter-colored hair, and he raised his eyes from the paper to meet hers.

She turned away, uselessly straightening one of the dozen doilies Jessie had draped on the furniture.

"You don't have to stay here tonight," she told him. "Jessie doesn't have to know. We'll just tell her you did."

"No. It's settled."

She shrugged and kept toying with the foolish doilie. "I'd really—really rather you didn't stay. I can take care of myself."

"Louise Brodnik brought Peyton here. Two days later she's found dead, her house set afire. Jessie's sensed trouble all along. I'll stay."

Eden gave a chilly little laugh at the idiocy of it. "If you're worried about us, just loan me a gun."

"You can shoot?"

"Of course I can shoot," she answered. "I grew up in the country. I've shot rats and copperheads and once a timber rattler. He was as long as your arm. Well—almost."

"How much gunslinging have you done since you ran off to Hollywood?"

"None. But—"

"I'll stay," he told her.

Still she didn't look at him. Desperately, she searched for something to say. "Have you called the police?" she asked. "To tell them what Peyton said about Mrs. Stangblood in Michigan?"

"Yes," he said. "Here and in Sedonia."

"And?"

"And they'll get back to us. In their own sweet time."

"I *hate* bureaucracy." Eden raked a hand through her bangs. "That's all? They'll get back to us?"

"That's all. In the meantime, I've been on the phone to Detroit information."

Her shoulders sagged slightly. Of course he had been on the phone; he was not a man to sit back waiting for others to do the work.

"Asking about listings for Stangbloods?" she asked, throat tight. She studied the crocheted pattern in the doilie, one loop knotting into the next and the next.

"Yeah," he said without emotion.

"This isn't even your problem, you know."

"I know. I made the calls on my cell phone. Don't worry. Jessie won't have to pay."

She turned to face him. "I'll pay you back."

"You don't have to," he said.

"I insist."

The air between them seemed to leap with an electrical charge that had nothing to do with phone bills or who paid them. He could feel it, too, she could tell.

He moved across the room, as if purposely putting

more distance between them. His eyes were no longer on her, for which she was grateful.

He glanced at the list, one dark brow crooked in a frown. "There are more Stangbloods in Detroit than you'd think. Seven listed. I reached four. They didn't know anything."

She clenched the back of Jessie's armchair. "The other three?"

"They don't answer. Yet. I'll try again tomorrow. It's after ten in Detroit now. I need to call Alvin Swinnerton about that security system, too."

"You worry about us too much."

He glanced up. As always, the blueness of his eyes jolted her. "I could use a drink."

She said, "Brandy?"

He nodded, went into the kitchen, and she trailed behind him. He opened the kitchen cupboard beside the sink and drew out the bottle of brandy. "You want any?"

"No," she said. "Thanks."

She glanced down at the kitchen table and saw Peyton's open tablet. The child had drawn a picture of a burning plane. Quickly Eden turned it facedown, went to the counter, and poured herself a cup of coffee.

Owen took down a glass and half filled it with brandy. "You'd be better off with this than that damned coffee."

"I don't drink," Eden said stubbornly. "Not with my family history. I'll stick to coffee."

He shrugged and leaned against the counter again, glass in hand. He took an economical sip, savored it. "So who drank?" he asked. "Besides Mimi?"

Eden shrugged ruefully. "Who didn't? Well, Jessie didn't. But her husband did, my grandfather. She married him when she was fifteen to get out of the delta country. She didn't know he was, in her words, 'a no-good sot.'"

Owen gazed at her over the edge of his glass. "He died young, right? When she was pregnant with your mother. I know that much. And that's about all. She never talks about your mother."

He gazed at her over the edge of his glass, something like challenge in his eyes.

"My mother—" Eden still struggled for the right words, after all these years. "My mother—started drinking when she was very young. She was a lovable person— but not stable. She and Jessie were estranged early on."

He made no reply, waiting for her to go on. His gaze was unwavering and thoughtful.

Eden swallowed hard. "She married somebody too much like herself. Charming, but, well, unbalanced. It's a miracle the marriage lasted as long as it did—five years, off and on. Then he disappeared. Just disappeared."

Owen frowned. "You don't know what happened to him?"

She shook her head and stared down at her ringless hands. She had her mother's hands, slender, fine-boned. "We never saw him again. And our mother was killed when I was ten and Mimi was six. She was hit by a car. Outside a bar. It was night, she was jaywalking. She wasn't—quite—sober. We lived in Little Rock. I didn't even know I had a grandmother. Our mother never told us about her. But suddenly, there was Jessie. And she brought us here. Now Mimi's sent Peyton here. And the same old twisted story just keeps going on and on."

Something fragile, something stretched too thin, broke in Eden. She curled her hand into a fist and pressed it against her forehead. She gave a small, stifled hiccough of a sob, and tears, unbidden, flowed down her cheeks.

Owen was at her side, his hands on her arms, raising her to her feet.

"I'm sorry," she said fiercely. "Usually I never cry. *Never.*"

He pulled her close and put his arms around her. "Stop apologizing and just cry, will you?"

"I'm *afraid* for my sister," she choked out, furious at herself for weeping. "I'm terrified for her. And what about Peyton? She's been through so much—maybe her life's already hopelessly screwed up."

"Eden," he said, lacing a hand through her hair. "Don't—"

"I'm not feeling sorry for myself," she insisted, her voice shaking. "It's her. It's not fair. Why should she—she didn't ask to be born into a mess like this—she didn't ask to be born at all—she—"

He drew back slightly, tipped her face up to his. Then he bent nearer, his eyes severe, his mouth twisted at the corner. His voice was a growl, deep and harsh in his throat. "I said 'Don't.' "

Then his lips were on hers. She tasted brandy and something like despair in his kiss, and she clung to him, kissing him back, desperate herself.

There was nothing studied, nothing artful in the way he kissed her. Everything in his touch was filled with immediacy and undisguised hunger.

His body arched against hers, taut as a bow. He pressed her to him even more tightly, and his chest was hard against her breasts.

Eden thrust herself against him recklessly, her hands gripping his shoulders, fingers avid for the feel of his strength. She felt like someone being hauled from a dark, depthless space toward a life-giving force. She wanted that force from him, she needed it, she gave herself up to it.

This is quite insane, she told herself, then let the thought fall away into the emptiness she was escaping. The world was cold, but he was warm.

It was intoxicating to give in to desire, to become lost in it. His hands were under her sweater, exploring the curves and angles of her bare back. When he touched her naked flesh, rationality returned to her with a chilling swoop.

She tried to draw away, turn her face, but he pressed his lips against the pulse of her throat. "What if Peyton sees us?" she whispered, her breath uneven.

"We'll go into the bedroom," he said, mouth warm against her skin.

"She could—walk in on us," she gasped. He was undoing the complex fastening of her bra.

"We'll lock the door." The bra came loose, and beneath her sweater, he touched her bare breasts. She shuddered with the pleasure of it.

"We—we shouldn't do this with a child in the place."

"Married people do it all the time."

This logic seemed infallible to Eden. Then his lips were on her breast, and logic ceased to matter.

He lay on his back, staring up at the darkness, heart pounding, body damp with sweat, one arm around her cool shoulders. She was curled motionless against him, her head on his chest. Her hair felt silky against his flesh and it tickled. He could feel her diamond earring like a pinprick over his drumming heart.

He ran his hand down her arm and back again. She stirred softly and nestled closer to him, and he brushed his lips against her hair. She laid her hand on his stomach, just above the navel. Her touch went through him like a sweet, desired knife.

"I should go to the other bedroom," she said. "In case Peyton wakes up."

"Not yet," he said. He drew her closer, kissed her hair again.

She sighed, her breath warm against his skin.

He was silent, glad simply to hold her, touch her. He had not had such a compulsion to touch a woman since Laurie. He didn't understand the urge, he had only followed it.

"I can't believe this," she said. "We did it in my grandmother's bed."

"Believe it," he said.

She drew her hand away, and he felt her body subtly tense. "I suppose this had to happen," she said. "I mean, we're two healthy, unattached adults. We're cooped up together. Things have been intense. It's—only natural."

She edged away from him minutely, moved her head from his chest to the pillow. He realized that the subtle distance she put between them was more than physical. It snaked between them like a crack that would widen until it yawned into an unbridgeable abyss.

"I mean," she said, turning so she lay facing away from him, "I suppose it's something we had to get out of the way."

Something we had to get out of the way. That puts me in my place, doesn't it?

"I suppose," he said.

"I don't want you to think I expect anything from

you," she said. "I don't. We probably won't see each other when this is over."

"No," he said. "You'll go. I'll stay."

"Yes," she said.

He withdrew his arm, stared up into the darkness again. "Tell me something," he said. "What you said about your family. Is that why you never married, had kids?"

"My gene pool is mined," she said. "Eccentrics and drunks. I don't think I should reproduce. The odds are bad."

"You don't get close to anyone, do you?"

"Not really."

She paused. "You don't, either."

"No."

They were both silent. At last she said, "You don't like Peyton, do you?"

"No."

"Is it because she's different?"

He sighed harshly. "Don't harp on that. I don't like kids. Period."

"Why?"

"My wife wanted kids," he said. "She couldn't have them. And then she died of—what all went wrong."

She sat up, drew the sheet up over her breasts. He closed his eyes in sudden weariness. The words had explained nothing. They never did.

She said, "I guess 'I'm sorry' is too easy to say."

"Yeah," he said. "It is."

"But I am sorry."

"So am I."

"I understand."

"Do you? I don't."

"I didn't mean . . ." her voice trailed off. She was

silent for a long moment. Then, quietly she said, "I should go."

"Yeah. You should."

She stood. He heard her gather up her clothes, slip into them with a whisper-soft rustling. He felt her sit on the edge of the bed again. She leaned over, lightly kissed him on the cheekbone. "I think both of us just needed someone tonight," she said. "Thank you."

He wanted to turn to her, haul her down into the bed again, strip her clothes off, make love with her until the sun rose. Instead, he said, "You're welcome. Anytime. Send your friends."

He felt her stiffen in resentment. She rose and quietly left the room, shutting the door behind her.

You're a prince, Charteris, he told himself. *A goddamn prince.*

He pulled up the sheet around his body, settled bitterly into the bed. What did he care about her? Soon enough she would be gone for good, and with luck she'd take that troubling kid with her. He would be safely solitary again, with only his private ghosts and his dying dog and one old fortune-teller for company.

It was forty minutes past midnight in Branson.

Outside the motel office, the neon sign flickered fitfully. It was supposed to say "Pleasant Inn—Vacancies," but several letters had burned out, so that instead it read "P easant Inn—Vacanc es."

The motel was off the main highway, in a trashy lakeside section near the edge of town. It looked right, it felt right, and Drace had a sense of certainty so mystically strong his heart hammered with it.

Yes, he thought. *Yes, yes, yes.*

"Yeah," said the night clerk, nodding at the snapshot of Mimi in Raylene's hand. "We got somebody like that. In unit ten."

He pushed the register toward them. Immediately Drace recognized Mimi's spiky, nervous handwriting, even though the name she'd signed was "Constance Caine" and not her own.

"You're sure?" Raylene asked, still holding the picture out for the man's inspection.

"I remember the frizzy hair."

The clerk was a rummy-looking older man with a bad shave, a worse haircut, and nothing but a scar where his left ear should have been.

He was slightly wall-eyed, but his crooked gaze was no longer on the photo. He kept it hungrily fixed on the shadowy cleft of Raylene's cleavage, which was just visible at the V-neck outline of her pink sweater.

Drace's heart galloped in triumph, but he said nothing, he let Raylene handle it. She leaned forward a little, so the clerk could see farther down her sweater.

She touched the sleeve of his grimy shirt, and she had tears in her eyes, God love her.

"She's our cousin," she said in a choked, vulnerable little voice. "She's not very stable, and if she stops taking her medication, well, she can get very depressed."

She leaned farther toward him still, and Drace could see the old man wanted to climb right down her neckline and gobble her tits whole.

"She drinks," Raylene confessed. "She goes off like this, and we worry that she'll drink herself to *death*. That someday a maid in some place like this is going to unlock the door and find her dead."

Raylene drew back her hands and pressed them together prayerlike to her chest, so that her breasts thrust out on either side. "We don't want to make any trouble for you, honest," she said earnestly. "We don't want to bring the law into it, either."

She nodded at Drace. "My brother here is with the police himself."

Drace flashed the old man the badge in its official wallet. It was a U.S. Air Force Security Police badge, and he had ordered both badge and wallet out of a mail-order catalog.

But the old man wasn't nearly as interested in the badge as he was Raylene. He licked his dry lips. "What do you want me to do?" he asked.

Raylene licked her lips, too. The tears rose, shimmering in her blue eyes, and her voice quavered. "We just want to keep it quiet, take her home. No scandal, no report. Her father's a minister, you know?"

She took a deep breath. She kept one hand clenched between her breasts and put the other over the clerk's gnarled hand resting on the counter.

"We've handled this before," she said. "Just let us in. And let us take her home where she belongs. Please."

"I can't do that," he said, his Adam's apple bobbing.

"Please," she begged. "My brother will make it worth your time. I promise."

"I'll pay her bill," Drace said, reaching for his other wallet. "I doubt that she can do it herself. And there'll be a bonus for you." He drew out a fifty-dollar bill. He handed it to Raylene.

She pressed it into the man's palm, holding the money there, bill against his palm, between her two hands.

He hesitated, and she leaned nearer to him.

"Nobody has to know about this," Raylene assured him in the sweetest, most irresistible of whispers.

• • •

Drace and Raylene moved the van in front of unit ten and got out, leaving it unlocked. The night clerk was waiting.

Beside Drace, Raylene held her breath as the clerk thrust the key in the keyhole and turned it. As soon as she heard the lock click, she pushed herself closer to the man.

"Let my brother handle it from here," she said softly, crowding against him. "Go back to the office—please. Please."

"There's a security chain on the door," the man said, but he did not move away from her.

"My brother can handle it," Raylene told him. "He's police. Go back now. If we need help, I'll come for you."

She edged away from him. He looked her up and down, then reluctantly moved back toward the office. He reminded her of a hobbling old dog that had uselessly followed a young female too far and now had to limp home.

Drace could get into the room, she knew. The chain lock didn't worry her. The door looked flimsy, and he had bolt cutters in the van.

Raylene could see inside. The room was mostly dark, but a dim light from the bathroom fell through its partly open door. A woman lay motionless on the narrow bed, her back to them. A half-empty jug of wine was on the table beside her. She was fully clothed and on top of the bedspread.

Raylene recognized the thin body, the flyaway hair, even in the shadows: Mimi. Hate slithered through her, cold and absolute.

You came into our house, when I didn't want you, Raylene thought. *You slept with my man, and I let you, I had no choice. We shared everything with you, even our plans, when I didn't trust you. Now you betrayed us, and I will gladly, gladly kill you.*

Moving quietly, Drace took the bolt cutters from the van. Raylene unzipped the purse that hung over her shoulder. It held handcuffs, duct tape, a knife.

Drace easily cut the chain lock and pushed the door open. The two of them stepped inside. Drace shut the door behind them and drew a small revolver from his ankle holster, a snub-nosed .38.

He nodded to Raylene. She took the handcuffs from her handbag and approached the bed. Drace switched on the overhead light.

"Hello, Mimi," he said softly. "We came to take you hunting. For Peyton."

Raylene thought it would be simple to take Mimi prisoner. She was probably too drunk even to wake fully. Raylene could clamp on the cuffs and gag her with the tape, and Mimi would be too groggy to struggle.

If she did awake enough to fight, Drace could subdue her in seconds with a choke hold and pressure on her carotid artery. They could hustle her into the van and take her someplace safe and isolated. There they could twist the truth out of her: where had she sent Peyton?

Drace moved to clap his hand over Mimi's mouth in case she came to, and Raylene seized her left hand and snapped the cuff shut.

But both of them were caught by surprise when Mimi reacted both swiftly and violently. She did not scream, but kicking and flailing, she somehow sprang to her feet, wild as a cornered animal.

She shoved Raylene with her right hand so hard that Raylene was knocked off balance and hit the metal dresser, hurting her ribs.

Mimi's left arm lashed out, and the swinging handcuff caught Drace across the wrist as he lunged for her. He swore and took an involuntary step backward.

"Get her!" he ordered Raylene.

Mimi had darted into the bathroom, slamming the door behind her.

"Shit," Drace said angrily. He threw himself against the door, but Mimi fought from her side to keep it shut. Raylene, teeth clenched, threw her weight against the door to help him.

For a moment, Mimi's strength to ward them off seemed unnatural, superhuman. But then the door gave way, swung inward. Raylene tumbled into the room first, and she'd meant to seize Mimi by the hair and strike her head against the sink.

But Mimi, foot raised, kicked Raylene in the stomach, knocking her backward into Drace, who kept her from falling.

Mimi had snatched up a bottle of something from the sink and unscrewed its top.

"Stop," Drace ordered, supporting Raylene with one arm and using the other to aim the gun at Mimi. Raylene couldn't get her breath, and she was swept with a nausea that made her half-faint. But rage kept her focused, and she glared at Mimi, wanting to kill her.

But Mimi quickly raised the bottle to her lips and drank, and as soon as she drank, she gave a strangled cry and lurched backward, throwing the bottle toward them, and falling to her knees. Then she collapsed onto her side, writhing and holding her mouth and throat.

"Christ!" Drace breathed. The bottle had missed them, bounced off the wall and spilled in a pool beneath the sink. Mimi lay twisting on the floor in agony, and the muffled sounds she made were low, but terrible to hear.

"What's she done?" cried Raylene, clutching at Drace.

Drace pushed her away and knelt beside Mimi, pulling her hands away from her mouth. Her lips were mottled, white and bluish and raw red, and they were swollen and covered with glistening blisters.

Mimi thrashed, whipping her head back and forth, pounding it against the dirty linoleum.

"What's she done?" Raylene repeated, watching in horror.

Drace poked at the fallen bottle cautiously with the barrel of his gun. He shook his head in disgust and dismay. "Drain cleaner," he said. "She drank drain cleaner."

"Oh, Jesus," Raylene said. She closed her eyes and leaned her head against the bathroom door. She did not feel sickened by the sight of Mimi's pain, only cheated by it, jealous that she had not inflicted it herself.

"She was trying to commit suicide, the dumb bitch," he said. "She told me once that was the way to kill yourself if you meant it. If you made a mistake and it didn't kill you fast, it'd kill you slow."

Raylene opened her eyes and stared down at the twitching body, the contorted face with its burned mouth. "Is she going to die?"

"I don't know. I don't know how much she drank."

He hauled Mimi to her feet and thrust her face under the sink faucet, turned the water on full force. "Open your mouth, you dumb bitch. Clean it out."

Mimi's legs buckled beneath her, her body convulsed, but Drace held her face in the rushing water, trying to pry open her mouth.

"Don't burn your hands," Raylene warned Drace.

He swore and wrenched Mimi's jaws apart, but when he did so, she convulsed again and fainted.

For a long time, he kept her jaw forced open and the water flooding over her, but finally he let her slip back to the floor again, fighting hoarsely for breath.

Raylene stared down at her. "Well, this is a fine turn of events," she said bitterly. "How's she going to tell us anything *now*?"

"We'll see," Drace said. He knelt and frisked Mimi, even as she spasmed and clutched unconsciously at her mouth and throat. He drew out the wad of crumpled money. He drew out the worn wallet.

He rose. The wallet contained no identification, no photos, no credit cards, only one tattered scrap of newsprint. On the floor, Mimi moaned and gurgled.

"Shut her up, gag her," Drace told Raylene, almost absently.

Reluctantly, fearful of burning her hands, Raylene knelt by Mimi, cut off a piece of the duct tape and plastered it over the raw and blistered lips. She seized Mimi's right hand and fastened the other cuff on it. Mimi groaned, her eyelids fluttered half-open, but her bloodshot gaze seemed trained on nothing.

"Well," Drace said with ironic satisfaction, "look at this. She's told us something, after all."

He handed Raylene the scrap of paper. It was an ad that looked as if it had been torn from a newspaper. It said:

YOUR PERSONAL PSYCHIC! The real thing! Sister Jessie Buddress, God's Gifted Seer and Healer. Clairvoyant, Spiritualist, and GENUINE Medium. $3.99 a minute. 1-900-555-6631, Endor, AR.

Raylene was stunned, half with fright, half with plea-sure. "Jessie of Endor—you found her."

"Check the receipt for the room," Drace said from between his teeth. "There were long-distance calls on it. Are they the same?"

Raylene dug the receipt out of the pocket of her slacks. The phone numbers were listed on the printout. There were three:

> 1-900-555-6631—5 min. 06 sec.
> 1-900-555-6631—6 min. 32 sec.
> 1-900-555-6631—4 min. 49 sec.

A psychic, she thought numbly. *She's talking to a bloody psychic. What's she said? What's she told? Christ, she could betray us all.*

"They're the same," she breathed, voice choked with apprehension. "But why? Why send the kid to a psychic, for God's sake?"

"I don't know," Drace said. He looked down at Mimi, his face impassive. He knelt and dug his thumb into the tape where it covered the corner of her blistered mouth. Her body knotted in pain.

"This Jessie in Endor," he asked, leaning over her. "Is she 'your people'? Your 'blood kin'? Shake your head yes or no, or I'll pour the damn drain cleaner in your eyes."

But Mimi only struck her head against the floor again in a frenzy. She arched her back and made an ago-nized gargling sound deep in her chest. Then once more she went limp and still.

"Is she dead?" Raylene asked, half hoping she was.

"No," Drace said. "She's still breathing."

"Will she die?"

Drace looked at her, something almost like amusement in his eyes. "Eventually, of course."

"I want her to last," Raylene said bitterly. "I want her to suffer. I want her to see Peyton die."

Drace gazed down at the still woman. Blood was seeping from beneath the tape, and her breathing was labored, cracked and irregular. "So do I," he said.

FIFTEEN

<hr>

THE PHONE RINGING BESIDE JESSIE'S BED WOKE OWEN. HE groaned and glanced at the curtained window. The narrow ribbon of light at its edges was dim; morning had barely dawned.

Next to the telephone, Jessie's clock radio showed the time in red letters: 5:14. The phone shrilled again. He swore, groaned, and answered it, hoping it hadn't awakened the kid.

"Buddress residence. Owen Charteris speaking."

"Charteris, this is Mulcahy. We got more on Louise Brodnik. Her oldest daughter got in this morning from Germany."

Owen rubbed his hand across his grainy eyes. "Yes?"

"She talked long-distance to her mother last Friday. She said her mother had agreed to help some woman with a kid. She thought the woman was mixed up with a bunch of hippies or paramilitaries or a cult or something on a farm outside of Sedonia."

Owen sat up straight, suddenly awake. "Hippies? Cult? *Paramilitary?*"

Mulcahy said, "A young guy named Yount took over a farmhouse and some land here for an uncle who went into a nursing home. He lives there with four or five other people. Louise Brodnik thought the woman was one of them."

"Was she?"

"We don't know," said Mulcahy. "The next shift'll check it out. I'm sorry to call so early. I thought you'd want to know as soon as possible."

"I appreciate it," Owen said. "But what's this paramilitary business?"

"We don't have much on it. People complain about hearing explosions. But there's a small quarry on the land. They could be blasting rocks. But who knows? They keep to themselves. The guy who took over the farm, Yount, came here driving a car with Michigan plates."

The back of Owen's neck prickled. "Mimi Storey came from Michigan. The kid was born there."

"I know. How's the kid? Can you ask her about this Yount? Maybe I should come down there and question her."

"The kid won't talk. She's scared to. You have anything concrete on these people?"

"Nothing. They've broken no laws. We can question them about Mimi Storey, but it's only hearsay she was with them."

"You still don't know where Louise Brodnik was Sunday and Monday night?"

"We've got no idea."

Owen frowned. "Can you get a warrant to search that farmhouse?"

"Not without probable cause. No judge would grant it. We could if the kid confirmed she was there."

The kid won't confirm anything, Owen thought in frustration. *We wouldn't have a problem if the kid would talk.*

"I'll do what I can," he said.

"Right," said Mulcahy. "If you find out anything else, let me know."

"Done." Owen hung up, swung his legs over the edge of the bed. Where in hell were his clothes? He'd torn them off and flung them out of the way, desperate to have his body naked next to Eden's.

Naked they'd been, he thought with a caustic ruefulness, but only in body. Emotions they'd kept covered as if the obscene parts of humans were the emotions; don't show *that,* keep *that* hidden.

He rose and found his Jockey shorts under Jessie's rocking chair, one sock beneath the window, one in the closet doorway. His jeans were at the foot of the bed, his shirt beside its head. One boot lay in the farthest corner, the other stood next to the bedroom door like a lonely sentinel.

He dressed, moved quietly down the hall, and eased open the door to Eden's room. She lay still and slender under the coverlet, her boyishly cut hair neat even in sleep.

The kid had climbed into bed with her again, a little black-haired bundle half curled, half sprawled next to her, looking anything but tidy.

Peyton sighed noisily and snuggled more deeply into her pillow. He shut the door and left the house, locking the door behind him.

He crossed the yard and unlocked his own house, which seemed to echo with emptiness. It held no homeyness for him and never would.

The beautiful old white farmhouse where he and Laurie had lived was sold. He never visited it, he never drove past it if he could avoid it. He'd sent the furniture off to auction.

Since then he'd moved from one of his family's rental properties to another, rebuilding, restoring. He always brought as little with him as possible, wanting nothing that was burdened by memories. Now he switched on his overhead light and walked into the kitchen.

One of the few things Owen had brought from the old house was the dog's bed. It was an ancient cushion covered in red and green plaid, and it always smelled like the dog, rank and sick.

The dog hadn't heard him come in; it was deaf as a stone. It lay curled up, nose beneath its scraggly plume of a tail.

As soon as he touched it, he knew it was dead. Its small body was cold and immobile with the terrible fixity of death. Its fur seemed to have lost what poor luster it had, its bones to have grown smaller and more fragile.

He had never much liked the dog, it was a fancy, fuzzy, yapping thing, but Laurie had loved it with all her sentimental heart.

Now that it was dead, a peculiar hollowness settled in his chest, tightened his throat. He picked up the little body. It seemed to weigh no more than a toy made of cloth and rags.

Hell, he thought bleakly, he should have saved one of Laurie's sweaters or blouses to wrap the old boy in, but he had none. What did the dog care? he asked himself coldly. The dog could never fucking care about anything again.

Still, he stripped off his own shirt and wrapped it around the still body. It was an irrational act, but Laurie had always insisted the dog was comforted by the scents of its loved ones.

Owen went to the basement and got a pick and shovel. He carried the dog to a spot among the oaks with their yellowing leaves.

He laid the dog among the fallen leaves and began to dig. The ground was hard; the Arkansas earth was more rock and root than dirt. He wanted the hole deep so that no animal would disturb the corpse.

The morning sun was starting to beat down with unseasonable heat. He was sweating by the time the hole was large enough to suit him. He layered dead leaves on the bottom and laid the dog on them. Then he covered it with dirt, and after that a large rock to protect the raw earth.

It would be sentimental and foolish to say words over a worn-out old dog, even to think them, and there was nothing to say, nothing to think.

Eden had awakened before Peyton and carefully crept from the bed. She put on her robe and went barefoot into the kitchen to start the coffee. She wanted a taste that was black and scalding and strong enough to burn away any misgivings she had about last night.

While the coffee brewed, she would take a shower and wash the memory of Owen from her body. A faint, ghostly tingle of excitement still ran over her flesh, and she resented it.

She had used Owen, he had used her. Neither of

them wanted to be involved; they'd gotten involved anyway. And, oh, he'd been sweet and exciting and athletic
in bed; he had been just *fine* in bed, thank you. It was
afterward, he'd turned cool. Let him, she thought. She
knew a thing or two about coolness herself.

But she glanced out the kitchen window and saw
him, bare chested, heading toward the edge of the woods,
carrying a bundle wrapped in blue as well as a pick and a
shovel. When she saw him lay down the bundle, she realized that at last the old dog had died.

A pang of sympathy wrenched through her. She
knew the dog had belonged to his late wife. He didn't
seem fond of the animal, but it must have been a strong
and intimate connection to the memory of the woman
he'd loved. Another link gone.

She saw him strain to push the stone atop the dog's
grave, then pick up his tools and walk back toward Jessie's. His tall body was lean and fit and strong, and the
silver of his hair seemed at odds with it.

She forgot about her shower. She poured two mugs
of coffee, and when she heard him enter the front door,
she stood waiting for him, feeling almost tremulous.

When he came into the kitchen, his face was expressionless, his blue eyes steady. He carried Jessie's morning
paper and handed it to her without remark.

"Hi," she said. "I've got coffee made."

He shrugged. The sweat on his shoulders gleamed,
and she could see the bullet scar across his breastbone.

"I don't need anything," he said. A long smear of
dirt marred his flat stomach, crumbs of dirt and broken
leaf clung to his jeans.

"Please sit down for a minute with me," she said. "I
want to talk to you."

He frowned. "I want to talk to you, too. John Mulcahy called from Sedonia."

An odd little shock of foreboding ran through her. She looked at him expectantly. "The detective? Yes?"

Owen told her what Louise Brodnik's daughter had said about Mimi living at a farmhouse and her suspicions about the people she'd lived with.

"My God, Owen, paramilitary? Or a cult?" Eden clutched her robe more tightly shut, as if chilled by the news.

"You're going to have to try to ask Peyton some more questions."

He turned from her, went to the sink. She watched him as he leaned on the counter, staring out the window toward the dog's grave.

"Before you talk to her," he said, "let me see if I can find out anything more about this Mrs. Stangblood. The more we know, the less the kid'll have to say."

He washed his hands at the sink and dried them. She watched the intricate play of muscles in his back and arms. He turned to face her again.

New, confused emotions roiled within her. "Sit down," she said, in order to say anything. "Your coffee'll get cold."

He sat down opposite from her, and they studied each other almost warily, like two opponents unsure about negotiating.

"Try not to worry," he said at last. "We'll unravel it. I promise you."

She gazed down at the black liquid in her cup but did not drink. "I—I saw you from the window," she said. "The dog died, didn't he?"

"It was for the best. He was worn out."

"I know," she said, with a helpless gesture. "But I'm sorry. It was your wife's dog, wasn't it?"

He nodded, said nothing, took a drink of coffee. He didn't want to talk about it, she knew.

She said, "I'm sorry I asked you about her last night. It's none of my business."

"No," he said. "I was the one out of line. I'm sorry."

She stared at him in surprise.

"You were right," he said. "We both needed somebody. That was all."

She traced the flowered pattern on her coffee mug with her fingertip. *That was all. That was all it meant. Only that, no more.*

"Sometimes these things happen," she said. "People just have to be adult about it."

She hoped to God she sounded adult.

Then Peyton appeared in the kitchen doorway, and Eden knew all adult conversation would have to be postponed until later.

At eight o'clock, Endor time, Owen went into Jessie's bedroom with his cell phone and began to dial the numbers remaining on his list of Stangbloods.

He was shaved, showered, dressed in clean jeans and a T-shirt, but a faint, maddening perfume of sex still hung in the air of the bedroom. He tried to ignore it.

Eden was in the living room now, keeping Peyton occupied by coloring with her in a coloring book. The child was still quiet with sleepiness, but the woman seemed upbeat, cheery, completely confident and at ease. "Seemed" was the operative word, for he knew under her smooth façade she dreaded the coming ordeal for Peyton.

Maybe, he thought, teeth set as he dialed, the fates

would send him a Detroit Stangblood who could answer all the questions, solve all the riddles, put everything to rights.

Instead, the fates gave him Yvonne Wannebacker. She was the tenth and last name on his list.

When he asked to speak to Yvonne Stangblood, she sounded put-upon and waspish. "This is Yvonne Wannebacker, formerly Stangblood. What do you want?"

"Ms. Wannebacker, my name is Owen Charteris. I'm calling from Endor, Arkansas. A six-year-old girl named Peyton Storey was abandoned here, and we need background information so we can locate her mother, Miriam Storey. We believe that recently the child and her mother lived in Detroit and knew a Mrs. Stangblood. Any information would be welcome."

"I'm not a Mrs. Stangblood any longer," the woman said acidly. "Thank God."

Owen gritted his teeth. "I'm sorry. Still, we have this child. Any information you could—"

"I don't know anything about a child," she said brusquely.

"The child mentioned a friend named Mrs. Stangblood. It's one of the few facts we can get out of her."

"I don't know anything about a child," Yvonne Wannebacker repeated. "I do know Stangbloods shouldn't be allowed to reproduce. There ought to be a law against it. They should send 'em all to the planet Mars."

Owen kept his voice calm, reasonable. "There's no reason to think the child's an actual relative. The Mrs. Stangblood might have been a neighbor, a family friend, a baby-sitter or caregiver of some kind."

"The only one that ever baby-sat was my ex-mother-in-law. It wasn't enough for her to screw up her own kids. Oh, no, she had to screw up other people's, too. Jeez, what a piece of work *she* was."

Owen's nerve ends prickled. "What's this woman's name?"

"Filumena, can you believe that? Filumena, with an *f.* As in 'fathead.'"

Owen frowned. Nobody he'd spoken to had mentioned such a woman. "Information didn't give me a listing for a Filumena Stangblood. Would she be unlisted? Or in the book under her husband's name?"

The Wannebacker woman laughed. "Her husband had the good sense to die off years ago. But you won't find Filumena, either, unless you got a hot line to hell. That woman was such a slob it was criminal."

"You mean she's dead?"

"That's what I mean," she answered with obvious satisfaction. "Maybe she looked in the mirror and scared herself to death. Fat? We're talking boxcar here."

Owen tried to nudge her back to the subject. "Ms. Wannebacker, do you remember if your mother-in-law ever baby-sat for a little black-haired girl named Peyton? Likes to draw, a picky eater—"

"She better not be picky if she stayed with Filumena. The woman could do about two things in the kitchen, and one was to boil water. When I was going with Ronald he took me over there for Christmas dinner. You know what she had? Pizza! Can you imagine it? We're sitting there, surrounded by Little Caesar's boxes, eating off TV trays, watching *It's a Wonderful Life.* Christ, I shoulda known then they were all crazy as coots."

Owen's pulses quickened. "This child is very striking. Extremely dark hair and eyes. May have worn large gold earrings—"

"I told you, I don't know. I had as little to do with

the woman as possible. The place was bad enough with just her in it. You think I'd go there with rugrats screaming and running all over? Christ, I saw a cockroach there the size of a rottweiler."

"What about her neighbors? Friends? Other relatives?"

"The person she was thickest with was her daughter. There was a prize pair, let me tell you—you get 'em together, they looked like two cans of lard."

"Could you give me the daughter's name, Ms. Wannebacker? It's important. Is she in Detroit?"

"She's in Detroit, all right," the woman said. "You know how I can tell? Every so often, I feel the ground shaking, so I know she's out there, walking around like Godzilla. Wham. *Wham.*"

Owen gritted his teeth. "Her name?"

"Her name's Theresa Bigby. Theresa Big-Butt is what it should be. I don't know her phone number; I've, like, erased it from my memory. Her husband's name is Warren. Warren the Moron."

Owen scribbled down "Theresa Warren-Bigby, Detroit." He said, "Thank you, Ms. Wannebacker. I think this may be just what we need."

"Is there money at stake here?" she asked suspiciously. "Is there a reward?"

"The only reward is helping a fellow human being," Owen said, almost managing to keep the sarcasm out of his voice. He said good-bye and hung up.

He called Information, got the phone number of Warren Bigby, and dialed it, hoping like hell that Theresa Bigby was at home.

She was.

She had a sweet, shy, hesitant voice that had little trace of education in it. She sounded blandly languid, but as soon as he told her of the abandoned child and began to describe Peyton, she grew excited.

"I remember her!" Theresa Bigby said. "I know her!"

Owen's heart clenched like a fist in his chest. "Yes?"

"Mama *kept* her," Theresa said. "A long time. Months. Maybe even a year. She lived at Mama's."

Bingo! Owen thought with a heady sense of triumph. "Tell me everything you can remember, Mrs. Bigby."

"Well . . ." she said, rather breathlessly. "This woman said somebody told her about Mama, and so she come to Mama and said she's gotta work nights and sleep days, so could Mama take care of Peyton."

"You're talking about Peyton's mother," Owen said carefully. "About Mimi. Miriam Storey."

"That's the name. That's her."

He took a deep breath, like a man preparing for a steep dive. "Mrs. Bigby, do you recall anything unusual about Mimi Storey's voice? Anything at all?"

"Why, yes. She was all hoarse and creaky. She had a scar across her neck. From a car wreck, she said. If it hadn't been for that car wreck, she mighta been a singer, she said. She was, like, bitter about it."

He exhaled between gritted teeth. *Eden, you were right. You knew.*

"Mama loved that child," Theresa Bigby said, a tremor in her voice. "That child needed a lot of love, and Mama gave it to her."

"What do you mean, she needed a lot of love?"

"I mean she was—what's the word?—unsecure. Unsecure is what she was. She wetted the bed a lot, and always she was sucking on her thumb."

That's our girl, thought Owen. He said, "Did she ever talk about the past?"

"She said she wanted to go back somewhere. Maybe

it was Deerborn. Or Flint. She was homesick for the longest time."

"Could it have been Holland?"

"Maybe. Anyway, she'd climb up on Mama's lap to watch television. And Mama would just hold her and sit and watch the cartoons and things with her. Mama had a big, soft lap."

"And Mimi would take the girl on weekends?"

Theresa Bigby paused again. "She did at *first*. And then she didn't do it so much. And then she didn't do it at all. She didn't take her for Thanksgiving or Christmas or nothing. It got so the little girl didn't even ask if she was coming."

"What was the problem? Do you know?"

"Well, Mama was a sweet person, and Mama, she didn't like gossip, but she got the feeling that there was a man mixed up in it, is what. That this man, he didn't like the little girl, and she didn't like him, neither."

"Do you know who he was?"

"He come with Mimi once to pick up Peyton for the weekend. I never saw him. Mama said he looked like that Cuban person. Not Ricky Ricardo, the other one, that Castro. He was dressed in army-colored clothes and he had a scraggy old beard."

"Did Peyton ever talk about him?"

"She *wouldn't* talk about him. Only once. The first time she come back from with them, she said he wouldn't give her nothing to eat. Just chicken and mashed potatoes and stuff she don't like. And he got mean about it."

"Mean? How?"

"Just mean," she said vaguely. "Mama always give Peyton what she liked to eat. She wouldn't make her eat things she didn't like, she was too tenderhearted. Mama was always tenderhearted."

"I'm sure she was," Owen said.

"A lotta times Mimi owed her money. Mama should've called her up and said 'Come get this child,' but she wouldn't do that. Mama loved that child, and she was a very easygoing person besides."

"I see. This man she was involved with—did you ever hear his name?"

"Not that I remember. Anyway, late last spring Mimi—that's her name?—shows up with an altogether different man and said she and Peyton are going off with *him* now. It like to broke Mama's heart. But she was sick by that time anyhow. Her heart, you know."

"I'm sorry to hear it."

"She couldn't get around. She couldn't wash dishes or make the beds or nothing. Peyton was the only child she was keeping because she couldn't bear to give her up. The kitchen bugs was about to run off with the place."

Owen winced in spite of himself. He had a vision of Peyton in the lap of an obese and dying woman, in a place strewn with filth and overrun with cockroaches.

"This new man," he said, "what do you know about him?"

"Well, him I saw with my own two eyes," Theresa said proudly. "I went over to straighten Mama's house. I tried to do it every two weeks or so, but she was clear cross town, and me with three children of my own, it wears me out. I got bad asthma, you know."

"Sorry to hear it. But the man, Mrs. Bigby?"

"He seemed like a very nice man, very polite, and he was very handsome, blond and almost pretty like a girl. And he paid Mama everything she was owed and ten dollars besides. And they took Peyton off with them, and we never saw her again. Mama nearly cried herself to death after that child walked out the door."

"This blond man, did Mimi introduce him? Do you remember a name?"

"No. Except it was a funny first name, different. But I'll tell you something about him," Theresa said.

"Yes?"

"When he smiled, he looked so good, I forgot for a minute I was a married woman. He smiled like an angel or a movie star or somebody, you know? I thought, Why, I'd follow *him* anywhere. And I said to myself 'That Mimi is one lucky woman.' I guess it was too good to be true, eh? Too good to last."

Owen said, "I guess maybe it was."

For the sake of politeness, he chatted with her a few moments longer, lied about how well Peyton was doing, then thanked her and hung up.

He rose and, leaving the phone behind him, walked down the hall. Eden was still on the floor before the television set, coloring with Peyton.

She looked up at him, hope and apprehension mixing in her eyes.

"Come into the office a minute," he said.

She nodded and led the way. She closed the door, then stood, shoulders squared, looking at him warily.

When he told her about Mrs. Stangblood, tears rose in her eyes.

"I'm sorry," he said. "But there's something else. The woman on the phone—with the hoarse voice. You're right. It's your sister.

Eden listened, horror in her eyes, to what Theresa Bigby had said about the accident. "My God, poor

Mimi," she said tightly. "Oh, Owen, what kind of trouble is she in? I'm scared."

He took her in his arms, and she didn't resist. Instead her arms went around his neck as if she actually needed him. He held her.

SIXTEEN

———◦◦◦———

TWICE DURING THE NIGHT, MIMI HAD SEEMED CLOSE TO death. She kept fainting from pain, and when she revived, she couldn't talk and seemed half-delirious. But she hung on.

The skinny little bitch was tough, Drace thought. She might be dying, but she was dying hard.

At nine o'clock, Drace had left the van parked near Endor's small city library. Raylene stayed, watching over Mimi's suffering with a cold air of satisfaction.

Drace went into the library in search of a pay phone and found one in the lobby. Calls from the cell phone could be intercepted, and didn't want to use it unless absolutely necessary. Inserting one of his anonymous phone credit cards, he dialed the number of Sister Jessie Buddress's psychic phone line.

On the third ring, she answered. "Sister Jessie," said a woman's deep and resonant voice. "God's gifted seer. What can I do for you this morning?"

Drace hung up. All he'd wanted to do was establish she was there. He smiled tightly to himself and headed out the library doors, past all the colorful children's drawings pinned to the bulletin boards and the poster of the Cat in the Hat.

He made his way to the main street of Endor, cloaking himself with invisibility. He had once read of a great and famous actor who could appear, undisguised, on the street and no one would recognize him. The actor made himself seem so ordinary, so inconspicous, that no one noticed him; in essence, he became invisible. Drace willed himself to do the same.

He had looked earlier in the local phone book for Jessie Buddress's name and home phone number and address, but she was unlisted. Still, he knew with godlike certainty that he would find her, and he knew how.

Just off Main Street, on Pecan Street, was a row of shops. He and Raylene had seen them early this morning. The buildings were small and narrow, made of weathered redbrick. Each store had an identical old-fashioned green awning.

In the midst of these shops was one with a publike sign over the door. A yellow crescent moon with a human profile smiled fatuously over letters that spelled out MOONGLOW GIFTS. They had seen a lone woman unlocking the front door.

Now he opened that same door, which set off the mellow ringing of chimes. The air was thick with the churchlike scent of incense.

The shop was cluttered with every sort of New Age trapping and trinket—candles, scented oils, crystals, bells, beads, charms, packets of strange powders. A tape of eerie, tuneless music played.

Besides Drace, the only other person in the shop was the woman, who was thirtyish, plain, and had long dull-blond hair.

She wore a long, shapeless dress with an Indian print, beat-up Birkenstock sandals, and a lot of cheap bracelets and necklaces. She looked half-stoned and had a delicate silver ring piercing her nose.

"Can I help you?" the woman asked.

Drace stopped being invisible and unleashed his charm. He gave her his most beguiling smile, boyish and shy. "Actually you might," he said. "I'm looking for someone."

"Aren't we all?" said the woman.

Drace's smile widened into a grin that was both bashful and seductive. "I've talked to this woman a bunch of times," he said. "She's a psychic. I thought maybe somebody in here might know her. Sister Jessie Buddress?"

"Hey—synchronicity!" exclaimed the woman. "Sister Jessie? Yeah. I know her well."

"Really?" he said with pleasure. He was looking deep into her eyes and would continue to do so.

"Really," said the clerk. "I've known her for years. She's a very spiritual woman. I took this job on her advice. She says my aura's really purified since I been here."

"She's amazing," Drace said in his soft voice.

"Yeah, she is. You're one of her phone clients?"

Drace nodded. "I'm from Oklahoma City. I had to drive over this way on business."

He reached into his shirt pocket and drew out a business card. He collected such cards, for at times like this they were valuable. It read "L. Robert 'Bob' Dinsmore" and identified him as the owner of Dinsmore's Rare Books and Documents, Oklahoma City, Oklahoma.

He handed her the card. She read it and looked impressed. "Rare books," she said. "Gee. I *love* books."

"I do, too," Drace said, turning more solemn. "But I was ready to give up on it. I just wasn't making a living."

She cocked her head sympathetically.

He said, "I'd been calling Sister Jessie, and she said to be patient, that things would turn around in September. But by the first of October, nothing had happened."

The woman made a sound like *tsk-tsk*.

"So now," Drace said earnestly, "comes the *strange* part. I called her on the second of October for another reading. I said the first one hadn't come true, and I was desperate."

The woman nodded, obviously enthralled.

Drace dropped his voice in awe. "But she said, 'It's come true. You just don't know it yet.' "

The woman's eyes widened.

"The week before I'd bought some books at an estate auction. There were a couple of boxes, and nobody was bidding, so I'd bought them blind, without even looking at them. I put them in my trunk and forgot about them."

"Oh, my God," the woman said, shaking her head. "I *know* what you're going to say."

Drace grinned again and nodded. "There were some newer novels on top, Book-of-the-Month stuff. But underneath, I found *five* novels by Ernest Hemingway. All first editions. All autographed. And a sort of album. In it were eleven *letters* from Hemingway."

"Oh, my Ga-awd," she said, putting a hand to her cheek.

"It was like striking gold. I sold the whole collection for over twenty thousand dollars—can you believe it?"

"That's incredible, it gives me *chills*," the woman said in awe. "I have goose bumps, I really do."

"I was going to phone her, but I was driving this way, and I decided to thank her in person. And bring her a present. I've got a beautiful leather-bound copy of the prophecies of Nostradamus I want to give her."

"Look at me," the woman said, pointing to her eyes. "Tears. I got tears. This is all too beautiful."

Drace smiled as if he were deeply touched. "The problem is, I don't know where she lives. I got her business number but not her home one. She's not in the phone book."

"Oh, I know where she lives," the woman said. "Out Churchyard Road. You go west, toward Huntsville, then take County Road Seventy-six. It's the next-to-last house before the parkland starts. You can't miss it. Little white house. I'll draw you a map."

"That'd be *great*," Drace said, beaming.

He watched as she drew on pale blue paper decorated with silver stars. "Do me a favor and don't mention this to anyone for a couple of days, will you?" he said. "I want to make sure I surprise her. If I don't catch her at home today, I'll try again tomorrow on my way back."

The woman stopped drawing her map. An odd expression, like doubt or guilt, crossed her face.

"I mean, I just want to surprise her," Drace said, watching her carefully. "So if I don't get there until tomorrow . . ."

"I understand," she said, still looking somehow crestfallen. "But I forgot. She's not home, she's in the hospital."

The euphoric mood that Drace had enjoyed so deeply and sweetly, collapsed. "What?" he demanded.

"She's been in the hospital all week. She fell down her front steps and broke her leg."

"What?" Drace repeated, numb with disbelief. "She hasn't been home? Since when?"

The woman paused, as if counting. "Since Monday," she said. "Yeah. Monday."

It's impossible, Drace thought, stunned to his marrow. *She's there. I just talked to her.* And Mimi, who had disappeared early Monday morning, had talked to her three times at that number.

"She hasn't been there? Since Monday?" he asked, as if the woman had made some incredibly stupid mistake.

She shook her head. "Her granddaughter's staying out there now. There's a little girl that has to be took care of, or something. They're looking for the kid's mother." She gave a dismissive wave of her hand. "It's complicated. My sister knows more about it than I do. She works at the hospital."

Drace could only stare at her, dumbfounded. *Peyton's there. But they're trying to find her mother—shit.*

The woman smiled kindly. "Don't take it so hard. Jessie's not going to die or anything. She's a tough old girl. You can probably go see her at the hospital. I think she can have visitors."

"I—I don't like hospitals," Drace said shortly.

She gave him a peculiar look. "Oh. Well, maybe you could just leave the book at her house. With the granddaughter. She's an actress. From L.A. She was a year behind me in school. My brush with fame."

An actress, Drace thought. *A fucking actress. They're trying to find the kid's mother, and I talked to a fucking actress.*

"Yes," he said stiffly. "I could do that. The map—you were showing me how to get there."

She took up her pencil again. She drew two *x*'s on the paper, a large one and a small one.

"Okay, over here's the park, right next to her. There's two houses, kind of all to themselves. One's big, looks torn up, it's being worked on. The other's little and white. That's Jessie's.

Drace pointed to it. "She's clear out there all by herself?"

"No, no," the woman said with a smile, drawing a circle around the larger *x*. "Owen Charteris lives there, and it's a good thing. He called the ambulance when she fell. He's like her guardian angel."

"Guardian angel?" Drace echoed.

"Listen," the woman said. "You think your story about Jessie is strange? You should hear *his*. I mean, it's like very spooky. You got a minute or two?"

"Sure," Drace said, willing his stampeding heartbeat to slow down. "Sure. I've got a minute."

She looked into his face, her eyes shining. "He was with the police, a detective, see . . ."

Detective. Drace's heart knocked as if it were he, not Mimi, who had been mortally poisoned.

After crying in Owen's arms, Eden had dried her eyes and drawn away from him. She needed to plug in the office phone in case Mimi tried to call again.

But it was almost ten o'clock now, and there had been only two calls. One caller was a lovelorn Oklahoma construction worker, and the other had hung up without speaking.

Owen told her to take a break, that he'd poured her a cup of coffee. Now she and he stood by the kitchen counter, and the silence between them seemed both uneasy and tender.

From the living room she could hear the sound of the television, a bouncy jingle being played on a cartoon show.

"I shouldn't put it off any longer," she said. "I should talk to Peyton."

He nodded. "It'd be easier if I wasn't here. I'll go see Jessie."

She put her hand on his upper arm, a gesture not only of gratitude, but of an affection that half frightened her.

He put his hand over hers and looked into her eyes. "I'll be back as soon as I can."

Her heart lurched crazily. *Why do I feel this way? This shouldn't be happening,* she told herself. She managed a shaky smile.

Suddenly he bent and kissed her lips. "Good-bye," he whispered. "Take care."

Then he was gone, out the back door. She moved to the window and saw him crossing the yard toward his car, a tall, lean figure.

Her chest tightened with unexpected longing. Her lips tingled, and with a dizzying rush, she remembered last night, her naked body against his own. She knew it would be that way again tonight, that she wanted it, and so did he.

She turned from the window and ran her hand nervously through her thick bangs. She shouldn't be thinking of Owen, she scolded herself. She had to question Peyton and, for once, get some answers from the child.

She marched purposefully into the office and unhooked the tape recorder. She checked to see if it could record like an ordinary machine. It could.

Carrying it, she went into the kitchen and took a tea towel from the rack. Then, shoulders squared, she made her way back to the living room. Peyton lay on her stomach before the television set, drawing another burning airplane. It was shaped like a crude cross and surrounded by bright orange flames in a blue sky.

Eden sucked in her breath. *Oh, Mimi,* she thought, *don't let it be as bad as I'm afraid it is.* But she kept her face a cheerful blank.

The television droned inanely about the softness of clothes washed in Lambkins Liquid Cold Water Wash. Eden turned on the tape recorder, and placed it atop the television.

Then she sat down cross-legged beside Peyton and switched the set off.

Peyton stared at her in hurt surprise. "Hey," she said accusingly.

"I need to talk to Fearless Fran," she said as brightly as she could. She draped the tea towel around Peyton's shoulders. "Hi, Fearless," she said in her friendliest, most guileless voice.

Peyton pulled the tea towel off and stared at it unhappily. "Fearless doesn't want to talk," she said.

"Where's Henry today?" Eden asked. "I'd love to hear about him. He's Peyton's special friend, isn't he?"

Peyton's face grew moodier. But she sat up, crosslegged, like Eden and put the tea towel back on her shoulders and tucked its corners into her collar.

"Fearless!" said Eden in the same enthusiastic voice. "I'm so glad you're here. Tell me. Why's Henry's hair blue?"

"Because it is, that's all," Peyton said brusquely in the Fearless Fran voice. She set her chin at a defiant tilt.

"Does Henry always go where Peyton goes?" Eden asked, trying to start the conversation on neutral ground.

"Always," Peyton said firmly.

"Where does he sleep at night?"

"Under her bed."

"So he can take care of her?"

"Yes."

"Did he always live with Peyton?"

The child slowly shook her head.

"When did he come to stay with her?" Eden asked.

"I don't know. He just came one day."

"Where was Peyton when he came?"

"In the dark place."

Eden tilted her head curiously. "What dark place? It's okay for *you* to tell, Fearless."

Peyton's dark little brows drew together in a frown. "The closet," she said from between her teeth.

Eden blinked in surprise, and a sinister ripple snaked up her spine. "Why was Peyton in the closet?"

"She was bad again. I don't like this game. I'm going away." She snatched the towel away again and flung it aside. Her face crumpled and she looked as if she were going to cry.

Eden stared at her in concern. She leaned over and took Peyton by the arms. "Get up," she said. "Let's go to Granny's chair, and you sit in my lap."

Owen had said Peyton had enjoyed sitting in Filumena Stangblood's lap and watching television. She rose and drew the child to her feet. She turned the television back on, but kept the sound so low it was nearly inaudible.

She led Peyton to the chair, picked her up, hugged her tightly, and sat down, holding the child close. Peyton nestled against her, sucking her thumb.

"Peyton," Eden said, rocking the chair gently, "I didn't mean to upset you. I'm sorry."

Peyton said nothing. She held the sleeve of Eden's blouse, gripping it so tightly her knuckles were pale. It was as if she feared Eden would vanish if she let her go.

Eden laid her cheek against the child's hair. "I told you the truth, though. We have to talk. You don't have to be afraid."

She felt the little body stiffen with tension. "You don't have to hide anything. I—I'm going to take care of you. And I won't let anybody hurt you."

"What if somebody hurts *you*?" Peyton demanded. Her voice was muffled because her face was pressed against Eden's breast.

The question startled Eden, but didn't frighten her. "Nobody's going to hurt me or you," she assured the child, rubbing her back. "Mr.—Mr. Charteris is helping take care of us. He's—protecting us."

"I don't like him," Peyton said, her voice trembling.

"Why? Why don't you like him? He's a good man."

"You'll go away with him. You'll leave me."

"I *won't* go away with him. And if I have to go away, and your mother's not back, I'll take you with me. That's a promise. How's that?"

Dear God, why'd I say that? Eden wondered in despair. But she found herself holding the child even more tightly, and kept rocking at a steady, comforting rhythm.

She took a deep breath. "Now listen," she said. "We know some things about you now. You didn't tell them, we found out, so it's okay. I know you came here from Sedonia, Missouri, with Mrs. Brodnik. Mrs. Brodnik was her name, wasn't it?"

Peyton drew back and stared at her almost fiercely. Tears swam in her dark eyes.

Eden put her hands on the girl's shoulders, clasped them firmly. "It doesn't matter if you tell, Peyton, because we already *know*. We know, love."

Peyton blinked the tears back, but her face was taut, full of accusation.

"You and your mother went away from Mrs. Stangblood with a blond man. We know that now."

Peyton gasped. "I didn't tell you that!" she cried.

"Sweetheart, I know you didn't. But we found out. Now we need you to tell us the rest. So we can take care of you. And find your mother."

"I want to go back to Detroit," Peyton said, her eyes welling with fresh tears and her chin trembling.

"Sweety, I know—"

"I miss Mrs. Stangblood," Peyton wailed, bursting into tears. "I want her."

Oh, God, what have I done? Eden thought. How could she explain that Mrs. Stangblood was dead when this child wept so wildly for her?

She pulled Peyton close to her. "Don't cry, don't cry," she begged. "Just tell me, when you went to Missouri, did you and your mother live on a farm?"

"Yes," Peyton cried.

"Were there people there besides you and your mother? Men, like you drew in your pictures?"

"Yes." The girl shuddered convulsively against her.

"Was a lady besides your mother there? With yellow hair?"

"Yes."

"Peyton, did these people have guns? Did they ever talk about blowing things up? Like that plane in Florida?"

"Yes! Yes! Yes!" Peyton screamed. Then she jerked

away from Eden's embrace and put her hands over her ears. "Stop it! Stop it!"

"Oh, Peyton," Eden said, struck to the heart.

But it was too late. The child was going into hysterics, and Eden had driven her there. The tape machine, its red light on, whirled on, setting it down like a relentless recording angel.

Eden sat alone at Jessie's desk, her head in her hands. Peyton had finally wept herself into a state of exhaustion and was asleep on her bed. Eden could not forgive herself for inflicting such distress on the child.

The phone rang. She raised her head and shot it a miserable glare. It rang again, as if to spite her.

She had plugged it in and reattached it to the tape recorder, done it numbly, mechanically, simply to do something. Now it rang a third time.

"Show time," she muttered bitterly and cocked her head at a determined angle. She picked up the receiver, praying she didn't sound as if she had been crying. "Sister Jessie," she recited, "God's gifted seer."

"Hello," said a man's soft voice. "I got a question, and I want psychic advice. What do I do? I've never done this before."

His voice was young, almost boyish, a pleasant and friendly voice with a midwestern accent.

"Give me your birthdate," she said. "I got to have it, it's the law. So I know you're of age."

"November thirteenth, 1969," he said.

"A Scorpio," she said. "You want me to do your horoscope? Read the tarot cards for you?"

"How do I know you're qualified to do all that?" he asked. "I mean, how much experience you got at it?"

She drew herself up and tried to answer as Jessie would. "I been doing this for fifty-five years. Is that enough experience for you?"

"Fifty-five years?" he said. "How old *are* you? You don't sound all that old."

"I am seventy-one years young," Eden intoned, "and I have been reading the stars and the cards since my sixteenth year and seeing visions all my life."

"Wow," he said, sounding impressed. "You've seen a lot of history. You ever predict any great historical event?"

He's a chatty one, thought Eden, but tried to shrug it off. It was his money, she told herself, and he could waste it if he wanted.

"I predicted the death of Franklin Delano Roosevelt," Eden lied. "I predicted the Korean War and the suicide of Marilyn Monroe and lots of other things."

"Wow," he said again. "So I guess you got a lot of experience with life, then."

"Indeed I have," Eden said, again puzzled by his aimless chatter. "So what can Sister Jessie do for you today?"

"Oh," he said. "Well, it's like hunting season just opened, and I wondered if I was going to be lucky. What do you think?"

The question made her oddly uneasy. She found herself staring into Jessie's crystal ball, which sat beside the phone. In it, she saw a shadowy reflection of herself, upside down, a woman suspended in a topsy-turvy world.

"You're asking just a yes or no question?"

"Yeah," he said, almost lazily. "Hunting. Will I be lucky?"

"For yes or no questions, I consult the crystal pendant," she said. She opened Jessie's drawer to find the pendant, a cone of polished quartz fastened to a silver chain.

"Just a second," she said. "I can't find the dad-gum thing."

"Never mind," he said. "Somebody wants me. I got to get off the phone. I'll call back."

He hung up. How odd, thought Eden, he had used up a good three minutes of phone time, at least twelve dollars' worth, then hadn't even waited for an answer.

She glanced at the caller ID machine. Its readout window had gone blank again, so she pressed the review button, expecting the usual information, "Number Unavailable."

But this time a number appeared, with the local area code and an Endor exchange. Beneath it were the words "Pay Phone."

She frowned in surprise. Why would someone call her from a local pay phone? She hadn't heard coins drop—had he used a phone credit card? Why? A frisson of mistrust quivered through her.

She pushed the review button on the caller ID. Her first call of the day had also been from a local pay phone, although a different one. That caller had hung up as soon as she'd answered. What did it mean? Or did it mean nothing?

But almost immediately the phone rang again. "Sister Jessie, God's gifted seer," Eden said, bone-weary of her deceptions.

It was the demanding Mrs. Eberhart, making her daily call from Miami. Eden sighed and reached for the cards, her other caller forgotten.

•   •   •

Drace stood at the pay phone outside a convenience store, his heart hammering. He opened the phone book, dialed the hospital, and asked to talk to Mrs. Buddress.

The connection was made, a phone rang and was answered by a low, sonorous voice identical to the one he'd just spoken to.

His breathing grew shallow, but he forced warmth and a smile into his voice and kept it steady. "Mrs. Buddress," he said with neighborly cheer, "this is Bill Phillips of the First Baptist Church. I'm on the Sunshine Committee. We were sorry to hear about your accident."

"I'm not a Baptist," said the woman.

"Why, you don't have to be," Drace said. "The Sunshine Committee doesn't care what your particular faith is. We're just people reaching out to people. We want you to know we're here if you need us."

"I never heard of no Sunshine Committee," she said suspiciously.

"It's relatively new and completely nondenominational," lied Drace. "It's times like now when we want to help any way we can. And I believe I heard you have a little girl to take care of, a granddaughter."

"A great-granddaughter," she corrected.

"Peyton?" he asked brightly. "Isn't that her name?"

"Hmmph. How come you know so much?"

"Several people in our congregation work at the hospital, Mrs. Buddress. Do you have family nearby to care for the child? To visit you, help you out?"

"My granddaughter is here from Los Angeles," Jessie said rather loftily.

"Just one person?" Drace asked with sympathy.

"And my neighbor," she retorted. "Company just walked in my door. I can't talk. Good-bye."

She hung up, and Drace stood listening to the silence

of a line gone dead. He swore under his breath and slammed the receiver back into place.

He stood by the pay phone, feeling as if his head were full of fire. He wanted to press his forehead against the phone's cool steel, but knew such an act would call attention to him. The pulses in his temples banged like drums.

Why in God's name is the granddaughter impersonating the old woman?

Be calm, be calm. The bitch at the store said, "The granddaughter's staying out there now . . . they're trying to find the kid's mother."

But why is an ex-cop mixed up in it?

Be calm, be calm. Because the real cops don't care, they know nothing. Be calm, be calm.

How much has Peyton told them? How much has Mimi?

Be calm, be calm. They can't know much. Or you wouldn't be walking around free, would you?

Yet, like an animal, he sensed a trap, a dangerous one, being set. Like a soldier, a strategist, he knew he must not merely avoid it, but destroy it.

Destroy it. It was that simple. It was a military problem, that was all, a tactician's job.

He straightened up from the phone. From his shirt pocket he drew out the map the woman at the New Age shop had drawn him. He wiped the sweat from his upper lip.

It was time to reconnoiter the enemy.

SEVENTEEN

━━━◦◦◦◦━━━

By the time Owen returned to the house, Eden's heart seemed wizened into something small, self-loathing, and frightened. Filled with self-recrimination, she recounted what Peyton had said.

"I feel awful," she told him. "If Mimi's really mixed up in something this bad, what will happen to her? What will it do to Peyton? And Jessie? My God."

"Let me hear the tape," he said.

In the office, while he listened, Eden moved to the window and stared out, her face taut and bloodless. The tape went silent at last. He switched it off. A silence that seemed impossibly heavy filled the room.

Eden turned to him. "Owen, if Mimi has something to do with that explosion in Miami, we have to tell the police. I don't want to, but we have to."

"They won't believe it," he told her. "Don't borrow trouble. Not yet."

She put her fingertips to her forehead in frustration. "I hardly believe it myself. But Peyton said these people—"

"Peyton said nothing," he said sternly. "Nothing but 'yes' when you asked questions. She's six years old and she was getting hysterical. What she said *proves* nothing."

Eden didn't understand the legal distinctions; she could see only the moral dilemma. "But Peyton said— Peyton drew—"

He cut her off, making an impatient slicing gesture with his hand. "It won't hold up. Any attorney worth his salt would say your questions were leading."

"Leading to what?" she demanded.

"Leading her to answer the way she did. She didn't volunteer the information. You put it in her mouth. Do you think the police will take that seriously? No."

"But there's Mimi, too," she said almost desperately. "If it *is* Mimi. We have tapes of her. She talked about the plane, too."

He gripped her shoulders more tightly. "What she said is ambiguous. It'd never hold up in court. So what are you left with? No credible evidence. The bombing is an FBI case. And you've got nothing they could use."

"Then what should we do?" she asked.

"I'm not sure I'm the guy you should ask," he said. "I'm just a washed-up, small-town ex-cop. I'm nobody."

"You're not nobody," she protested with passion. "You're an honorable man, an intelligent man—"

I could love you, she almost said and was appalled and fascinated by the thought. *My God, isn't that the cream of the jest? I think I could love you.*

He searched her face. "If you want, I'll tell Mulcahy. Maybe he can use it. Maybe not. Will that satisfy you?"

He kissed her. She kissed him back.

But then they heard Peyton stirring in the bedroom and broke apart. They looked at each other with wariness, guilt, and amazement.

Owen gathered up the phone-psychic tapes of Constance to rerecord them on a single cassette. He worked alone in Jessie's bedroom.

He frowned as he listened. The desperation in the woman's hoarse, breathy voice troubled him. Was this frightened woman with her slurred words actually connected to the terrorism in Miami? Or was she bound to its violence only by a sick fantasy?

He listened to Eden, impersonating Jessie, telling about the blond woman with fire in her hand and "a flag burning inside her."

"*Oh, my God—oh, my God,*" the woman had said in her broken voice.

"*Miami,*" she had said. "*You know about Miami?*"

Owen cracked his knuckles in frustration. This woman sounded frightened, she sounded guilty, but what she said was proof of nothing.

He spread Peyton's drawings across Jessie's bed and studied the primitive figures, the jarring colors. There was the crude house with the red door standing in the middle of nowhere, radiating anger. There were the planes shaped like burning crosses.

Hell, he thought, shaking his head in disgust, nobody would believe this as evidence. They'd think he'd lost his mind. He had a few taped conversations with a hoarse, breathy, irrational woman, a couple of creepy drawings, and a few ominous words uttered by a six-year-old.

Only a damned fool would carry such a flimsy story to the FBI or the police. He shrugged and thought, *All right. I'll play the fool.* He reached for the cell phone and hoped he wasn't waking up the insomniac John Mulcahy.

With luck Mulcahy would not think Owen completely mad.

As Owen dialed, he glanced out Jessie's bedroom window and could see Eden and Peyton collecting colored leaves. He'd told her, just to be on the safe side, not to leave the yard without him.

Peyton seemed to have forgiven Eden, even if Eden hadn't forgiven herself. The child crouched on the ground beneath the yard's one sugar maple, sorting through the red leaves, looking for the prettiest.

Eden knelt beside her, smiling and holding a cardboard box. The afternoon sun glinted on their hair, Peyton's ebony dark, Eden's brown and highlighted with gold.

As he listened to Mulcahy's phone ring, he kept his eyes on the two figures like a watchman. It did him good to have them in view, to see their faces gilded by the fragile sunlight.

The park was serene with autumn, and the van was alone, parked near the play area with its slides and swings and brightly colored plastic animals.

Drace, his face tense, was dressing in his camouflage. Raylene watched him, frightened and dismayed by the news he'd brought.

Mimi lay on one of the bunks, her chest rattling as she fought for air. They'd had to take the gag off so that she could breathe. Her mouth was blackened by sores and crusted with blisters. Her eyes were rolled up so that the whites showed.

She'd been unable, of course, to tell them anything about the old woman being in the hospital or her sister being at the house. She'd reacted only to Peyton's name, which had torn a raw, incoherent groan from her.

Raylene had no pity for her, only abhorrence. She didn't even look at Mimi, but kept her eyes fastened on Drace, whom Mimi had so endangered. "Oh, be careful," she said to him, breathing the words like a prayer.

A black watch cap hid his silky blond hair. He expertly daubed camouflage paint on his face. "I'll stick to the woods, stay out of sight," he said. "I've got to check the layout of the place, that's all."

"If somebody sees you?"

"I'll take the twenty-two, say I'm hunting."

Her heart beat so hard that it rattled her ribs. "And then? After you've checked it?"

"Then I'll decide the best way to take them."

He's smart, he's brilliant, he can do it, she told herself. But the idea that Peyton was with a lawman of any kind, even a former lawman, terrified her.

"You have a plan?" she asked.

"A tentative one," he said. "Get me the twenty-two, will you?"

She knelt obediently, lifted the strip of carpeting that hid the panel of plywood.

He lit a cigarette, inhaled deeply. "I'd like to ambush them. They'll go out sooner or later to see the old lady. When they come back, we surprise them."

She nodded numbly as she shifted aside the wooden panel. "What about her? The old lady?"

"We'll cross that bridge when we come to it. Old

ladies aren't hard to kill. They practically kill themselves. Remember Brodnik?"

On the cot, Mimi twisted and groaned.

Drace glanced at her, exhaling smoke. "Oh, shut the fuck up," he said, almost absently.

Raylene picked up the twenty-two with both hands and lifted it toward him like an offering. "Be careful," she said, pleading in her voice.

He clasped the rifle, but for a moment he didn't take it, he merely held it, his hands touching hers. He looked into her eyes, and her pulses leaped with love and fear for him.

He smiled mischievously. "I'd kiss you for luck, but I'd get makeup on you."

"That's usually my line," she said and gave him a shaky smile.

"Ray," he said with affection. He took the rifle in one hand, touched her face with the other.

From the cot, Mimi whimpered, but Raylene and Drace kept staring into each other's eyes and paid her no heed.

Owen could not reach Mulcahy, so he called Swinnerton again at GuardLok Security Systems. "Alvin," he said, "this is Owen Charteris again. What's it take to get you out to Jessie Buddress's house? A frigging court order?"

Swinnerton's voice was full of apology. "Owen, we're shorthanded this week *and* busy as the devil. I feel awful we ain't got to you yet."

"I'm worried about this woman and kid out here. You said you'd be here Wednesday. You weren't. You said you'd be here yesterday. You weren't. If you can't make it today, forget it. I'm calling AlarmTronic."

"Now, now, Owen, don't do that. I'll have somebody there if I have to come do it myself."

"Alvin, I want it in place by *tonight*."

"I'll come do it myself, even if it's overtime. I swear it. You have my solemn word."

Owen could no longer see Eden and Peyton through the window. For no reason, he was getting an eerie, anxious feeling, as if tiny ants ran beneath his skin.

"Words are cheap, Alvin," he said and hung up.

He stood to go check on Eden's whereabouts, but then he heard the back door open and close and the sound of her voice in the kitchen. He heard Peyton say something about Henry.

He sighed, sat down again, and picked up the phone. His gaze lingered on the bed where he and Eden had made love last night. Pacing the room, he dialed Mulcahy's number again.

Mulcahy answered this time, on the second ring. "I was just going to call you," he said in his dour voice.

Owen stopped pacing. "Why? You got something new?"

"Not much," Mulcahy said. "We sent a pair of men out to the Wheaton place this morning. They couldn't raise anybody. Place seemed deserted."

"That's all?"

"They went back later. There was a truck parked in the drive this time. They saw a man at the window, but nobody answered the door. After about ten minutes, a rottweiler came out of somewhere. It was in a bad mood. They left. Tried again an hour later. Same thing."

"Did they run the truck's plate through DMV?"

"Yeah. Registered to a William Stanek. He doesn't seem to want to talk to us."

"Did they try the phone?"

"All they got was an answering machine. Which is weird. The place is a mess, a wreck. Not the kind of place you'd expect to have fancy phone options."

"Standard message?" Owen asked, frowning.

"Standard. 'You have reached such-and-such a number. Nobody's here now. Leave your message.' That's it."

"Shit," Owen muttered.

"Whoever's in there's not going to talk to us, and we can't make him talk without a subpoena. We can't get a subpoena without probable cause. Has the kid said anything?"

Owen rose from the bed and started pacing. He told Mulcahy of the conversation with Theresa Bigby about Mrs. Stangblood, told him of how Peyton had become hysterical when Eden asked her about the farm, the plane, the guns.

He drew a deep breath. He could feel the imaginary ants swarming under his skin again.

"We think Mimi's been calling here," Owen said. He told about Mimi's ruined voice, the calls from the woman claiming to be Constance and what she'd said about the plane and Miami. "We've got them on tape," he finished. "For what it's worth."

Mulcahy was silent for a long moment. Then he said, "It's interesting. But as far as the law's concerned, it's not worth crap."

"I know," Owen said grimly.

"But I want to hear the tapes."

"I'll send them."

"Keep the phone near," Mulcahy said. "I'll stay in touch."

• • •

When Drace came back to the van after his preliminary scouting of Jessie's house, he was in high spirits.

"It's a piece of cake," he told Raylene. "I'll keep watch over there until they go out. Then I'll get inside and call you from there. We'll take them when they get back."

"Inside?" Raylene asked, fear in her eyes. She touched his sleeve.

Mimi lay silent and motionless on the cot. Either she had fallen asleep or passed out again.

Drace put his hand over Raylene's. "It's the best way. We've got to get them to talk. To find out how much they know. And if they've told anyone else."

"Can you get in?" Raylene's face was full of care and concern. "What if there's an alarm system or something?"

"There's not," he said. He patted his binocular case. "I scoped it out."

"What if they don't come out?" she asked.

"We'll wait until they're in bed and go in after them," he said. "It's not a problem. The place is a crackerbox. Just like Brodnik's."

Raylene didn't look reassured.

"And guess what?" he asked in a teasing tone.

"What?" she asked, her lovely face paling.

"I saw Peyton. Outside. With a woman. It must be the sister."

They both looked at Mimi's motionless body. Drace knew what Raylene was thinking. She wished he'd killed Peyton and the sister when he'd seen them and that they could kill Mimi now.

"I couldn't get a clear shot at the third one, the man," he soothed her. "I only saw him once, on the porch. Besides, we need to find out what they know.

Having our little hostage here will help. They'll be more talkative."

Raylene looked almost petulant. "I wish it was over."

He ran his forefinger along her satiny lower lip. "It won't be long now, puss," he promised.

Then he kissed her and bid her good-bye. For just a little while.

Early that evening, as Eden got Peyton ready to visit Jessie, a white GuardLok truck pulled into the yard.

Alvin Swinnerton swaggered in, lugging his toolbox and hearty with his own virtue. "See?" he said. "I came myself, even though it's overtime."

He assured them they could go to the hospital and he would have everything in place by the time they got back.

"I'll put the control panels right beside the doors," he said, laying his hand on the wall next to the light switch at the entrance. "You know how it works, Owen. Just give me a code number to program. Four digits. And when you come in, hit it."

"Pick a number," Owen told Eden. A number came into her mind. She forced herself to sound brisk and businesslike. "How about one-two-one-four?"

Swinnerton nodded and repeated it. He had no way of knowing that she had picked it because it was Mimi's birthday—the fourteenth of December.

"When you get home, it'll be set," Alvin Swinnerton said. "Ready to go. Ain't gonna be nobody get in that you don't want in. When this thing goes off, it immediately signals us and we send the police department out, they come in a flash. You're safe as can be."

"Wonderful," Eden said brightly. She darted Owen a look that said, *See? Now there's nothing to worry about.*

He looked unconvinced, slightly stormy. For no particular reason he had been uneasy all afternoon.

"Come on," she said to Peyton. "Let's go see Granny." She reached out, took the child's small, warm hand in hers, and led her from the house.

The blood thundered in Drace's ears. In disbelief he'd watched the truck pull up to the house and park. He could clearly see the sign on the side, GUARDLOK SECURITY. In dismay he'd seen the overweight, uniformed man clamber from the truck carrying his tools.

Drace had wanted to be able to get inside the house with no complications, and now the fat bastard was going to install a security system before Drace's very eyes—it was the stuff of nightmares, a terrible cosmic joke.

What could he do? Could he walk up to the house while daylight still lit the sky and try to take everyone prisoner now, by himself? Or just throw open the door and start shooting, hoping to take them down one by one?

Christ, Drace thought in despair, he had to do *something*—he couldn't just hide in the shadows and watch while the fat man secured the house against attack.

And then the gods smiled on him. A tall gray-haired man, the woman, and kid got into the car. He thought of trying to take them down by sniper fire, but he didn't have a clear shot and he only had the twenty-two, and the fat bastard was still in the house, free to call for help.

He gritted his teeth. He would have to improvise, follow his gut instincts. He waited until the car drove off and was out of sight. Then he walked around the house, a wide semicircle. He descended a small ravine and followed it until he could emerge at the edge of the woods by the curve of the drive.

He strolled down the driveway easily, his rifle casually over his shoulder, like a young hunter stopping at a house to ask permission to shoot on the property.

He mounted the steps of the front porch quietly. The lights were on inside, and he could not see the man, but he could hear a radio loudly playing country music.

Drace looked about. The main road was not visible from here, not even a glimpse of it. From the trees came the chatter of starlings noisily roosting for the night. He opened the screen door, raised his rifle, and entered the house.

A portable radio sat on the living-room floor, playing a staticky version of Garth Brooks's warbling "The Dance." From down the hall came the sound of an electric drill. Light from a room, a bedroom perhaps, spilled out into the hall. He walked toward it.

He stopped at the edge of the door, stole a glance inside. The fat man was engrossed in mounting a control box unit in a closet. His back was to Drace. He wore a khaki uniform that stretched tightly over his wide, womanish hips.

He sang along with the radio in a slightly out-of-tune tenor voice. Drace silently raised the barrel and sighted along it, aiming at the wrinkle in the man's thick neck near the base of his skull.

He squeezed the trigger. The rifle crashed and kicked. The man gave a gargled gasp and his blood spattered and gushed onto the clothes in the closet in bright red streamers.

The control unit fell to the floor with a clang, and the man staggered backward, grasping convulsively at a woman's white dress on a hanger. Then he fell, settling into the perfect stillness of death, the dress still in his hand, blotched now with crimson.

Drace stepped backward so he wouldn't stain his boots. His heart was beating with violent swiftness. He turned from the room and went back into the living room where he'd seen a telephone.

He dialed the number of the cell phone in the van. His hand was steady.

Raylene answered, sounding worried and nervous.

"It's me," Drace said. "I'm in the house. Something's happened. Get here fast as you can."

Jessie was glowering malevolently at a square of orange Jell-O on her tray when Eden, Owen, and Peyton came to her room. Eden had worked all afternoon with Peyton to help the child overcome her fear of the hospital.

Now Peyton clutched a small vase of flowers that they had bought for Jessie at the grocery store. "Look what I got for you, Granny," she said with shy pride, offering them up.

"Ain't they pretty?" beamed Jessie. "Thank you, honey. Eden, take these and set 'em on the dresser, so I can look right at 'em. Owen, flush this damn Jell-O down the toilet before I sling it at the wall."

Owen smiled and removed the offending Jell-O. Peyton followed him into the bathroom to watch its interesting demise.

Jessie cocked her head in the direction of the bathroom. "Has she taken any more to him yet?"

Eden sighed. "Not really. I don't think she likes men in general. Probably because of Mimi's boyfriends."

Jessie patted the perfect braided crown of her hair.

"Mimi's going to settle down after this. She'll be a proper mama to that little gal."

"Jessie," Eden warned, "you promised not to talk about that."

"Not in front of Peyton," Jessie said righteously. "And I didn't. But here's my honeyduck. You want to come up and sit by Granny? My, what a nice haircut you got."

Owen lifted Peyton to sit on the edge of Jessie's bed. "It's like Eden's," Peyton said proudly. She pointed at her ears. "And I got new earrings. They're like Eden's, too."

"Hmm," said Jessie. "You don't try to be like Eden. You be your own sweet self instead."

"I *am* like her," said Peyton. "I'm going to be an actress, too. I'm going to do voices. Meoww. Meeowwwr. That's a cat."

"It's an excellent cat," Eden said, for it was true. The child had talent.

"Eden," Jessie said, "don't try to give this little girl a big head. Don't try to make her over in your own image."

Eden bit back a reply and was glad that Peyton chattered on. "I know a secret," Peyton said, grinning at Jessie mischievously.

Jessie feigned delight at the news. "A secret? Tell Grannie."

"I got to whisper it," said Peyton. Jessie smiled at the sweetness of the gesture as Peyton leaned and whispered into her ear.

Jessie's smile instantly dropped from her lips, and she shot Owen a killing glance. "A security system? I don't want no security system. No sir!"

"Peyton!" Eden scolded. "I told you it was a secret."

"You didn't say not to tell it to *her*," Peyton argued.

"We'll discuss this later, young lady," Eden told her.

"I don't want all those bells and sirens in my house," Jessie said stubbornly.

Owen's face went implacable. "You got 'em. Alvin Swinnerton's installing it right now."

"I'll call him and tell him to get out of my house," Jessie said, stretching her hand toward the phone.

Owen set the phone out of her reach.

"Then I'll call him tomorrow and tell him to go back and rip it out," Jessie insisted. "I don't like them things. You make one mistake, you set one button wrong, and it sounds like the Last Judgment's coming down on you."

"Jessie, it's a perfectly simple system," Owen said. "You'll get used to it in no time. And if you don't, just deactivate it. But I want it on while Eden and Peyton are there. The house is isolated, and you know it."

Jessie crossed her arms again and said nothing.

"Besides," he added, "you asked me to watch out for them. The system's part of it."

Jessie looked placated, but not completely. "It'll scare the Holy Ghost right out of the house."

"A ghost lives there?" Peyton asked in a small voice.

"No, Peyton, absolutely not," Eden said firmly. "Granny made a joke, that's all. Let's go downstairs. I'll buy you an ice-cream sandwich out of the machine."

Peyton, her expression nervous, nodded. She stretched out her arms and Eden lifted her down from the bed and set her on the ground. They left the room hand in hand.

Jessie stared after them. "The two of them are getting mighty thick." She sighed. "That's good, I guess. That's good."

There was weariness in her voice. Owen narrowed his eyes at her. "Are you all right?"

She sighed again and shook her head, the corners of her mouth turned down. "I'm fine. Only—"

"Only what?" he asked. She slumped back against her pillows, put her hand to her forehead. "Before this, I been sensing danger. But today, all day it's been like fog is closed round me."

He frowned. "What kind of fog?"

"Just fog," she said, "and nothing's clear. Not one thing. But then, the fog opens, and I see Mimi walking toward me. In dreams lately I hear her footsteps on the porch. I hear her knock at the door. This afternoon I dreamt I was in my house, and I looked down on the bathroom sink, and there was her hairbrush. With her curly long hairs stuck in it, just like old times. And I thought 'It's true. She's home at last, safe.'"

"Let's hope it happens," he said gruffly.

She turned her stare to him. "It *will* happen. And when it does, the danger's past. I know that. When she's home, then everything'll be put right again."

He said nothing.

"Thank Eden for me," she said tiredly. "Thank her for all she's doing. I'd try to do it myself, but it won't come out right. It never does. I don't know why. Tell her that . . . I'm sorry."

He was touched. She hated saying she was sorry, and he knew how much the words hurt her pride.

"I will. But you've got to take it easy."

"I know," she said, then added irritably, "Where'd Eden go? Is she going to spend all night at that ice-cream machine? Where's she took my honeyduck?"

She put her hand at her forehead. "I didn't mean to

snap at you of all people. It's just this fog. I can't see nothing clear. It's like God pulled down the curtain."

Again Owen felt the nameless apprehension that had haunted him all day. *Some things,* he thought, *we aren't meant to see, aren't meant to know.*

He said, "I'll bring your girls to you, Jessie."

EIGHTEEN

⚊⚍⚊

DRACE MOVED THROUGH THE LITTLE HOUSE, SEARCHING, probing.

In the strange room decked out as an office, he was shaken with anger to find labeled tape cassettes, one marked "Peyton," another marked "Constance/Mimi."

What were these fuckers doing? Nothing made sense; it was too bizarre, too unexpected. He felt as if, far away, an unseen edge of his plans had unraveled, and he did not know how dangerous the damage was or could be.

But he acted, swiftly and with purpose. He pocketed the tapes, cut the phone lines, and drove the security truck deep into the trees where it could not be seen. He plotted the most efficient way to take the enemy by surprise.

He heard a vehicle approaching the house. His muscles tautened and his heart slammed in anticipation.

Adrenaline surging, he moved to the living room, peered out between the drapes, and saw the van, its lights cut, wheeling past the house.

Raylene. He smiled tightly as the van rolled past the graveled parking spot and around the corner of the drive, as he'd told her. She was to park the van behind the house where it could not be seen from the drive.

Drace hurried to the kitchen door and eased it open. In the gathering darkness, he saw Raylene's trim figure climbing out of the driver's seat.

Her face was a pale glimmer and her hair a ghostly silver. She wore her fitted camouflage pants and a matching jacket. She moved to him and seized his hands in hers.

"What about Mimi?" she asked tensely.

He could feel the anxiety coursing through her. "Did you take your Xanax?" he asked with concern.

She nodded, squeezing his hands more tightly. Somehow she looked younger to him tonight, almost girlish, and animated by a shaky elation that gave a fragile edge to her beauty.

"Frightened?" he asked.

She shook her head with conviction. "Not with you here."

"We'll take her in," he said softly. "She'll have her uses. And I want her to see."

Raylene nodded and tossed her hair. Drace released her hands and slid open the van's back door. He stepped inside and came out hauling Mimi, who stumbled. Her hands were still cuffed behind her back.

Drace pushed her toward Raylene and handed

Raylene the twenty-two. "Take her inside," Drace ordered. "Secure her."

He climbed back into the van, peeled up the strip of carpet, and slid open the floor panel to the cache of weapons and ammunition.

Raylene pushed the staggering Mimi into the house. Drace snatched up the two assault rifles, the ammunition belts, the handguns, and closed the compartment again.

He went inside the little house. Raylene had Mimi sitting on the living-room floor, legs crossed, prisoner-of-war style. She looked barely conscious, so stupefied she seemed lumpish and bestial to him.

He went to Raylene, handed her one of the Sierras and one of the holstered handguns. She buckled on the holster.

"I want you out there, up on that hill overlooking the house," he told her. "You cover the drive. And keep it covered."

He saw the dismay in her eyes. "But—" she protested.

"It's safer," he said firmly.

"But you'll be all alone in here when they come," she said, laying her hand on his arm.

Behind them, Mimi's breath rattled and choked.

He smiled down at Raylene. "Don't argue. Mind me." He tugged at a lock of her blond hair. "Put on your ski mask, soldier girl."

Once off the main highway, the route to Jessie's was crooked and deserted, with the forested mountains rising so steeply on either side that the road seemed to snake through a nearly featureless maze of black.

Owen reached for the cell phone and punched out the number of the GuardLok office.

"GuardLok Security Systems," answered a man who sounded deeply bored. "Bill Joe Wilmer speaking."

Owen recognized the name and voice. Wilmer was a former traffic officer with the city police.

Owen spoke quietly, so as not to wake Peyton, who slept in the backseat. "Bill Joe, this is Owen Charteris. Alvin was at Jessie Buddress's house installing a system. Is it in place—working?"

"I just come on duty. Let me check." There was a long pause, then Bill Joe said, "Sorry, Owen. It's not done."

Owen's nerves snapped to attention. "What do you mean, not done?"

"Well," Bill Joe said, "Alvin logged in by radio that he got there, but he never done the tests. We haven't had a peep out of him. It's not connected. No."

Owen frowned. "He got there almost two hours ago. He hasn't even run one test?"

"No sir. I got a note here his wife called, wanting him to phone home. But they couldn't raise him by radio, and the phone at the Buddress house was dead. He maybe hit a glitch. It happens."

"Then he's still there?"

"I reckon."

"You reckon. But you don't know?"

"Hell, Owen, maybe something come up. You never know."

Owen didn't like this. "I'm going to be there in a few minutes," he told him. "If he's not there, I'll be in touch." He hit the switch hook and dialed Jessie's home number. He was answered by nothing, by silence.

He folded the phone shut and stared at the serpentine road winding ever more deeply into the darkness.

"What's wrong?" Eden asked.

"Jessie's phone line is dead," he answered. "That means the security system's not installed yet."

She shrugged. "Well, these things take time, don't they?"

"Yeah," he replied, not liking his own train of thought. "They take time."

"I forgot how dark it gets out here," Eden said pensively, gazing out at the night. "How empty it is."

Owen glanced sideways at her. "Miss the bright lights, big city?" he asked.

She didn't meet his eyes. "I think I was born missing them."

"Yeah," he said tonelessly. "Well."

"And when I'm gone from here, I'll miss you," she said.

"Well. Yeah," he repeated. "I'll miss you, too."

They were silent a long moment, and the silence was laden with all they would not, could not, say to each other.

He nodded toward Peyton. "She's sound asleep?" he asked just to have something to say.

"Yes," she said. "With luck we'll get her in the house and in her own bed without waking up."

And then? he thought, saying nothing.

"And then," she said, moving her hand to his arm, "if we can be discreet about it, I'd love to make love again."

His heart took an unexpected curving flight at her words, at her touch. "I'm a discreet guy," he said.

He turned down the lane that led to Jessie's house and his.

• • •

In the living room, Drace stood at the window, looking through the slit between the drapes, his weapon ready. His gaze was fixed on the lawn's rise and the shadowy stand of mimosas, where he had sent Raylene to cover the drive.

Only the light from the hall spilled into the room. Behind him Mimi sat on the floor, cuffed and helpless, in the semidarkness.

She was weak and sick with agony, but on some dim level she realized Drace and Raylene were waiting for her family. Her sister—how, she wondered in confusion, did Eden get mixed up in this? And Owen Charteris. In her pain, she could barely remember Owen Charteris.

But then there was her daughter.

Peyton, she thought, and the name was like a distant gleam of light. *Peyton.*

On the couch lay Peyton's familiar tattered yellow bear with its unraveled mouth. There was a brand-new doll beside it, a Raggedy Ann with a sparkling clean pinafore.

Somebody bought her a new doll, Mimi thought dazedly. *Somebody's taking care of her. My sister. Why my sister?*

She thought of being with Eden in the backyard, behind Jessie's trailer when they were children. Eden was trying to draw Mimi out of some deep fit of childish sadness.

Eden had knelt in the grass, holding a dandelion to Mimi's chin.

"This turns your chin yellow if you like butter," she said in her resonant voice. *"Do you?"*

Mimi had ducked her head, refusing to look at her. *"No. No. I don't like butter."*

Eden tickled her chin with the flower, leaving a faint golden smear of pollen.

"*Yes, you do, too,*" she teased. "*Go look in the mirror. You'll see.*"

She had played so many games like that with Mimi when Mimi was a little girl, trying to stop her from crying. Mimi was crying because of Mama. Always because of Mama. Mama didn't love them, did she? And so there was no place to be safe.

"*Don't cry,*" Eden had said. "*Don't. Shh. Shh. Do you like butter?*"

The soft, cool brush of dandelion petals beneath Mimi's chin, the scent of grass, the warmth of May, the bluejays quarreling in the mimosa trees.

Eden, take care of me. Eden, take care of me.

Mimi wanted to reach out for the Raggedy Ann doll, to hug it, hold it tight. But her hands, bruised and swollen, were pinioned behind her.

I am a prisoner of war, Mimi thought. *I am a traitor. They will kill Peyton. They will kill Eden. They will kill us all.*

She straightened one leg. Drace did not seem to notice. She straightened her other leg. She edged toward the couch.

"Be still," snapped Drace.

She thought, *I could get to my knees. I don't know if I could stand.*

"Mimi," he said, "if you go moving around, I'll break your goddamn knees for you."

And she thought, *Eden would not like this. Grandma would not want this. Peyton, Peyton, Peyton, I let it all go wrong.*

Her throat burned like fire, but she felt Eden's presence. She felt a cool, ghostly tickle under her chin.

•   •   •

Peyton shifted in the backseat, made a small, unhappy sound. Eden glanced back at the child in concern.

"Are we home yet?" Peyton asked sleepily. She plucked irritably at the buckle of her seat belt.

"Almost," Eden said. "Leave your seat belt on until we stop."

They rounded a curve and Jessie's house came into sight, almost, but not quite, dark. Alvin Swinnerton had apparently left the hall light switched on for them.

Owen said, "His truck's gone."

He picked up the cell phone again, punched in a number.

"What are you doing?" she asked.

He frowned, shook his head. "Jessie's line's still dead. It shouldn't be."

"He probably just got called away," she said mildly.

He pulled up before the house, but didn't stop the motor or cut his lights. Still frowning, he stared at the little house.

"What's wrong?" she asked.

"Nothing," he said, but he was troubled. Alvin must have quit mid-job, but why? Didn't he know he'd knocked out the phone line? He had to know.

He realized he was holding his breath. He still did not turn off the lights or motor.

"Stay here," he told her. "Let me check the house first."

She looked at him questioningly.

He shrugged, not fully knowing his own motives. He opened the door of the Blazer.

He heard the dog's shrill, silly bark, and it was full of alarm.

He frowned, wondering why the dog was barking. The dog never barked.

Then he thought, *The dog is dead.*

At the same split second, across the years, he remembered Laurie's soft voice warning him. He heard her say, *"Take care. Take care."*

His reaction was immediate and instinctive. He leaped back into the car, slammed the door, cut the lights. He threw the car into reverse, and the tires rasped wildly against the gravel. The Blazer lurched backward so swiftly that Eden screamed.

He wrenched it into drive and floored the accelerator.

"Owen!" Eden cried as the car leaped forward.

A bullet crashed through the rear window on the passenger side, and he screamed, "Get down! Get down! Get down!"

Raylene, panicked, kept firing. What was this man doing? Why had he started to leave the car with the motor still running, then changed his mind?

Why had he cut his lights, as if suddenly he knew he was on the defensive? Somehow he *had* known. Somehow he was trying to escape.

Drace had fired first, and Raylene had immediately joined in the attack. Desperately she'd kept her night sight trained on the car, emptying round after round at it.

She must have hit a tire, for she saw the car veer out of control, swerve off the drive and into a grove of trees and brush. She heard the scream of metal, the splitting of wood. The Blazer must have caromed off a tree, a big one. The crash shook the air. And then all was silent. Ominously silent.

Raylene, so rigid with tension she trembled, kept her barrel trained on the grove. She could barely make out the car's dark bulk in its midst. But nothing moved. After the gunfire, the silence seemed enormous.

Raylene thought, *Now what? Now what?*

Someone's shooting. At first, the realization had filled Eden more with wonder than fear. Then she'd felt a sinister thump shake the front wheel, felt the car bolt out of control.

The Blazer spun halfway around and crashed into the grove. Its rear side must have smashed against one of the larger trees, and the impact was deafening, it shook her to her marrow, it literally rattled her teeth.

She was hurled forward, but the seat belt caught her back so sharply that the air was knocked from her lungs. She was conscious of the airbags looming up like a hallucination, just as suddenly deflating.

Then came silence, punctuated only by a strange ticking from somewhere deep in the car's engine, as if a large insect was trapped there, dying.

"Peyton?" Eden whispered fearfully. "Owen?"

He swore under his breath, "I'm okay. Are you?"

"Yes—Peyton?"

Peyton moaned weakly, stirred in the backseat. Eden tore off her seat belt and was reaching for the door handle, but Owen's hand seized hers.

"Don't open the door," he whispered harshly between his teeth. "The light'll go on. They'll see you."

"But I have to go to her," she pleaded tearfully.

"Be quiet," he warned. "They're out there with guns."

Oh, Jesus, she thought, closing her eyes. Her head swam, blood pounded in her ears, and she fought back the mindless terror that rose in her, that wanted to sweep her away.

Out in the darkness, she heard a man shout, but she could not tell what he said.

Owen glanced into the backseat. "She's awfully still. Maybe just stunned. Get back there, make sure. Can you make it?"

She nodded grimly and half clambered, half slithered between the high front seats. With horror she saw that Peyton had apparently undone her seat belt. She lay back against the seat at an odd angle, silent and motionless.

In panic Eden felt the child's forehead. It was cool, clammy, and her fingers came away slightly sticky. "Oh, God, Owen, she's hit her head."

Wildly Eden ran her hand over Peyton's limp body. One small foot was pinned between the seat and the back door, which had buckled in the crash. Eden's stomach wrenched. Her hands shook and tears blinded her eyes.

"She's *pinned,*" she said in horror. "Good God, she's *pinned.*"

"Is she breathing all right?"

"I think so."

"Is she bleeding?"

"A little from the head—" Eden swallowed hard. "I—I can't tell anywhere else."

"Don't try to move her. Understand? Whatever you do, don't move her."

Eden couldn't speak. She stroked Peyton's forehead and fumbled for her pulse.

"Eden, listen," Owen whispered tensely. "They'll come for us. Just stay calm."

"Owen—the phone—call 911."

"You call. I've got to move. Reach back into the hatch. Hand me the crossbow."

What he said made no sense. It was mad, out of a nightmare. She heard the hum of the window rolling down.

He repeated, very calmly, very softly, "Reach into the hatch. Hand me the crossbow. Hurry."

The crossbow? she thought, dazed with disbelief. But she obeyed blindly, groped in the hatch area and found the sling. The weapon with its built-in quiver of bolts was heavier than she'd imagined, but she dragged it out and handed it over to him.

Peyton moaned brokenly. Eden started to turn back to her, but Owen seized her hand. "I'm going out through the window. There was fire from two directions, the hill and the house. They'll be coming for us. I need your help."

Peyton whimpered and tried to shift, but flinched when she couldn't move her leg, then moaned.

"Help? How?" Eden begged. "Owen, don't—"

"Shh," he ordered. "When I'm out of sight, you scream for all you're worth, baby. Scream that I'm dead. Got it? I'm dead and you and the kid are hurt. Keep it up. Not steady, just at intervals. And call 911."

Scream, she thought dazedly. *I can do that.*

"Keep down," he ordered. "The car's pointed toward the house. I don't think the guy there can get a clear shot. If he opens up, the engine's between you and him. It should shield you. Just stay down, baby."

He leaned back out the window, gripped the roof of the car, and in one surprisingly fluid movement, hoisted himself outside and onto his feet. He reached back inside, snatched up the bow, and in only seconds, it seemed, he disappeared into the deeper shadows.

Peyton whimpered softly again. Eden stroked her face. "I'm sorry, honey," she whispered. "I'm so sorry."

Dear God, she thought, *help her. Save her.*

She took a deep breath from the diaphragm. She drew back her head and screamed with all the raw power and volume she possessed. "Oh, God, he's dead! He's dead!"

She pitched her voice even more shrilly. "Help me!" she wailed. "He's dead, the child's hurt, and I can't move my legs. Help! For God's sake, help me!"

She split the darkness with another high-pitched animal howl of unbearable suffering. And another. And another.

The screams unnerved Raylene. She gripped her rifle more tightly.

The door of the house flew open. Drace shouted at her. "Ray, stay back! Shoot if you see anything move."

Raylene swallowed hard. Training and logic told her to check the car. It made sense for her to do it; she was closer to it by seventy yards than Drace, and she could move under the cover of the trees, which he could not. If he told her to stay back, it was only to protect her. She did not want that. She wanted to be his best lieutenant, always, braver and better than any man.

Holding the gun at combat ready, she drew a deep breath and began to move, slowly, cautiously, toward the stilled car. She kept as deeply in cover as she could.

At first the silence of the night had disquieted her. But now with the woman screaming so terribly, Raylene

fervently wished for the silence back. That first godfor-
saken screech startled her so badly that her stomach
lurched.

The first screams were nearly unbearable to her, but
somehow they grew even worse, even wilder, almost supernatural.

The man's dead, she told herself. *The man's dead and
she's helpless. It's almost over now. It's almost over. Hurry.
Move. Move. Move.*

But that demented howling kept her from hurrying.
She moved more slowly, more carefully, hoping if she
took her time, the woman would die—or at least pass
out—before Raylene could reach her.

"Ray!" Drace's voice came from the house, jarring in
its intensity. "Stay put! Wait her out!"

The woman fell silent, and Raylene hoped it was forever. She was just starting to breathe easier when the
woman began again, pleading now with God. "Please,
God—kill me—it hurts too much!' and then the screams
again, those tormented cries that no longer sounded human.

Raylene forced herself to quicken her steps. *Maybe
she'll die. She'll die and so will Peyton. Then it's over, it's
over, it's over, and we'll get out of here.*

She edged toward the grove, and could barely make
out the darkened Blazer within it. She could not see
movement of any sort. The screams had reached a sort of
crescendo she had not thought possible. She put her rifle
in a firmer position and stepped closer.

Owen saw that the gunman was small, hardly larger than
a boy, and with his rifle ready he was making his way
slowly toward the Blazer's window.

Age, size, didn't matter, Owen told himself. He stood in the shadows ready, the bow cocked, the safety off.

He held his breath, his heart knocking at his ribs. But his arms were steady, and his aim, he knew from instinct, was good.

He wanted to kill this gunman, wanted it so much it was like a seductive drug spreading through his veins. But he aimed for the shoulder of the bastard's gun arm.

In the sniper's next two steps, for the space of perhaps three seconds, Owen would have a clear shot.

The figure moved temporarily into the open. Owen did not hesitate or waver. He pulled the bow's trigger, and the bolt sprang from the groove.

But as he shot, the figure unexpectedly turned. The arrow buried itself in the upper chest of the camouflage jacket, next to the sternum. The sniper made a surprised, gagging sound and staggered, then fell heavily to a kneeling position, left hand scrabbling at the feathered shaft.

Christ, Owen thought, *I hit him too low, too close to the heart.*

He dropped the bow and hurled himself at the kneeling figure, grabbing from behind in a tight left-armed choke hold, so there could be no cry. At first his prisoner bucked feebly, trying to struggle free, but Owen, teeth gritted, tightened the hold. With his right hand, he took hold of the feathered shaft and gave it a small, deep twist.

The sniper lunged wildly, as if hauled upward by an invisible hook, then fell back.

"You want more, you son of a bitch?" Owen whispered fiercely. "How many of you are there? Tell me."

"Go to hell," she panted.

Owen's heart lurched sickly. A wave of nausea seized him. He suddenly realized how slight and rounded the sniper's body was, not a man's, not even a boy's.

Swearing, he stripped off the ski mask, and the woman's hair spilled free, a shimmer of pale blondness.

I've shot a woman, he thought, stunned and repelled. But another part of his mind told him, it didn't matter; she had tried to kill them all.

He shook her. "I said how many of you are there? Tell me—or I give that arrow another twist." He put his hand on the shaft again.

"Two!" the woman grimaced. "Two—for God's sake, don't."

"Both in the house?" Owen asked.

"Yes—yes—"

"Both armed?"

"No," she said in a quavering, tearful voice. "One's a prisoner. A woman."

Jesus, Owen thought. *A woman. A prisoner. As if we didn't have enough problems.*

"Who is she?" he hissed and shook her again.

"M-M-Mimi," she stammered. "M-M-Mimi S-S-Sto—" Her voice stuttered into silence. Her body lurched, then twitched weakly.

Mimi, he thought, and the nausea came sweeping back. Its taste rose bitterly in the back of his throat, like poison. He swallowed it down, ground his teeth. "Who's the other one? I heard him. Who is he?"

A man's voice called from the house. "Ray? Are you all right?"

The woman fought with sudden wildness to sit up, her hands flailing, her mouth working convulsively. She'd begun to shiver.

"I want him," she said with a strange desperation, clutching at Owen's shirtfront. "Please—I want him—I want—"

She went limp, sagged forward. He felt for the pulse in her throat. It was erratic, weakening.

Owen swore again and tasted salt. He didn't know if it was from sweat or tears.

He tried to work mechanically, not to think. He stripped the woman of her sidearm, stuck it in his belt. He took the assault rifle, slung it over his own shoulder.

From the house he heard the man call, "Ray? Raylene, what's happening?"

Owen rose, wiping his bloodied hands on the legs of his jeans. He bent and hauled the woman to her feet, then hoisted her into his arms. A plan had formed in his mind. It was desperate and dangerous, but he knew he had little choice. He licked his upper lip.

The woman stirred in his arms, sank back, and shuddered against his body. He carried her through the shadowy grove toward the house.

"Raylene?" yelled the voice from Jessie's house. "Answer me and get back. I'll fire on the car. I'll rip it fucking apart. *Raylene?*"

NINETEEN

———⟡———

EACH TIME THE WOMAN SCREAMED, THE SCREAM WAS LIKE a long, poisoned needle jammed into Mimi's body, tearing her innards and making her sicker. It was like more fire being poured down her throat.

And Eden kept screaming those terrible words: *He's dead and the child's hurt, and I can't move my legs. The child's hurt   the child's hurt   the child's hurt.*

Not all Eden's cries were coherent, sometimes they were only sounds, but terrible sounds. Out in the night, Peyton was suffering, and Mimi thought, *I tried not to do this, but I did, I made it happen.*

Eden kept screaming.

"Ray!" Drace yelled angrily. "Stay back. I'm going to fucking open fire. I'll rip that car apart. So stand back. Hear me? Raylene?"

There was no answer.

He waited. "One more minute," he said as if assuring himself. "One more minute."

Peyton, forgive me
Eden, forgive me
Jessie, forgive me
I'm so sorry so sorry so sorry

The minute took an eon to pass.

Drace moved to the northeast window of the house, peered out and swore. "Frigging bushes," he said. But he smashed out the glass from the window with his rifle butt, and aimed out the window.

He squeezed the trigger, and fired repeatedly. Mimi heard the clangorous din of bullets tearing metal. The image of Peyton trapped in that barrage shook her to her heart. She thought, *Hell is like this. I'm in hell.*

Then the volley stopped, and a deathlike stillness fell. Only the leaves in the dark wind rustled and whispered.

Mimi kept her eyes tightly shut. She could not breathe and her mouth and throat burned, but she no longer felt the pain. She hated Drace so much it crowded out the pain. *You've killed them, you bastard,* she thought. *My baby. My sister. You bastard.*

Then, like a demon riding on the night, Eden's cry came again.

Drace cursed it with such malice that Mimi was glad it tormented him. He pointed the rifle, aiming again toward the car.

But suddenly, inexplicably, the single light in the house went out.

Blackness embraced them. Mimi's heart leaped in astonishment.

"What the fuck?" Drace snapped.

The darkness pulsed around them. The unseen leaves

rustled, they whispered, and in the distance a woman moaned and then fell silent.

A noise, a heavy scuttling, came from the back porch, and Mimi thought, *My God, somebody's there, somebody's at the back door, somebody's trying to get in.*

She turned instinctively toward the kitchen. The scuttle, a kind of indistinct rasping and thudding, sounded again. Drace was beside her, hauling her to her feet, holding her as a shield before him.

A burst of noise split the silence, and a small, bright storm of gunfire blazed at the lock as the back door was shot away.

The door itself flew open, a voice—a man's voice—shouted something incomprehensible, and someone was hurling through the doorway toward them. Drace fired.

He fired repeatedly, and Mimi cringed as the kitchen windows shattered and the bullets ripped the walls.

She had the befuddled sense that the man who had entered the kitchen stumbled and then fell. But Drace kept shooting, almost insanely, even though no answering fire came.

Even when he must have realized his attacker had fallen, he still kept squeezing off rounds as if possessed. He swept his arc of fire across the kitchen floor, strafing it until he was sure the intruder was dead.

Then he stopped. He was shaking.

"Crazy son of a bitch," he said. "He walked right into it. Crazy. Crazy."

He fumbled in his pocket for his lighter, flicked it on. The figure, sheeted in blood, lay on its side on the floor. Mimi gasped brokenly, sickened because Drace's bullets had savaged the corpse.

One booted foot was severed from the shattered legs, and lay beyond them. The shots had struck mostly in the lower body, which looked as if it had been partially shredded by the teeth of some terrible machine.

Yet something was odd about the body. The hands, hardly touched by gunfire, were small, even delicate. The clothing, which had once been the mixed colors of camouflage, was darkly soaked with blood.

The night was quiet now. Eden had stopped screaming.

Drace stared at the corpse, transfixed. His hand trembled as he drew the lighter nearer the head. A large piece of skull had been shot loose and lay in the pool of blood, red soaking the pale hair.

But the face itself, turned sideways, was untouched by bullets. A cobalt-blue eye stared fixedly at nothing. The face was flecked with blood, like a disguise, yet Mimi recognized it. Before them, dead and shattered by Drace's gunfire, lay Raylene.

From her chest was inexplicably thrust the feathered shaft of an arrow.

The blond woman was dead by the time Owen had reached the house. She had died as he carried her. He told himself it was best that way. That way his choice was easy.

When he shot the lock off the back door, the force of the bullets shuddered the door and simultaneously forced it to swing inward.

He half shoved, half threw the woman's body into the dark kitchen, then instantly dropped to the concrete porch, shoulder-rolling across it. Even as he hit the dirt, he heard a wild fusillade of shots.

He sprang into a crouch and dodged behind the parked van, the assault rifle raised. Clouds were thinning, the night growing brighter. The van was lousy cover, but it was better than none.

When he had first seen the van, his heart had leaped with a hope that was both joyful and barbarous. If he could flush out the man inside the house, the bastard would have to go for the van. It was his only means of escape.

Now Owen, breathing hard, trained the sight of the captured rifle on the back door. Its wood ripped and splintered by bullets, the door swung slightly in the cool night wind, back and forth.

Raylene. That had been the name shouted from the house, the name of the woman he had captured. *Raylene,* he thought, breathing hard.

He hadn't enjoyed the thought of sacrificing her. Neither had he flinched from it. He had Eden and Peyton to protect. The bastard in the house was opening fire on them again, and the revelation of the hostage had put a desperate spin on everything.

With enough ammunition and a hostage, the son of a bitch could barricade himself in the house indefinitely. He could keep back the police cars and the ambulance, and stand off the police and even the fucking FBI.

Suddenly a very small and unsteady light flared within the kitchen; the bastard must have lit a match. The light flickered for a moment, then went out. He must know he was alone now, except for his prisoner.

Owen licked his upper lip and tasted the warm salt. He shouted, "Put down your weapon and come outside, asshole. It's over now."

For a few seconds there was silence. Then from within came a man's voice, so harsh and raw it sounded crazed. "Get back, you motherfucker. I still got a woman here, a hostage. Stay back or I kill her."

Owen gritted his teeth. He thought of Mimi, but mostly he thought of Eden. He prayed that she and the kid were safe; her name kept drumming through him like his own blood. *Eden. Eden.*

The man's voice tore through the night again, and it sounded dangerous with despair and rage. "I said I got a woman. Stay back or I kill her."

Owen's heart pounded, but he willed his own voice to be steady and flat. "How do I know you got her? Let me hear her talk."

Another silence.

"She can't talk," the man cried in frenzy. "But she can scream—listen."

Owen heard a woman's cracked, agonized moan. He thought, *Jesus, what's he done to her?*

The man shouted, "I'm coming out. I'm getting in the van and driving out of here. Make a move, and I'll blow her fucking head off."

Owen stepped back from the van and looked for cover. There was little. A few pale stars had pierced the thinning veils of cloud overhead. In their faint light he was visible, a clear target. He edged toward a patch of immature scrub cedars. They would provide conceal-ment, but no cover.

The man burst out of the door, pushing the woman before him. He held an automatic to her temple, and he had an assault rifle slung over his shoulder. Owen kept edging as quietly as he could into the cedars. He cursed under his breath; the bastard was too headlong, too rash.

The man paused on the porch, peering out into the night. The woman's head was twisted at an odd angle; he seemed to be gripping her by the hair. Her hands seemed to be bound behind her, and she looked as if she were barely able to stand. She was slender, that was all Owen could tell. He couldn't see the man's face.

Owen crouched, aiming at the gunman, but the woman was in the way. The man must have wrenched her hair, for her head jerked to an even more unnatural angle.

The man began to move across the small porch, to descend its two concrete stairs. The woman struggled. She tried to cry out something, but her voice was ragged and incomprehensible.

"Let her go," Owen shouted, "or I shoot you both."

It was an empty threat, and he knew it, but he kept the sights on the struggling pair.

The man, wrestling Mimi down the stairs, suddenly swung the rifle's barrel in an arc across the backyard, squeezing off a series of shots. Owen felt something knock him to the earth, biting into his ribs like a snake.

Mimi seemed to rise out of her own body, to look down and see herself and Drace as if she floated above the two of them. At the sound of the man's voice in the night, Drace had swept his aim across the yard, strafing it.

Now he had forced her almost to the door of the van and for some reason he was aiming at a shadowy little stand of trees. His hand was near her head and

I don't have to let him, Peyton, I don't have to

and she saw how near Drace's hand was and she heard him fire again and *I won't let him Eden, I don't have to* and she sank her teeth into Drace's wrist as if she were an animal, and although it hurt her burning jaws, she bit and bit.

She bit until hot blood bathed her mouth and her teeth ground hard against the bone.

Drace released her hair, shoved at her as if fending her off, and she stumbled away from him, trying to run, trying to hide because suddenly she was

free
running toward Peyton
running toward Eden
running toward home

Afterward, when Owen remembered it, it seemed to happen in a jerking blur, as if a very old piece of movie film had gone awry.

He'd been hit. It felt like somebody had jabbed a burning spike between his ribs, deep into his innards, knocking him to the ground. He recovered himself enough to get the rifle aimed again from a lying position, but the woman was still in the way.

The gunman aimed toward the cedars again. Owen gritted his teeth in pain and kept his aim as steady as he could.

Then, somehow the woman, Mimi, broke away, and he had a clear shot at the gunman, and he fired again and again. But the man shot, too, and the shot hit Mimi in the back and she fell, even as the man crumpled beside the van's closed door.

Owen knew immediately that he'd mortally wounded the gunman. He'd hit him at least three times, and one shot had struck squarely in the center of the chest, ripping it open.

The man had screamed out a single anguished syllable, the name Ray. He'd drawn out that howl until he began to choke on his own blood, and then he'd fallen and gone silent. The body lay motionless.

The girl didn't move, either. Owen started to rise, to

go to her. He intended to keep the rifle aimed at the man, just in case, but he found he could not get to his feet. He simply could not.

His legs felt like dead weight and would not obey him. He ended up dragging himself to her, still awkwardly holding the rifle, like a soldier crawling through the dirt.

As soon as he was close enough to touch her, he knew she was dead. He turned her over and saw that something terrible had happened to her mouth. Yet the rest of her face seemed strangely peaceful, almost placid, even with dirt and blades of dead grass clinging to it.

Her eyes were open and reflected the light from the stars that were starting to shine overhead. Did he imagine it, or were they extremely lovely eyes?

He tried to close them, but then the pain overcame him, and he passed into unconsciousness.

He lay bleeding beside her, his fingers still touching her upturned face, the starlight still shining in her eyes.

Crouched in the backseat of the Blazer, her hand pressed against Peyton's damp brow, Eden used her other hand to dial 911 for the third time.

Tears ran down her face, but she did not realize it. Again the laconic officer answered her, the voice absolutely empty of emotion.

"This is Eden Storey again," she said, her voice shaking. "Where *are* you people?"

"Ma'am, hang on. We've got a SWAT team and an ambulance on the way. I'm surprised you don't hear the sirens by now."

"There's been more shooting up there," she said.

Peyton moaned slightly, and her small body twitched, then shuddered. Eden sucked in her breath and thought, *Hold on, Peyton. Hold on, sweetheart.*

"Shooting exactly where, ma'am?" the officer asked in his bored voice.

"At the house. He went up there. Owen Charteris. There was shooting. A lot of shooting. It's stopped now. I—he might be dead. Where *are* you?"

"There was more gunfire?"

"Yes."

"But it's stopped."

"Yes. Yes."

"I'm going to keep the officers informed, ma'am. Now, how long since you heard anything?"

"I don't know," she said in frustration, staring at Peyton's small, shadowy face. "A long time. I can't tell."

"Five minutes, ma'am?"

Peyton made a sound of pain. "I don't *know,*" Eden repeated. It seemed like fifty years, all spent in darkness and fear.

"All right, ma'am. Now I'm going to switch your call, keep you on the line with someone. Help you wait this out."

"I need someone who knows first aid," she said. "There's a child hurt here. Badly hurt. Nobody says anything but 'Don't move her.'"

"I'm going to switch you to another officer. He'll keep talking to you."

"This child is pinned. Her leg is pinned. She's unconscious."

"I'm switching you now, ma'am. Stay calm."

In the distance, she heard the sirens. For a moment she was blinded by her own tears of relief. But they seemed far away, so far.

• • •

Although Peyton had a broken ankle and a concussion, Owen was still more seriously hurt.

The shot had hit the edge of his spleen, then exited between his eighth and ninth ribs next to his spine, nicking it badly. Eden was terrified because at first he could not move his legs.

But by his third day in the hospital, he could walk again, although rather unsteadily and not far. But Eden had not been able truly to celebrate his recovery. She was still stunned, in shock at her sister's death.

It was as if Mimi, absent so long in life, had become ever present to her in death, a close and faithful ghost. A host of shifting memories took possession of Eden, yet she still did not know what had happened to bring Mimi to such a violent death.

She hardly had time to grieve, only to be haunted. She stayed with Peyton as much as she could. The child had not yet been told Mimi was dead, and Eden dreaded telling her.

She herself was numbed. Alone she made the decision to have Mimi's body cremated, alone she had gone to the mortuary to pick up the paper box of ashes. Not knowing what else to do, she put the box in a safe-deposit drawer at the bank, thinking, *Someday we'll have a ceremony. Not now.*

Eden could console herself only by vowing that life would treat Peyton better than it had her mother; she herself would fight to make it so.

On the third day after the shootings, she was sitting beside Peyton's bed, trying to amuse the child with paper dolls. The telephone rang.

"Eden? It's Owen. Can you come to my room? There's someone here who wants to talk to you."

She kissed Peyton's cheek, promised to be back shortly, and went to the second floor to Owen's room. It seemed she had spent the last three days moving from room to room to room in this hospital, from Peyton to Jessie to Owen. She was punchy from it, feeling in an unreal daze.

As she entered Owen's room, she was surprised to see two men in suits at his bedside. One was a tall, thin, dour-looking man with a balding head and sea-green eyes. The other was shorter, younger, and more squarely built, with a serious face and conservatively barbered dark hair.

Owen sat propped up in bed. He looked drawn, and although his eyes were alert, his expression seemed troubled. She tried her best to smile, but was not sure she'd succeeded. He reached for her hand and drew her to his bedside. "This is her," he said to the men. "Eden Storey."

They regarded her as solemnly as undertakers.

The balding man said, "Miss Storey, I'm Lieutenant John Mulcahy of the Missouri State Police. This is Agent Dennis Robey of the FBI."

Eden's nerves tautened. She had already talked to the police, she had already talked to other men from the FBI. In addition, both agencies had been all over Owen, badgering him with questions from the moment he could talk.

"I—I already gave my statement," she said.

"We know, ma'am," said Mulcahy. "I'm sorry about your experience the other night. How's the child?"

She could not shake off a deep anxiety, but she kept her voice level and controlled. "She's doing well. I'm taking her home tomorrow."

"No complications from the concussion?" Mulcahy asked.

Eden shook her head. "None they can see. They've been keeping her under observation, mostly. A headache at first, of course, but it's gone."

"No dizziness? No double vision?" Mulcahy asked. Despite his sour face, he seemed sincerely concerned.

"No. She's been very—" She started to say "lucky," but the word seemed ill-chosen. Peyton's luck, in her short life, had run about as badly as it could. "She's been recovering well," she amended.

"Her ankle injury?" asked Mulcahy.

"She's proud to have a cast like her granny's."

"Does she remember the car crashing? Or the aftermath?"

"No. The last thing she remembers is talking to her granny in the hospital."

Mulcahy nodded sympathetically. "That's a blessing."

"Yes. It is," said Eden, but she thought, *I'll remember. To my grave I'll remember.*

"You're taking her back to your grandmother's house?" she asked.

"No," she said. "Not yet. I have another place for right now."

Eden swallowed. Men were at work on Jessie's house today, cleaning it, replacing the ruined kitchen floor, patching the walls. She was staying in a furnished apartment that Owen had untenanted.

She and Jessie had argued over the house. Jessie wanted to go back to it, and she wanted Eden and Peyton to be with her. Eden had not thought she could bear to return, but Jessie was so adamant that at last, reluctantly, she'd agreed.

Mulcahy dropped his gaze. Dennis Robey, the FBI agent, looked less than comfortable. He cleared his throat.

"Miss Storey, we have some news for you," he said. "A man named Yount has talked. We know your sister's history now. And the people that she was involved with, we know about them, too."

TWENTY

———⟨ɘ/ɘ⟩———

Robey's words filled Eden with apprehension. "Yes?" she said.

Robey said, "Your sister met Drace Johansen in an outpatient group, a sort of counseling session in Detroit. They'd been ordered there separately, each as part of probation."

Owen gripped her hand more tightly.

"Mimi'd been in court for an incident in a bar," said Robey. "It started with a political quarrel, ended with her resisting arrest, making a lot of wild threats."

Eden stared at him, unable to speak.

Robey squared his shoulders, set his big jaw. "Drace Johansen had made threats, too, to a black liberal city council member. He'd been ordered to attend the same sessions."

Robey paused, his expression blankly stoic. "Your sister was rebellious and a little militant. This guy was rebellious and *very* militant. He had a whole ideology, even followers—a few. A kind of family or commune. He looked at Mimi and saw a potential convert. He could be a spellbinder when he chose to. He wanted Mimi and he got her."

Mulcahy spoke, his mouth twisted. "Our friend James Yount came into some property in Missouri. Drace Johansen decided they'd all go there. By that time he was going only by the name Drace. It means 'dragon,' as in the dragon of the Apocalypse."

Eden's heart constricted. She held on to Owen's hand tightly and tried to keep her expression severely controlled.

Robey shook his head. "Yount said at first your sister knew very little. She thought Drace was some kind of demigod, that he had all the answers. But after the move to Missouri, he and his cousin—the woman—Raylene Johansen—decided on less rhetoric and more action. They planned a series of antigovernment bombings, beginning with the Bahamian plane. In the beginning, Mimi thought it was just talk. By the time she knew it wasn't, she felt that she was implicated up to her neck. She protested. She became the group's black sheep, its scapegoat. Raylene in particular had always resented her."

"B-but," Eden stammered in frustration, "who were these people? Where did they come from? Why did they hate the government? I don't understand."

Mulcahy spoke again, his thin face harsh. "As a child, Drace was sent to live with Raylene's family. His father had been an army officer, killed in Vietnam. Raylene's father was career army, too, and a sort of petty tyrant.

They moved a lot, didn't put down roots. Raylene and Drace—became close."

Robey said, "The family had money. It also had a long tradition with the military. Drace went to military school, but got expelled. Raylene's older brother went to the Gulf War, died of leukemia a few years later. They believed it was Gulf War syndrome.

"They both resented the father. They came to resent the army, the government itself. They fed each other's suspicions and created new ones. They began seeing cover-ups and collusions and conspiracies everywhere. So they decided to strike back. And they did."

Eden listened with a sort of sickened fascination.

Owen said, "But why the Bahamian airline? Why not a U.S. target?"

Robey opened his empty hand, a gesture of futility. "Yount says Drace and Raylene claimed Bahamian banks were laundering money for illegal CIA schemes. But Yount thinks it was partly because security on that particular airline was so lax they thought they could pull it off. It was vulnerable, so they hit it."

Mulcahy's green eyes searched Eden's face. "For what it's worth, Miss Storey, Yount says Mimi opposed the plan. But by then she knew too much for them to let her go. She was close to being their prisoner. The child, too."

Robey nodded. "Your sister did the best she could to get herself and the kid out. But Yount says she was scared, and he also says, to put it kindly, ma'am, her thinking wasn't always . . . clear."

Owen said, "She had the courage to defy them, Eden. She was trying to free Peyton. But she couldn't come with her. By that time she was guilty of conspiracy."

"Your sister stopped in Branson," Robey said. "From

what we can piece together, she meant to have a kind of last fling, then die on her own terms."

"Die?" Eden repeated, stunned. "You mean to kill herself?"

"Yes, ma'am," Robey said gruffly. "I imagine she thought she was out of options."

All this information seemed to fall on Eden like a tangled net. She could not speak.

"I'm sorry," Robey said.

"I'm sorry, too," said Mulcahy and stared out the window.

Owen drew her nearer. "Peyton's yours," he said.

She's both Mimi's and mine, thought Eden. She drew away from him, put her face in her hands, and wept at the complexity of her own emotions.

Jessie had taken Mimi's death hard. For the first time in Eden's life, she had seen her grandmother openly weep.

She saw Jessie weep again, just as hard, when she learned of Mimi's flight from Drace and Raylene. The old woman's shoulders shook, and she covered her eyes.

At last she dropped her hand, clenching her handkerchief, into her lap and raised her head. "Peyton still doesn't know that Mimi's—still doesn't know?"

Eden swallowed hard and shook her head. "She only knows she isn't coming back. The rest, I think, she should be told little by little. I want professional help with this."

"Mimi," Jessie said brokenly. To Eden the name seemed to reverberate with an infinite sense of loss.

Jessie bowed her head and cried again. Then she wiped her eyes, squared her jaw, and said, "Tears never cured nothing. We got to get on with things. We got to take care of our own."

"I'm taking Peyton to California with me," Eden said. "I—I'll adopt her."

Jessie moved her shoulders as if irritated. "Don't keep her all to yourself. I'll be wanting to see her, you know. But I ain't getting on no airplane to do it, nosirree bob. And I ain't riding a bus all the way out there, neither. I truly despise a bus ride."

"I'll bring her back to see you," Eden said. "And we'll talk on the phone more. I promise. We're all the family she's got, Jessie. She'll need you, as well as me."

Jessie crossed her arms. "Hmmph. Us—a family. I never thought I'd hear you say that."

Neither did I, thought Eden. *But we are, aren't we?*

Owen was the last out of the hospital. He knew Eden's hands were not simply full, but crammed, running over with responsibilities. But when the day of his release came, he asked her to leave Peyton and Jessie for an hour and drive him home. They were all back in Jessie's house again, and he knew Eden had to pretend it didn't bother her.

She showed up at his door, brisk and cheerful and businesslike. Her hair slanted rakishly over her forehead, and the diamonds glittered at her ears. She looked like a million dollars.

Once inside the car, Eden arched one brow, and gave him a rueful smile. "You look moody for somebody homeward bound. What's the matter? Fall in love with hospital food?"

He shifted stiffly in his seat. He still had bandages

around his midsection and it was like being encased in
armor.

Her smile faded. "Still in pain?"

He shook his head. He could stand the pain.

"Then what's wrong?" she asked. She pretended to
concentrate on maneuvering out of the parking lot, but
he could see she was concerned, troubled, even.

"We haven't had much chance to talk," he said.

"I know," she said, keeping her eyes on the traffic.

He leaned back against the seat, his body rigid.
Whenever he'd get a minute alone with Eden, they'd kiss
almost shyly, then seem at a loss for words. They were
complex people for whom it was often difficult to show
even simple emotion, and Owen's emotions were far
from simple.

He wanted Eden, but he didn't know what she
wanted. She was pouring all her grief and energy and
nervousness into caring for Peyton and Jessie, especially
Peyton.

Now his sister Shannon, in full nursing mode, was
lurking in wait for him at home, a fate too gruesome to
contemplate. She was filling his unfinished house with
objects he didn't want, beds, chairs, *possessions*.

"Look," he said to Eden. "I know you're concerned
about Peyton. That you have to be."

"She needs a lot of attention now," she said, not
looking at him. "We're doing everything we can for her.
Time will tell."

What will time tell about you and me? he wanted to
ask. Instead he said, "How's Jessie doing?"

She smiled slightly. "Jessie's tough. But she's shaken,
she's even humbled a little."

They were both silent for an uneasy moment. Then
Eden said, "I can never thank you enough, you know.

You nearly got yourself killed for us. We owe you—everything."

A sharp, crooked little bolt of pain shot deep inside him, twisting and turning. He wished, for Eden's sake, that he could have saved Mimi, but in his heart he did not believe that Mimi had wanted to be saved.

Whenever he thought of the other woman, Raylene, and he thought of her often, a dark chill fell on his soul. His emotions about her were many and complex, but sorrow was not among them.

Eden kept her eyes straight ahead. "All this has changed Peyton," she said.

He nodded. "It would have to."

"She can talk about the past now. She doesn't like to, but she can. She saw and heard terrible things with those people. She *heard* them talk about bombing that plane."

"It's over now," he said. He reached over, rubbed her shoulder, even though the movement cost him pain.

"There's something else, too," she said, her pretty face looking haunted. "Henry's gone. Last night she said he's gone for good."

He nodded. "Maybe she doesn't need him now."

Eden said, "A psychologist talked to her at the hospital. He said she has a healthy sense of self and seems very intelligent. And strong. That should help."

"Yeah," he said, stroking her shoulder. "It should."

She glanced at him, smiled rather sadly. "I've thought about you so much and so often," she said. "But Jessie's needed me, and Peyton's needed me even more. Can you understand that?"

He caught her right hand, laced his fingers through hers. He took a deep breath. "Right now I've got my sister hanging around playing Florence Nightingale. You've got Jessie. But when we have time alone again—"

Her fingers tightened around his. "Owen, we're not going to have time alone together. I go back to L.A. Soon. Tomorrow."

Of course, he thought. *Of course.* Of all the things they hadn't talked about, that was the subject they had avoided most carefully. She must go back.

She withdrew her hand from his and placed it back on the steering wheel. She glanced in the rearview mirror.

"Everyone's anxious for you to get home," she said lightly. "They're all waiting for you. Jessie made you a lemon cake. That is, she bossed me around so that I made it to her orders. I don't know how it'll taste. I'm no cook."

He watched her. "Tomorrow. That's early, isn't it?"

She kept her chin high. "Not really. Jessie's set; I've hired a nurse to stay with her. She's there now, in fact. And I have to get Peyton settled."

"And you?" he asked, watching her profile. "Your memories of this—will they all be bad?"

She sidestepped the question. "I just mean the sooner she feels she has a permanent home, the better."

"I asked about you," he said.

She shrugged almost blithely. "Me? I've been too busy to let myself think. I had to set up an appointment with a psychologist for Peyton in L.A. I have to find a pediatrician—a hundred things. Then there's Jessie. Getting her a nurse, making sure she's taken care of."

"I'll see she's taken care of," he said gruffly. "She's going to hate to see you go so soon."

Eden shook her head. "She and I are already arguing about how to treat Peyton. Jessie—well, Jessie's set in her ways."

"Yeah," he said darkly, "people get set in their ways."

He gazed out at the woods. Many leaves had fallen while he was in the hospital; the trees were starting to look bare, winterlike.

She tossed him a careless smile. "I've got some big adjustments ahead. Life with a child is *not* simple. I'll have plenty to do."

"Yeah. I know how it is." He thought of the thousand and one responsibilities that nailed him to Endor.

"Plus," she said brightly, "rehearsal begins next week. I'm a working girl, remember?"

"You'll come back to see Jessie from time to time?" he asked as casually as he could. "You don't plan to wait another fifteen years?"

Her expression went wistful, but only for a moment. "Yes. Peyton's fond of her. But Jessie won't come to Los Angeles. She says it seems as far away as the moon."

It seemed farther to him. "Maybe I'll come see you," he said. "Someday."

She didn't seem to know how to take that. She flashed him a brief, insincere smile, then looked back at the road. "You should do that," she said pleasantly.

He thought, *I ought to step on the brakes. I ought to wrench that wheel out of her power, pull over to the side of the road, and kiss her until—*

Until what? he wondered. Then, it was too late to wonder. The car was pulling into Jessie's drive, and his sister was standing on the porch, holding the strings of a batch of metallic balloons that said things like "Welcome Home!" and "Cheers!"

Jessie sat in a wheelchair, beaming at him, a bouquet and a lemon cake on the wicker table beside her. Peyton sat demurely on the porch steps, holding a sign that someone had printed for her. It was white, and in red letters said WELCOME HOME, OWEN!!!

She had her pixie haircut and was wearing new clothes, pink overalls and a white T-shirt with pink trim. She looked like a normal kid, pretty, even, and he tried to force himself to smile at her.

Yet when his gaze met hers, she seemed to look through him as if he weren't there. It was Eden who brought the smile to her face, it was Eden she ran to meet and hugged.

He did not belong in the equation.

TWENTY-ONE

I T WAS A SNOWY AFTERNOON IN FEBRUARY. JESSIE SAT IN the living room, playing chess with Owen. She was a fierce and wily competitor, and she won as often as he did.

Four months had passed since Eden had returned to Los Angeles, taking Peyton with her.

This particular game was close, and Jessie studied the board craftily, plotting her next move. From down the hall came the sound of her office phone ringing.

"Oh, hellfire," Jessie grumbled and heaved herself to her feet. She shook her finger at Owen. "Don't you move nothing while I'm gone."

He gave her a wry, one-cornered smile. "I don't cheat, Jessie."

Jessie gave him a look that said, *You better not.* She

lumbered down the hall, leaning heavily on the ivory-headed cane Owen had given her.

She pulled out her chair and sat. She picked up the receiver. "Sister Jessie," she said. "God's gifted seer."

"Hello, Jessie," said a familiar voice. "It's Eden."

Jessie stiffened in surprise and disapproval. "Why you calling me on this line?" she scolded. "It's expensive. You'll waste all your money."

Eden laughed. "It's not wasted. It goes to you, doesn't it? Then you'll have money to call me. It works perfectly."

"You got no more financial sense than a rabbit," Jessie said, but she said it with brusque affection. She had never been able to believe that Eden was doing well in Los Angeles, but Owen said it was true, and Owen was expert in such matters.

"Consider this call a Valentine present, then," Eden said. "It's almost Valentine's Day. Besides, I'm in a celebrating mood. Guess what I got for Peyton today."

"What?" Jessie demanded.

"A puppy," Eden said triumphantly. "She's been wanting a puppy. A collie. It'll just be old enough to bring home on her birthday."

"It'll shed all over the place," Jessie said, although she was pleased that Peyton would be happy.

"It's genetically engineered not to shed," said Eden.

Jessie's nostrils flared in suspicion. "Is that a joke?"

"Yes," Eden said. "Anyway, I was excited and I wanted to call and tell you before she got home from school."

Jessie's heart softened. "Does my honeyduck still like school?"

"She loves it, Jessie. She's amazing. She's *hungry* to

learn. I think it's one of the things that's going to save her."

Jessie thought of what the child had been through and it gave her a troublesome lump in her throat. She tried to swallow it down. "How's she doing?"

Eden paused. "Emotionally? There've been ups and downs. But her psychologist is optimistic. And she's like you, Jessie. A survivor."

Jessie didn't like the idea of a psychologist at all, but it flattered her ego to hear that Peyton resembled her. "Does she ever talk about Mimi?" she asked.

"Not much," Eden said. "It's something she's still learning to deal with. But she understands that Mimi's dead, and we're working hard to make her understand that the death is in no way her fault."

"Well, it's certainly *not* her fault," Jessie countered. "She shouldn't think such hogwash for a minute."

Eden sighed. "The human mind is complicated, Jessie. And mysterious. But she's a strong little girl. She's going to make it."

"Of *course* she's going to make it," Jessie said, offended by the very thought the child might not prosper. "But she'll do better if you're not in the poorhouse. You hang up now. Call me back on my home phone some other time—when Peyton's there and she can talk to her old granny."

"I'm not ready to hang up yet," Eden said, an odd note entering her voice. "I had another reason for calling on this line."

"Well, what?" Jessie said impatiently.

"I need your professional opinion," Eden said. "Some psychic advice."

"You?" Jessie said dubiously.

"Me," said Eden.

Jessie had a sudden flash of intuition. "Ha," she said. "It's Owen, isn't it? He wants to come out there, don't he?"

"Did he tell you that?" Eden sounded wary.

"He didn't have to tell me," Jessie answered. "I got eyes in my head. I can see what he's thinking."

"Can you really?" Eden said, rather dryly.

"Yes I can," Jessie asserted. "He's thinking he's got responsibilities here, but it don't always have to be that way. He's thinking it's time he got on with his life, that's what."

"Jessie," Eden said, sounding nervous, "he phoned me. He's thinking of buying property in L.A. If he does, he'd have a reason to come out here regularly. And if he comes out here, he says he wants to see me, and—"

"And what?" Jessie demanded.

"And I told him I'd have to think about it."

Jessie paused. She had seen this coming, of course, she had expected for some time it would happen. It was possible that Owen could even move to Los Angeles. He could consolidate his family affairs somehow, manage everything from halfway across the country; in this day and age it was possible.

Jessie felt a strong and unpleasant twinge of jealousy. She herself would never leave Endor, she knew, and she loved Owen as if he were her own flesh and blood. She did not want to lose him. Her desires and loves fought a small, intense war within her breast.

"Jessie?" Eden said. "Did you hear? I told him I'd have to think about it, and I'm afraid of what I think."

"Have you got rocks in your head?" Jessie said harshly.

"What?" asked Eden, obviously taken aback.

"What's to think about?" Jessie asked pointedly.

"He's a good man, a fine man. You'd be lucky to have him. And he'd be wonderful for Peyton."

"But—Peyton never seemed to take to him, Jessie. That's one of the things that worries me."

"She will," Jessie said. "Just give her time."

"You think so?"

"I by God know so."

"How?" Eden asked with false lightness. "Can you see it in your crystal ball?"

Jessie eyed her crystal ball. It was full of deep and glassy shadows, and things danced in those shadows that seemed like indistinct forms trying to take shape.

"As a matter of fact, I can," she said. "I can, indeed."

ABOUT THE AUTHOR

BETHANY CAMPBELL was born and raised in Nebraska. She has taught at colleges and universities in Nebraska, Illinois, and New Hampshire. She and her husband make their home in Arkansas with three cats and a dog passionate about rodents and their pursuit.